SHOOTING
THE
MOON

SHOOTING
THE
MOON

V.M. JONES

ANDERSEN PRESS • LONDON

To my dearest aunt and friend Margaret 'Wheels' Mackenzie, who taught me that when the hill gets steeper, you just have to pedal harder.

Acknowledgements
I would like to express my gratitude to the people who have so generously shared their time and expertise with me during the writing of this book.
To Rob Campbell, Jules Day, Emma Hawke, Sue and Trevor Isett, George Nation and Aaron Regan, and to Lorain Day and Mandy Little: thank you.

First published in Great Britain in 2008 by
Andersen Press Limited
20 Vauxhall Bridge Road
London SW1V 2SA
www.andersenpress.co.uk

First published in 2006 in New Zealand by
HarperCollins Publishers (New Zealand) Limited

British Library Cataloguing in Publication Data available.

ISBN 978 184 270 738 8

Typesetting by Janine Brougham.
Printed in the UK by CPI Bookmarque, Croydon, CR0 4TD

The Valentine's Ball

'You're grounded!' roared Dad.

'But Dad —'

'Don't you *But Dad* me! A girl doesn't give a boy a black eye for no reason — and at your age the reason isn't hard to guess. That's it! Grounded! Period! Do you hear me?' The words puffed out at me through the open car window, misty in the frosty air. They might look harmless, but they weren't. This was Dad, and he was mad at me, and his words were as lethal as bullets. And, like bullets, they carried clear across the carpark to where the seniors were lounging in the shadow of the auditorium, enjoying an illicit cigarette before heading home.

A cherry glowed red in the darkness and a mocking voice echoed: *'But Daddy . . .'*

Jordan Archer — the very last person I wanted to think about. I slid into the passenger seat, rolled up the window and risked a sidelong glance at Dad, glowering in the driver's seat. Though my eye was swollen almost shut, I could read the signs. His mouth was invisible under his bushy black moustache, but his sandpaper-stubbled jaw was clenched, his black hair sticking up in angry tufts. The collar of his Homer Simpson PJs stuck up jauntily above the frayed V of his gardening pullover, pulled on for the drive, but there was nothing jaunty about the look on his face. There was no point arguing or trying to explain.

'Dad,' I said, 'can we go home?'

'No we can't! Where the hell's your brother?' Dad obviously hadn't seen what I had — the silhouette of Nick deep in the gaggle by the hall, plank-thin and unmistakable, wreathed in a haze of smoke.

'He said he'd get a ride with his friends, remember? Dad, *please . . .*'

Dad glared round the rapidly emptying carpark one final time, then started the engine with a roar and crunched the truck into gear. Bone-weary, I tugged Dad's borrowed tie down to half-mast and undid my top button, then leaned back and closed my eyes as the first wave of Dad's tirade broke over me. My soul was already so bruised that Dad getting his boot in wouldn't even leave a mark.

It would be a long ride home.

How had everything managed to go so wrong? We'd been counting down to the night of the formal ever since the notice had been read out in assembly in the first week of term. *The Valentine's Ball.* Every time I thought of it I got this knee-jerk reflex in my gut — a twang of excitement, nerves and sea-green nausea.

It was a world first for Greendale High: the first time in living memory Mr Gilroy had agreed to something like this. We'd never even had a fundraising disco, never mind a formal ball open to the whole school. We didn't call him Mr Killjoy for nothing.

The news was met by stunned disbelief, wild celebration — and then panic.

'What do we do?' I hissed at my best friend Michael in the first period after assembly, under cover of the chemistry experiment.

'What d'you mean, *do*? We go, of course.' Mike clunked the 2-litre bottle of soda for the experiment down on the bench and regarded it dreamily, thoughts elsewhere. 'We rent tuxedos and —'

'Tuxedos?' I squawked, dropping the roll of Mentos that was my contribution to science.

Doc Sweeney's voice crackled into our whispered discussion like static. 'Philip, would you kindly repeat what I have just been saying?'

Desperately I trawled for some clue to what it could possibly have been but there was nothing. Detention loomed. In desperation I glanced down at the two objects in front of me on the bench. 'You said we must . . . uh . . . put the Mentos in the soda, Sir?'

'Correct,' said Doc sourly. 'However, it is vital that you do not . . .' Tuning him out, I waited till his watery gaze had drifted safely elsewhere and continued my discussion with Mike, this time keeping my gaze firmly fixed on the whiteboard. 'But what about partners?'

'We find partners. It shouldn't be too difficult. There are girls all round us.' He was right, there were: heads down, scribbling notes. But the sight didn't fill me with much hope.

I peeled the foil off the end of the Mentos pack and prised two out, one for each of us. My ears registered the tinny crackle of Sweeney issuing yet another of the Hazard Alerts he was famous for: '. . . and most importantly, make sure you do not under any circumstances . . .'

As I sucked my Mento my eyes slid of their own accord to the end of the front bench, where the early morning sunlight slanted in. There she sat, chin resting on one loosely curled fist, gazing dreamily into middle-distance. Her lips were parted to reveal a glimpse of pearly teeth. A tendril of hair caught the sunlight like the purest filament of gold.

Katie Wood.

A year ago we'd been best mates. Then things changed.

Katie changed — transformed overnight into this other-worldly creature who made my heart behave as if it was linked to a pacemaker on steroids. For a while — though now that seemed impossible to believe — I'd hoped . . . but not for long. Along came reality in the form of Jordan Archer, with his swagger and car and careless drawl: 'a walking, talking chick magnet', as Mike ruefully put it, that no chick — especially Katie — was capable of resisting.

It all seemed light-years ago. This Katie was on a different planet — in a different solar system — from me, and I could barely remember how things had been before. The easy friendship; the shared chocolate bars; the secret bird-call we'd used to summon each other to the fence; the casual touches I'd never even noticed. If she touched me now it would burn my skin like a brand. But the days when Katie touched me, even acknowledged I existed, were long gone. Would I have had the courage to invite her to something like the Valentine's Ball, even way back then? I didn't know. It didn't matter. Because now one thing was for sure. Katie would be going with Jordan. They were an item.

I was used to it. I'd even finally managed to convince myself I didn't care. Katie was history, and I'd moved on. But now, watching her dreaming in the sunshine with that tiny smile on her perfect lips, I felt a sudden stab of pain.

I wrenched my eyes away, reached for the soda bottle and ripped off the lid with a savage twist. Back to business! We had a science experiment to do. The Mentos were already open; with a fluid motion worthy of Einstein himself I upended the whole lot into the open neck of the soda bottle, only half-registering Mike's expression of horror before there was a massive *WHOOSH!* and the world erupted, drenching everything and everyone in the lab in a super-charged explosion of flying fizz.

Partners

Beattie lowered me to the ground with a thump. 'So,' she said, 'what have you decided to do?'

Beattie, my climbing partner, was the best belayer around. It wasn't often she lost focus and dumped me in a heap on the floor — in fact I couldn't remember it ever happening before.

I picked myself up and gave her an injured look. 'Dunno. Like I was saying before, it isn't easy. There are girls around, but I don't know any of them well enough to . . . you know. And now there's only a week to go. I'm getting desperate.' I was talking to the back of Beattie's head, bent over her 8-knot. What was going on? We were constantly swapping goss on our two schools, scummy old Greendale High and swank Oriole Girls where Beattie went, and she'd been following the ongoing saga of the Valentine's Ball closely. So why wasn't she listening? I took a breath to ask her, and tackle the subject of my undignified dumping while I was at it — and suddenly my breath whoofed out and my mind flooded with blinding white light like Archimedes when he discovered the Principle of Displacement and raced outside butt-naked to tell the world. I'd had a revelation.

'Beattie,' I croaked, hardly able to believe it was true, 'I've just realised: you're a girl!'

'So,' I told Mike at photography club next day, 'it looks like my problem's solved. I'm taking Beattie. She isn't really what I'd call the *formal* type . . .' A sudden image of Beattie, small, dark and self-contained, popped into my mind. The first time I saw her she'd reminded me of a troll; now, picturing her as Michael would see her, she made me think of a beetle — practical, efficient, made-to-measure for the job at hand. The fact that for Beattie the job was climbing, not dancing, was something I'd try to ignore. 'But she's coming. So that just leaves you.'

'No it doesn't.' Mike was loading a new film, having more trouble than usual by the look of it. 'I'm sorted.'

'You've found someone? Who?'

'Tildy.'

'Tildy? Who the heck's Tildy?'

Mike's ear and the slab of cheek I could see turned a mottled radish-colour. 'Ballisha Hump,' he said indistinctly.

'What?'

He turned to face me, eyes glittering dangerously. 'Matilda Bunt,' he said, very slowly and clearly, articulating every syllable with exaggerated care.

I stared at him, the cogs in my brain making a ghastly grinding sound as they struggled to process this new piece of information. Matilda Bunt? Beattie was Paris Hilton compared to Matilda Bunt. Matilda was in our class, as much part of the furniture as the desks. She was dumpy, plain and almost completely silent, with thick glasses. She wore a shapeless second-hand blazer like a protective coat of armour, even in the height of summer. She had reddish-brown crinkly hair worn in a lumpy plait and spent every break in the library — alone, as far as I knew.

To the best of my knowledge Mike had never exchanged a single word with her.

At last, with a shudder and a shriek of metal, my brain ground back into action and processed the odd, defiant expression in my best mate's eyes.

I cranked my mouth closed and stretched it into a grin. 'Smooth move, Hot-shot! Looks like we won't have to dance with each other after all.'

The fact that I was only taking Beattie meant I could relax and enjoy myself. Still, I felt like a prize idiot as I stood in front of Mum's full-length mirror surveying myself gloomily. 'It's too tight,' I grumbled, tugging at the collar of my shirt. 'And the jacket's way too small — like a straitjacket. I won't be able to breathe, let alone dance. And the tie's all wrong.'

'You're nervous, Pippin. Stop hyperventilating.' Mum's face, reflected in the mirror, wore a crooked little smile. On her hip was Madeline, resplendent in saggy pyjamas, eyeing me distrustfully.

'Biffin mart,' she offered doubtfully.

'For your information, Philip McLeod, you look one hundred and ten per cent drop-dead gorgeous,' said Mum in her firmest don't-you-dare-argue-with-me voice. 'You'll have a wonderful time. Your first proper dance is a milestone — unforgettable.' Well, she had that right. She reached up and gave me a kiss, Madeline cringing away as if I was red-hot. Normally I'd have given my baby sister a hug, or blown air into her neck with the fart-sound that made her chortle with delight, but I could read the signs. If I got any closer I'd unleash The Shriek, Madeline's supersonic weapon against the world — and then the house would disintegrate around our ears and I wouldn't be going anywhere.

'Find Dad and tell him you're ready to go. And,' the no-nonsense note intensified, sending warning signals arcing through my brain, 'give Beattie this.'

'*No!* Mum, please no.'

Mum gave me a look. She was holding out a waxy flower with a pin stuck through it — so Beattie could stick it on her dress, I realised. Dress? Till now I'd imagined her wearing baggy old cargo pants . . .

Reality tightened like a noose round my neck.

I reached out and took the flower. 'Dad,' I croaked, 'I'm ready to go.'

But when Beattie walked through the door of her lounge she wasn't wearing the cargo pants, and I realised Mum's flower was right after all. She was still Beattie, but a Beattie I hadn't suspected existed. She'd had her fringe cut kind of ragged-looking as if Muddle'd had a go at it with Mum's pinking shears, and beneath it her eyes glowed in a way I'd never seen before. Nerves, I guessed. She had on a dress the colour of squished-up strawberries, with straps like ribbon noodles. Her bare arms were smooth and tanned. Staring at her, I thought: *If you asked me whether this girl could make it to the top of the Morning After, hardest climb in the Igloo, I'd say* No way! *But I'd be wrong.*

If Beattie was a surprise, Matilda Bunt was a total eye-opener. I should have guessed something was up when Mike met me outside the auditorium with a swagger and a sheepish grin, and when I saw his partner I thought he'd changed his plans at the last second.

Then I saw it was Matilda. Gone were the thick specs; because she wasn't crashing into things I guessed she must have contact lenses. Her hair was piled up on her head with corkscrew bits dangling down the side like one of Madeline's picture-book princesses. All the bits of Matilda Bunt that had seemed lumpy under the shapeless old blazer didn't look lumpy at all . . . and I realised what the protective armour was for.

For a horrible moment I thought we were going to go through the entire evening all staring dumbly at one another unable to think of a single word, but the band struck up and the mosaic globe in the centre of the ceiling began to turn and the bubble of glass we were all treading so awkwardly inside blew apart and we were pulling the girls onto the dance floor and laughing and I knew Mum was right: my first dance was going to be an experience I'd never forget.

The seniors

That's how it was, almost right to the very end.

We talked and laughed and guzzled enough Coke to send us into orbit. I danced with Beattie and Beattie danced with Mike and I danced with Tildy and Tildy danced with Beattie; Mike and I stopped short of dancing with each other, but only just — it was that kind of crazy night where anything went and everything was cool.

I didn't even realise what was missing. Or who.

I'd known the seniors had organised some kind of before-party. Nick was going with Barney and a bunch of other mates; when I'd asked him about a partner he muttered something about 'kids' stuff . . . cooler to just hang out'. Mum teased him gently about it, calling his group the 'bachelor herd' as if they were wild animals, but let it drop when she saw he wasn't in the mood.

I don't know what time they finally arrived. By then the hall was a disaster area, steamy with hundreds of wildly gyrating bodies, littered with crushed paper cups and chewing-gum wrappers, the air almost opaque with the accumulated sound-waves of four solid hours of hard-out music. My ears were ringing, my eyes were stinging and my feet felt numb, but my brain was singing and I was ready to party all night.

We were near the end of a dance called the Chattanooga Choo Choo — a long train gallumphing round the dance floor — when the double doors at the end of the hall flipped open on a gust of icy air. The seniors. In the time it took them to survey the scene and advance slowly and in some cases rather unsteadily into the room, all the fun and laughter drained away. What had been a blast before seemed silly and childish. Everyone made way, shuffling their feet, leaving a little no-man's-land of space round the seniors' group. I looked for Nick but didn't see him; for Katie, Jordan Archer . . . and then the band struck up again.

They'd played it once already, to a riotous reception and pleas for an instant encore; the band leader had promised it for later, with a grin. Now later had come: time for 'The Birdie Song'. Before, we'd hammed it up and laughed so hard we could barely stand, mirroring the actions of the lead singer, but now everyone except a few juniors backed off or headed for the wreckage of the drinks table.

Then a tall, broad-shouldered figure sauntered up to the stage. Jordan. The lead singer hunkered down to talk to him, then crossed to the band and exchanged a few words. I caught a glimpse of Jordan's face as he came back towards us; there was a sleek, self-satisfied expression on it that reminded me of one of Mum's sayings: 'the cat that ate the cream'.

The band struck up again, but this time the music was different. I knew the song — you couldn't not. It was on the radio 24/7: 'Girl of My Dreams', by Dark Angel. One of those smoochy, slow numbers with twangy notes that send shivers down your spine and bass tones that turn your bones hollow. I took a breath to suggest a drink — not that I wanted one. I wanted to watch Jordan and Katie . . . and at the same time I didn't. But Mike and Tildy were heading back into the fray, Mike holding Tildy's wrist, neither of them looking at the other, and what had been a fray moments ago was settling to a swaying expanse of bodies, moving with a completely different rhythm.

Beattie was watching me, eyes very bright. Even in those few seconds the music had seeped into my blood and was doing strange things, making me want to hold that crushed-strawberry close. We pushed our way through till we found an island of space and Beattie moved into my arms.

I'd never held a girl before. I wasn't sure where to put my hands. My heart was swelling inside me with a mixture of horror and something close to bliss. It was only Beattie. The stuff her dress was made of was as soft as one of Madeline's plush toys . . . but I didn't want to think of Madeline now. I hadn't realised how much taller than Beattie I was; her bent head was glossy and dark, and I could feel her breath on my neck. My tie was way too tight. I could smell a faint scent of apples in her hair, and beneath it a deeper note of something musky, like flowers in sunshine. My feet shuffled in a small circle, the only space we had. Hoping Beattie wouldn't notice, I took a shallow, unsteady breath.

And then I saw them.

Jordan's face had a smooth, swollen look, and his eyes were shut. His head was bent, nuzzling Katie's bare neck. And Katie . . . whatever she was wearing was held up by magic. It was the colour of electricity or the dark part of lightning, slinky and sinuous, shimmering as she swayed. Her head was tilted as if she was listening to some secret music the rest of us couldn't hear, the dapples of light from the silver globe drifting over her like snowflakes.

I stared, transfixed.

The crush of bodies between us shifted and parted. Now I could see that Katie's dress plunged in a deep V to where her back ended and the curve beneath it began. Jordan's hand was on that curve, pulling her tight against him. I wasn't turning now. I was shifting foot-to-foot, staring. As I watched, Jordan's other hand moved up to the soft fall of her hair and twisted itself into it like a rope. Katie was facing me again now, her eyes distant and unfocused. Then her gaze shifted and for a second our eyes met. Hers were deep as night, and there was something in them so foreign it made me flinch.

Rocking from foot to foot, oblivious of Beattie standing stiffly in my arms, I watched as Jordan pulled Katie's head back and his open mouth came down over hers like a shark.

Then Beattie was somehow outside the circle of my arms. I blinked, took a half-step back — and that's when it came, from nowhere: a left hook that caught me smack in the eye and knocked me flat on the floor with the spat-out gum and crumpled tissues.

I lay there stunned, shock and silver spangles of light spinning through my brain as Beattie whirled and marched away, the expanse of shocked faces parting for her like the Red Sea.

Katie Wood

I don't remember how I got out of the hall. All I remember is a mosaic of faces, bright against the darkness, staring, whispering, sniggering . . .

I stumbled to the boys' toilet and shouldered my way in. It was empty. I slammed into a cubicle, locked the door and leaned against it. My heart was turning over with a slow, sickening roll that echoed in my head, as if my eyeball was being slowly pumped up. For once, my brain had been shocked into silence — a hollow, ringing silence louder than a shout. I knew I'd done something terrible, unforgivable, but I didn't know what. I should go after Beattie, apologise, explain . . .

I couldn't. Staring at the stained wall, the oozing cistern, I kept seeing Katie's eyes slowly closing, her soft lips opening to Jordan's probing tongue.

Vomit surged in my throat. I clunked to my knees on the puddled floor, cradling the toilet rim. Spewed into the bowl, closing my eyes to the soggy paper and unflushed turds.

Dimly I heard the door bang open and wheeze shut. There was the flare of a match and the tang of sulphur, then smoke, deep voices, a bass burp. 'Ah, man, I needed that!' A voice I'd know anywhere. Him. I froze, hugging the bowl.

'Archer, you're an animal!'

There was a muttered response, followed by hoots of laughter. The rasp of a fly being lowered, then a gush of liquid like a camel pissing that went on and on.

'So: reckon you'll get lucky tonight, Arch?'

'Me, I'm lucky every night.'

'C'mon, you know what I mean. Man, she's one hot chick.'

'Not too hot for me to handle.'

'So what's the score?'

'Score?'

'Yeah — with Katie Wood.'

'With Katie? D'ya *really* wanna know?'

In slow motion I lowered myself to the filthy floor, slumping back against the door. Before I closed my eyes I saw a snake of smoke curl over the top of the door as if it was peering in at me.

I didn't want to know, but Jordan was going to tell me anyway.

'Let's just say this,' he drawled, 'it isn't Katie *Wood*; it's Katie *Does*.'

I realised my fists were clenched, my teeth clenched so tight they might splinter. I wanted to fling the door open and pound Jordan Archer's pretty face to pulp, but I didn't. I stayed where I was and prayed they wouldn't realise I was there. He was bigger than me, he had his friends with him, and I smelled of vomit.

So I sat there quiet as a mouse till at long, long last I heard the hiss of butts dropped into water, a final thunderous fart, and the sound of the door squeaking open and sighing shut behind them.

It was only after they'd gone that I realised there were tears on my cheeks.

Women

The second the truck lurched to a stop in our driveway I slid out and slunk into the house. Lights were blazing everywhere; Dad wasn't someone who tiptoed around, even at midnight. Behind me the front door slammed shut, the key rattling in the lock.

I'd hoped to make it to my room without bumping into Mum, but no such luck. Her face, smudged with sleep, sharpened to instant alert when she saw me. 'Pip! Whatever's happened?'

I pulled away, turning my face to the wall. 'Everything's fine. I just . . .'

'It's far from fine,' growled Dad. 'The boy's been up to something and he won't say what. Look at the state he's in. That girl — Beattie — pasted him one and went off home on her own, God knows how. *Or* why. But I'll —'

'Jim, enough.' Mum's voice, normally so gentle, could cut like a Samurai sword. Dad stomped off to bed, muttering. Without another word Mum shepherded me to my room and moments later I found myself tucked up in bed in my pyjamas, a bag of frozen peas pressed to my eye and a hot-water bottle warming my toes. Mum moved quietly round the room in the soft light from the bedside lamp, picking up my clothes. If she noticed the state they were in she didn't comment.

When everything was tidy she came across to me, took the peas away and brushed my hair off my forehead, the way she used to when I was little. 'Want to talk, Pippin?' I shook my head. What could I say? She took a breath, then gave me a tiny smile. 'Whatever it is,' she told me, 'it will seem better in the morning.'

But it didn't. Nor the next day, or the next. Because every day that passed took me closer to climbing training, when I'd be seeing Beattie again.

Tuesdays and Thursdays were climbing nights. Neither Beattie nor I had missed a single session I could remember, but this Tuesday five o'clock came and went, and Beattie didn't arrive.

'Looks like you're without a partner too, Fraser,' said Rob cheerfully. 'You and Phil team up today, OK?'

My mouth felt dry. 'What about Beattie?' I muttered, trying to sound offhand.

Rob shot me a narrow look. 'Didn't she tell you? She phoned earlier to say she's out of action for a day or two. Bruised hand, apparently.' His ice-blue gaze flicked to my eye and away again.

Rob would never ask. And ironically, that made him the single person in the entire universe I could possibly bear to tell.

Rob Gale was the coolest person I knew. He was lean and stringy and somehow ageless, with dirty-blond dreads and a stud earring and a wide mouth set in a self-mocking twist that stretched into an infectious grin. In all the time I'd known him he'd never come close to losing his cool; he seemed to exist in a dimension a degree removed from the rest of the world. Stuff that would leave a normal person gutted and writhing on the ground had a way of somehow sliding by Rob, as if he was surrounded by an invisible

21

barrier that made him untouchable. He was into Eastern philosophy and meditation and stuff like that; you could imagine him alone on a mountain somewhere, living on watery sunshine and a single grain of rice a day. If you told Rob you were a mass murderer on the run from Interpol he'd look at you with those faraway eyes and smile his crooked smile and say, 'Oh, yeah?'

So after training I hung around a bit and asked if he needed help with anything. 'You could put these up for me,' he said, handing me a sheaf of notices.

I mooched over to the notice board in the corridor, flipping through them as I went. There was a list of gear for sale and a couple of ads for climbing buddies, then an official-looking notice headed CLOSURE OF CLIMBING GYM that sent my heart into free fall till I read on: *The Igloo will be closing temporarily for upgrading . . . improvements to the existing climbing walls, as well as the addition of a new gallery-style café, the* Crag & Cornice . . .

My face cracked into a grin. This'd be the Igloo's answer to the swank new climbing gym, Summit, that had opened across town. Jordan Archer — a climber too, and a good one, much as I hated to admit it — had decamped there with his cronies the minute it opened its doors, on the principle that 'new and expensive' had to equal 'better'. But they didn't have Rob Gale, and we did. The Igloo didn't need to install a new café to make me stay, and anyhow, the improvements to the climbing walls interested me more. Dad always said competition was a healthy thing, though he said it less often now the new supermarket had taken away half his milk run customers.

Next came a job ad on the Igloo letterhead for a Fair Play Coordinator . . . and last of all something that brought me to a complete standstill. My eyes skidded over the words while my poor old brain stumbled along behind, battling to take them in.

UIAA-ICC World Youth Climbing Championships

National trials for the team touring to the UIAA-ICC
World Youth Climbing Championships will be held in March
this year. The most prestigious competition in the world
for youths and juniors will take place at the National Rock
Climbing Centre of Scotland in the Adventure Centre Ratho . . .

'Finished?'

Wordlessly I held the notice out to Rob. 'Oh,' he said casually — though there was a glint in his eyes that was anything but casual — 'I thought that might interest you. I know you've set your sights on making the Highlands team, but this is a whole notch higher. We'll be looking at country-wide talent, and I know you don't like to feel pushed.'

Pushed? 'Do I stand a chance?' My whole being latched onto the idea like one of those dogs that grab hanging tyres with their teeth and dangle there for days. '*Do I?*'

Rob looked down at me, eyes narrowed appraisingly. 'Yeah, you stand a chance. The trial will be informal anyhow, low-key and cruisey — very much your style. Good experience for you and Beattie either way.'

'Beattie . . .' I croaked.

Rob said nothing.

I told him everything.

'I don't even know what I did,' I finished miserably.

'Women,' said Rob, shaking his head. 'I don't pretend to be an expert, but I'd say maybe it's not a question of what you did, but what you didn't do.'

'Huh?'

'Exactly.'

'So what do I do now?'

Rob shrugged. 'What can you do? Only one thing, and you know what that is as well as I do.'

Thursday rolled round with sickening slowness. My eye felt better; the swelling had gone down, and the size was almost normal. But it looked worse: green and purple, as if the skin was rotting.

She was already there when I arrived, back to the door, pulling on her climbing shoes. I walked towards her like someone wading through treacle. Squatted down beside her and cleared my throat.

'Beattie . . .'

Her head whipped round so fast I half expected it to fall off. 'What.'

'Beattie, I'm sorry.'

'Sorry?' she snapped. 'What for? I'm the one who should be *sorry* — for being fool enough to go to the damn dance with you in the first place!'

She jumped up as if she had springs in her legs and crossed over to the bouldering wall, swarming up it like a spider.

After what felt like a long time I took a painful, shuddering breath. Out of the corner of my eye I could see Rob fiddling with ropes by the Midnight Run. At the same moment our heads turned and our eyes met, our shoulders lifting in a helpless shrug.

Women.

Brothers

After the milk run on Friday Dad and I headed to the Igloo to pick up Nick, who worked there after school as a soccer umpire. The Igloo wasn't only a climbing gym, it was a massive indoor sports complex with soccer, cricket and netball, a bowling alley and even an indoor pool. Something for everyone, even Madeline, who'd started going to a toddlers' Gymboree with Mum two mornings a week.

Mum must have had a word with Dad about the dance; he hadn't mentioned it again, contenting himself with giving me dark looks from under his eyebrows occasionally, but I was used to that. Today I sensed something else was on his mind; never chatty, he was more silent than usual while we did our rounds, his hands clenched on the steering wheel so tight I thought it would crack.

The digital clock read 7:58 when we pulled up in the parking lot. By 8:02 Dad was starting to fidget; 8:05 and he was shifting impatiently in his seat, making the milk float rock like a ship on a stormy sea. At 8:08 the muttering started, and two minutes later Dad exploded into action. 'This is ridiculous! We'll go and find him. And when we do . . .'

I bobbed along in Dad's wake like a tugboat as he ploughed through the waves of chattering kids at his usual breakneck pace, his limp doing nothing to slow him down. We headed for the court where Nick usually reffed, but instead of my brother's dark hair and craggy Dad-clone features there was a rounder, blonder guy, frowning anxiously as he hovered on the edges of the action with his whistle at the ready. Dad's frown darkened several shades; without breaking stride he forged on down the corridor towards the climbing gym — the one place Nick would never be. I was about to call him back when a familiar figure caught my eye. Nick, on Court 3 — the one they called Wembley — playing, not reffing. As I watched he pirouetted on his heel, feinted left and right, then dodged past the defender and smashed the ball into the goal, to whoops and high fives from his team-mates. Instinctively I checked over my shoulder. Dad wasn't going to like this, not one tiny bit — eight o'clock meant eight o'clock in his language, especially when he was hanging out for his dinner.

Dad was standing in front of the notice board, hands deep in his pockets, scowling. 'I've found him, Dad.'

'What? Who?'

Surely Dad couldn't find the contents of the notice board so fascinating he'd forgotten what he was here for? 'Nick,' I reminded him warily. I expected him to wheel on me in typical Dad-rant mode, reminded of Nick's lateness and taking it all out on me, but he didn't. Instead he lumbered round slowly, brow furrowed. 'Nick?' he repeated, as if dredging the name up from some dim and distant past. 'Oh, yes . . . Nick. Well, come on then, Son.'

Even when I pointed out Nick's scarecrow figure whirling about on Wembley like a dervish, Dad seemed unnaturally calm. 'Having a game, is he?' he grunted. 'Might as well watch, I suppose — but he'd better not be long. Your mother will have dinner waiting.'

Less than five minutes later Nick pushed his way over, sweaty-faced and grinning ear-to-ear. 'Sorry,' he said. 'They asked me at the last minute — one of their team's pulled out for the season. Five–one — not bad, huh? And I scored four of 'em!'

I'd've been grounded for life, but Nick was always able to get away with murder where Dad was concerned. And if it had to do with sport — especially soccer — Nick was on extra-solid ground. He was everything I wasn't: physical, aggressive, and, as Dad told anyone who'd listen, 'with more talent in his left toe than I ever had, even in my hey-day'. Which was Dad-speak for 'before my accident' — the accident that put paid to his career as a fireman, and taking part in active sport ever again.

Though some people — me for one — would call the way Dad carried on at soccer matches too active by half: his over-the-top 'encouragement' from the sidelines had destroyed any enjoyment I'd ever had for the game, and come close to wrecking our relationship. But all that was over now: I'd discovered climbing, a non-sport in Dad's book, and Dad had Nick, the soccer paragon, to focus on. This season I'd taken the final step of giving up soccer for photography club on Saturdays, ruling me out of the sporting equation completely where Dad was concerned.

Now I sat forgotten in the back seat while Dad and Nick dissected the game and analysed the players. 'So anyhow,' finished Nick with the elaborate casualness I knew heralded a blind-sider, though Dad seemed oblivious, 'I said I'd join the team, if you don't mind shelling out four bucks a week and picking me up those few minutes later.'

Any other reason and that four bucks would have been a king's ransom, the 'few minutes' the time-span from the Big Bang to the present day. But this was Nick, and sport. 'Good idea,' agreed Dad. 'It'll help your outdoor soccer too — build a parallel set of skills. I don't mind watching now and again.' Just try to stop him, I thought. Anything that might help Nick's quest — *Dad's* quest — to make the Highlands soccer team, and Dad would be right there on the sideline cheering him on. And Nick was almost there. Six months ago he'd been chosen for the elite Zone Team, and all summer he'd been training — in the special $250 hardground boots there was suddenly money enough to buy — with the rest of the hand-picked squad. A tournament had been held over the holidays; based on the performances there, the Highlands team was about to be selected, the letters of confirmation due any day now.

With Nick's usual luck, the question of joining an indoor soccer team couldn't have come at a better time.

'So,' said Dad, as we pulled into Contour Terrace, 'what's the team called, then?'

There was a second's hesitation before Nick replied. '*Hoof*,' he said, very slowly and distinctly, '*Hearted*. The teams all have real wacky names, Dad.'

'Wacky?' growled Dad. 'That's completely meaningless! You should have a proper name, like . . . *The Champions* or something. But *Hoof Hearted*? It's ridiculous!'

Nick was staring set-faced out of the window. Watching him, I saw his face give a convulsive twitch; then he gave a sudden snort, as if he was suppressing a sneeze.

'*Hoof Hearted*,' Dad was muttering as he opened the door. '*Hoof Hearted* indeed! We'll see what your mother has to say . . .'

The door finally slammed behind him, and Nick and I exploded. It was a long time before we dared hobble — with aching sides and streaming eyes — after Dad into the house. It had been a long time since the two of us had laughed together like that, like little kids. It felt good.

If I'd known what was ahead, I'd have hung on to it a lot tighter.

Two letters

To hear Dad, you'd have thought Mum would be pacing up and down in the kitchen brandishing a cleaver demanding to know what had kept us so long. But she was snuggled in her favourite chair in the lounge with Madeline on her lap, reading her a story. Mostly she read Madeline picture books, but recently she'd started reading her proper stories, fairy tales I remembered from when I was small. 'Isn't she too little to understand that, Mum?' Nick had asked once.

Mum just smiled. 'You're never too young for stories,' she told him, 'even if it's just the rhythm of the language she's absorbing.' Mum was an English teacher long ago, so she knew about that kind of stuff. And she was right: Madeline loved story-time, no matter what Mum read.

. . . the old woman sat on the porch in her rocking chair surrounded by the scent of roses. But her face was as sour as a lemon. 'Oh, what a pity! What a pity, pity, pity!' she complained. 'To think I have to make do with a tumbledown hovel like this! I should be living in a smart new house with lace curtains at the windows and a shiny brass knocker on the door!' Mum glanced up and smiled. 'Dinner in five minutes, Pippin. Put those socks away, would you?' *. . . The fairy was surprised. She would have liked a cosy little cottage to live in, instead of flying east and west, west and east her whole life long . . .*

I scooped up the pile of socks — five of them, rolled neatly into balls — and took them to my room, juggling them absent-mindedly on the way. One-two-three-four flew onto my bed; I stood frowning at the fifth. It was bigger and bulkier than the rest, and though it also smelled of Rain Forest fabric softener, I found myself wrinkling my nose. Nick's training socks. I took a breath to yell 'Nick! Come get your smelly socks!' But I could hear the shower running and I figured it wouldn't kill me to put them in his room this once.

As always, the door was wide open and it looked like an atom bomb had gone off inside. Clothes were strewn everywhere, rumpled socks, muddy shoes and shin pads fighting for floor-space with old towels, water bottles and kit bags. My room wasn't tidy, but it wasn't a tip like Nick's. Mum said our rooms were our business: we could keep them how we liked, as long as she wasn't expected to clean up after us. Dad took a different view, but then Dad would.

There was no way I was going in there — I'd vanish without a trace. I tossed Nick's socks onto his unmade bed, narrowly missing Horace's nose. Horace was the real head of an actual stag Nick shot on a hunting trip with Dad the year he turned 14, the age I was now. Dead as a doornail, stuffed and mounted on the wall, he gazed down at the shambles on the floor, a long-suffering look on his face. A pair of Nick's bright red Liverpool boxers dangled from one antler giving him a festive air, like one of Santa's reindeer.

I headed for the kitchen, suddenly aware that I was starving. Friday night was takeaway night for most of my friends, but not for us — especially now, with money a bit tight. Situation normal. I peered into the oven. Five fat golden pasties, one each, a corner for Madeline, and the rest of hers for Dad and Nick to argue over, though I knew who'd win.

Nick slammed in, instantly taking up more than his fair

share of space, oxygen and attention: 'If I had a cellphone I coulda let you know, but seeing as I don't — yum! Pies! So that's where the leftover stew went!' No leftovers were safe from Nick — he'd eat cold stew, soup, pasta, anything he could find straight out of the container, so long as Dad wasn't around to catch him.

I turned to the table — and then I saw it. I couldn't believe it had been there all that time without me noticing. A rectangular white envelope smack in the middle of my place-mat, doing handsprings and cartwheels and chirping 'Look at me! Look at me! Open me now, quick, before I self-destruct!'

But Nick's voice drowned it out. 'Well, how's about that! My letter's arrived — the final nod from Highlands Soccer!'

That's when I realised my envelope wasn't the only one on the table.

'Well, come on, open it! Don't keep us in suspense!' said Dad, making a grab for Nick's envelope. Nick snatched it away, laughing, backing off with it held high above his head. 'Oh no you don't, Dad — this is *my* moment of glory!'

'I don't suppose you could save your letters till after you've eaten,' said Mum.

Nick thumped down into his chair, hacked off a crispy corner of pie and shoved it in his mouth, then slid the greasy knife into the slit of his envelope and ripped. 'I can read and eat,' he said indistinctly. 'It's called multi-tasking.'

'Don't talk with your mouth full — and read that damn letter!' barked Dad. 'We haven't got all night!'

'Read tory *now!*' chipped in Madeline, banging on her high-chair table with her spoon.

'Yeah, read your letter, why don't'cha,' I muttered.

'Damn right I will, baby bro!' Nick's face was flushed with excitement, his damp hair sticking up haywire as if he'd been electrocuted, eyes blazing electric-blue like a circuit shorting. 'Listen up, sportsfans!' He cleared his throat, grinning round at us, then deepened his voice, put on a posh accent like a sports commentator, and began to read.

Highlands Soccer Union, yaadee yaadee yaa . . . *Dear Nicholas, thank you for your participation in the recent zone tournament. The high standard this year has made the selection of a 16-strong squad to represent the Highlands Region exceptionally difficult.*

Your physio-something *maturity, technical skills and tactical understanding of the game were noted by the selectors. As with any developing player, there is always scope for further improvement, in your case the adoption of a less individual focus, leading to a more holistic approach to what is in essence a team game* . . . 'What bollocks — sorry, Mum.'

The Highlands Soccer Union has identified you as a player with significant promise, and further opportunities will undoubtedly open to you in the future. However . . .'

'However?' echoed Dad.

Nick's face slammed shut. His eyes went flat as stones, his cheeks grainy-grey.

He grated his chair back and stood, as if he was struggling to find his balance in a world that was suddenly upside-down. Somehow he made it to the door, walking slowly and deliberately, the way I always imagined a sleepwalker would, and out.

But before he went he looked at Dad. The strangest, apologetic, almost furtive glimmer of a glance, like a little boy who'd done something wrong and didn't want to be found out.

But Dad didn't see. He was staring down at the letter, his face wiped clean of any expression at all.

The Old Woman
in the Vinegar Bottle

I lay on my bed with the door closed, my envelope in my hand. The life had gone out of it: it was just a normal piece of paper now, content to wait till I was ready to open it, however long that took.

I felt sorry for Nick — of course I did. But I felt sorry for me, too. Deep down, I felt angry. And deep, deep down — with a part of me I didn't even want to admit existed — I felt glad.

And ashamed.

I tore the envelope open and pulled the letter out. It was on a letterhead I hadn't seen before, headed Highlands Regional Sportclimbing Federation.

Dear Phil, it said: *It is with great pleasure that I am writing to advise you of your selection to represent the Highlands Region in the upcoming National Cup Series. As you may be aware* . . .

My eyes stuck there and wouldn't go any further. They wouldn't go past that first sentence: *It is with great pleasure that I am writing to advise you of your selection to represent the Highlands Region in the upcoming National Cup Series.*

This was it. I'd done it.

It would be me who'd be travelling round the country to compete, me who'd be billeted with strange families in places I'd never been before, my name Dad would be casually dropping into conversations with his friends: 'Of course, Pip — Phil — is away right now on the National Tour'; 'See that boy there? Phil knows him from the Highlands team'; 'Phil's climbing has come on a blue streak since he was selected for the Highlands team — and you know, there's a lot more to that sport than you'd think . . .' Even Mum would be in on it; I could just hear her over the fence to Mrs Wood: 'I wash Pip's Highlands track suit separately in cold water . . .'

Me, not Nick.

This was the moment I'd been dreaming of since that long-ago first climb up the Midnight Run. The goal I'd set myself, without even realising it at first, had been reached.

So why did I have such a strange feeling of emptiness?

There was a tap on the door and Mum popped her head round. 'Sweetheart?' In she came and perched on the edge of the bed; looked at the letter, open in my hand, and crinkled up her eyes in a smile. 'What does it say?'

'I've made the Highlands climbing team.'

'The Highlands team? What an achievement! Dad will be so proud of you! And so am I!' She gave me a hug. She was doing all the right things, saying all the words I wanted to hear; but at the same time I had the weirdest feeling Mum was play-acting: that deep down inside, she'd rather it was Nick.

Somehow my moment of triumph had turned to ashes, sifting down round me like nuclear fallout.

'It can be hard to take on board sometimes, can't it?' Mum was saying gently. 'When something you've dreamed of for so long actually happens. It takes time to get used to.'

I wanted to ask, 'Where's Dad? Why hasn't Dad come to ask about my letter?' But I didn't. I already knew the answer.

Mum paused at the door. An expression almost like

embarrassment snuck across her face. 'Oh, and Pippin. . .'

'Don't worry,' I said flatly. 'I won't talk about it in front of Nick.'

The door closed after her, and me and my letter were left alone.

Maybe Mum was right: maybe I just needed time to get used to the idea.

I lay and let my thoughts drift . . . and the story Mum had been reading Madeline bobbed into my brain. It had been one of my favourites when I was little: *The Old Woman in the Vinegar Bottle*. It's about this crotchety old lady who lives in a vinegar bottle, and grouches and groans about it all day long. Then one day along comes a fairy and overhears her, and what d'you know? In the morning the little old lady wakes up in a pretty thatched cottage. You'd think she'd live happily ever after, but no. Two minutes later she's grumbling again: the cottage isn't good enough for her. On it goes till at last she's queen, living in a palace with taps made of solid gold. But even this isn't enough: now she wants to be Empress of the Universe. But finally the fairy's patience has worn out. When the little old lady wakes up next morning, she's back in the vinegar bottle — and it serves her right.

When I was little I used to think the old woman was over-the-top unreasonable. I'd never be like that — not me! But now I knew the truth. I was exactly like her. Here I'd been given my heart's desire — a place on the Highlands team, and the Highlands track top I'd have sold my soul for — and before it was even hanging in my wardrobe I wanted more.

Now I wanted to be picked for the National team to go to the World Youth Climbing Championships in Scotland. I wanted it more than I'd ever wanted anything. And yet I was prepared to bet that before the letter was halfway out of the envelope I'd have dreamed up something new to want — to be Climbing Champion of the Galaxy or something.

And what would my own personal Good Fairy do then?

Suddenly the air in my room smelled stuffy and my news was busting to be told.

I half got up to phone Beattie, and then remembered. So, moving stiffly as an old man rather than with the fluid grace of a Highlands athlete, I mooched off to the deserted kitchen to look for some leftover pie and phone my trusty mate Mike.

The Terrible Twos

I didn't see Dad again till the next day. He had some meeting at the MooZical Milk headquarters in the morning and was already gone by the time I got up; Dairy Industry Executives, as Dad calls himself when he's in a good mood, keep different hours from other people, busy in the early morning and evening, with nothing much in between.

But Dad was busy at lunchtime too. I bumped into him when I was coming in from photography club; he was heading out again, dressed in his best grey slacks and Fire Department tie. I blinked. It was a special day — Madeline's second birthday — but it wasn't like Dad to dress up, or miss lunch.

Dad sometimes reminds me of a secret agent or a spy, coming and going and never saying where, and after 14 years I knew better than to ask. From the look on his face it was clear that whatever happened at the meeting hadn't been good.

We practically collided in the front doorway. I ducked aside to let him out, half-expecting him to ignore me completely. I could feel my heart clench into a cold clump. Mum must have told him my news, but whatever he was doing, wherever he was going, was more important.

But he stopped in mid-stride. I could almost hear the crunch as he forced himself to change mental gear, overdrive into reverse in a single shift that would have left any self-respecting gearbox smoking on the tarmac. He turned to face me, forcing a smile. 'So, Son,' he said gruffly, 'your mother tells me you've been selected for the climbing team. Highlands, eh? Well, that's a turn-up for the books. Pretty damn good. Congratulations.' He held out his hand and we shook. His eyes met mine and held them. I could see pride there, and love . . . and other things too, things I didn't have names for. Something flickered way down deep and for a second I thought he might pull me forward into a hug, but I guessed I was too big for that kind of stuff. Instead he gave a terse nod as if he was clinching some kind of business deal, gave my hand a final bone-crunching squeeze, and turned away.

I heard the birthday girl before I saw her. The Shriek rang through the house, making the windowpanes vibrate and the foundations tremble. I ventured into her room, hands over my ears.

Madeline was an unexpected baby: a girl following on the heels of two boys. And in our family times were always tight. So there were no girlie frills in the cupboard-sized hidey-hole Mum grandly called The Nursery: buttercup-yellow walls, farm-animal curtains from my own babyhood, an old workbench of Dad's as a changing table and a beat-up second-hand cot in one corner, swamped by the cuddly toys us big brothers had thankfully offloaded. But there was a brightly painted frieze of bunnies on the wall, and nursery-rhyme wrapping-paper posters, and sunshine.

In the midst of all this splendour Mum and Madeline were locked in combat.

'Don't be so silly, sweetheart,' Mum was cajoling between the shrieks. 'It's your birthday. You want to be a pretty girl on your special day, don't you? You want to be a party princess?'

'No!' shrieked the party princess, drumming her heels furiously on the bench-top. Her square face was red as a beet, smeared in snot and tears; her black eyelashes prickled out like drowning spider-legs. Every atom of her baby body was rigid with determination. 'No tarty dess!'

She saw me and gave a convulsive heave, dislodging Mum's grip and almost rolling off onto the floor. 'Biffin!' she whimpered pathetically, holding up her chubby arms. 'Biffin uppy tousers!'

My baby sister was the world expert in what Mum laughingly called Power Talking — where you only use the words that are absolutely essential to put your meaning across as forcefully as possible. But Mum wasn't laughing now. She looked worn to a shred.

I reached out my arms and Madeline scrambled into them like a little monkey, wrapping her arms round my neck and glaring at poor Mum. 'Why don't you let her wear trousers if she wants?' I suggested cautiously. 'It is her birthday, after all.'

'I suppose you're right. It's the beginning of the Terrible Twos, right on schedule. It seems wrong to give in to temper tantrums, though — and it is a shame. She wouldn't wear the dress for her toddler party yesterday either, and it wasn't cheap. It's so pretty.' Poor old Mum gave the dress a wistful glance, but personally I agreed with Madeline. I wouldn't have been seen dead in it.

'I'll get her ready if you want,' I offered. 'She can wear her pink T-shirt as a compromise. Hey, Muddle, whaddaya say? Want Biffin to get you ready for your tarty?'

She jounced up and down and chortled. 'Tarty dess poo!' she told me. 'Tarty-poo!'

'Yeah, whatever,' I mumbled with a wary glance at Mum. Madeline had yet to learn the art of gracious victory. Truth was, though, Madeline and I were comrades-in-arms. Right from the very beginning when I'd first clapped eyes on her little face, still crumpled with newness, we'd been on the same side against the world. Even before she said her first power-talk word (which happened to be 'No!') we'd spoken the same language. As far as I was concerned, what Madeline wanted, she got. And my birthday present to her — already wrapped and taking up half the space in my cupboard — was a prime example.

On the first day of the school holidays Nick and I had been packed off to the Fourways Mall for our traditional Christmas shopping expedition. Mum and Dad had a long drive planned — 'some together time, just the two of us,' Mum said romantically, but the worry-lines round her eyes told a different story.

But with fifty dollars from my bank account in my pocket and the prospect of McDonald's for lunch I was way too excited to worry about it. I tagged along behind Nick as he motored from shop to shop, unearthing bargains and sniffing out special deals while I goggled at all the expensive stuff I could sooner fly to the moon than afford.

Nick was Dad's son in every way but one: he'd inherited Mum's Killer Shopping Gene. 'Check this out, baby bro,' he said seconds into the expedition. 'Homer Simpson PJs at half price: *shop soiled*, it says. We'll get Mum to shove them in the wash before we give 'em to Dad, and they'll be good as new. Half price, a joint present — that's a three-quarter saving!'

In no time flat Nick had spent almost all his money and most of mine, making my head spin with his rapid-fire calculations. 'Nearly done!' he announced. 'Just Maddy to go.' He glanced at his watch. 'I'll make it, no problem.'

'Make it?' I echoed blankly. 'Make what?'

'The start of *Sexy Movie Two*,' he said with a devilish grin. 'Starts today, ten o'clock sharp.'

'But . . . but . . .'

'But what? But I'm not eighteen yet? Well,' he said, whipping a credit-card-sized ID from his pocket like a rabbit from a hat, 'according to this I am.'

I recoiled as if it might bite me. I didn't know what to say.

'So . . .' said Nick, scanning the shop fronts, 'what to get for my baby sister . . .' His gaze lit on a table set right in the gangway outside the bookstore. A small crowd had gathered there; a guy a couple of years older than Nick was just starting to hold forth. Nick homed in on it.

'Here we have the perfect gift for the special toddler in your life,' the dude was saying, 'guaranteed to develop creativity and latent artistic ability. Ten pens in an array of attractive colours, with a handy blowpipe. All you do . . .' a flick and a twist, and the pipe was on the end of one of the pens, 'is snap it on like this, and blow . . .' he demonstrated, 'like this . . . and using these state-of-the-art stencils you can create your very own work of art in moments . . .'

'How much?'

The guy looked up, startled. 'Well, I'm just about to — '

'*How much?* I'm on borrowed time here.'

'Well,' said the guy, 'my normal price is . . .' he saw the look on Nick's face and cut to the chase. They were two of a kind, even I could tell that. 'The blow paints plus the finger paints for a fiver.'

'And throw in that demo picture,' said Nick, pointing to one the guy must have done earlier, 'seeing I don't have time to watch.'

41

Meekly the guy handed it over, together with two rubber-banded boxes. 'Free gift wrapping over there,' he said sulkily. He had my brother sussed.

Nick swaggered off towards the gift wrap, smirking back at me over his shoulder. 'Christmas and birthday both,' he gloated, 'done and dusted — and change for popcorn. Maddy won't know the difference between Christmas and birthday paper, will she? Shame I don't have a fake ID for you too. Catch ya later.'

Which was how I'd had all the time in the world to find my own present for Madeline. And once I did, it was too special to give at Christmas, when even our tight-budget family was awash with presents. Way too special.

Like I said, Madeline and I spoke the same language. And I knew there was only one thing in the world Madeline really, truly wanted. She was fixated on them, obsessed, ever since she'd watched me and Nick dicing on the Segas at the games arcade.

Not finger paints or blow paints; not a tricycle or a doll's pram or even a scooter. Not my baby sister Madeline. She wanted a motorbike, and that's what I was giving her.

Closed doors

Madeline's motorbike was made of moulded black plastic, just the right height for her to sit astride and shove along with her feet. It was pretty basic really: plain black, solid-looking and indestructible. But it was unmistakably a motorbike, and when she tore the wrapping off her eyes went round as dinner-plates.

'Mopabite,' she said reverently. Then she plopped down onto the floor and sat and gazed at it.

Seeing she was the birthday girl, there was a respectful pause while everyone watched Madeline watching her motorbike. Then Mum said briskly, 'She's thrilled with it, Pippin. Now, Nick, do you want to give your present?'

'OK,' mumbled Nick. 'Here you go, Maddy.' He held out a rectangular package resplendent in shiny reindeer foil and red ribbon. But Madeline ignored him. Her eyes were still glued to her motorbike; slowly, inch by inch, she was hitching herself closer on her bum.

'She doesn't want my present, Mum,' said Nick.

There was an odd note in his voice that made me wish I'd saved the motorbike for last. 'Hey, Muddle, c'mon — Nick's got a present for you too. Look!'

But Madeline wasn't interested in any of her other presents. In the end Mum unwrapped them all for her while she straddled her motorbike with a look of glazed rapture on her face, rocking from side to side and making a continuous sputtering-engine noise that made spit dribble down her chin in a very un-princesslike way. Any attempt to take her off her 'mopabite' was met by the rising grizzle that heralded The Shriek.

Nick's blow paints, Mum's Baby Doll and Dad's Swingball set were completely ignored. The birthday cake Mum had made specially, cram-jammed with Madeline's favourite raisins, hardly rated a second glance.

I guess I should have been glad she liked it so much — and I was. But I also felt a bit sad for Nick, even though he hadn't taken much trouble over his present. It was as if, without meaning to, Madeline was getting the boot in when Nick was already down from the soccer thing. But he didn't say anything, just sloped off to his room muttering something about studying for his maths test, without even staying for cake.

I figured I'd make up for it by helping Muddle do him a special picture with the blow paints to show how much she liked them. I planned to copy the demo picture to get the hang of the technique. It was a random mish-mash of things that didn't really go together: a penguin in the desert with a Christmas tree and a rainbow, and 'Merry Xmas' across one corner. I'd figured we could change that to 'Thank you', but wouldn't you know, there was no stencil for that.

Adding to my problems, Madeline had promoted herself from Birthday Princess to Birthday Dictator of the Solar System. Whether it was the presents or the fizzy lemonade, an overdose of raisins or the start of the Terrible Twos, she was over-the-top hyped up and hell-bent on getting her own way with everything. First her motorbike had to be balanced on a chair beside her like some kind of imaginary friend. Then she wanted to dabble her fingers in the wet paint, and when finally she got the hang of blowing instead of smearing, she wouldn't let me show her how to use the stencils. 'Mine! *My* bowtaints!' she insisted, grabbing hold of the pen and tugging.

'OK, OK,' I said, letting go before she pulled it in two. 'Now what you do, Madeline, is choose a picture — this cute little penguin —'

'No pendin! Mopabite!'

'Well, yeah, but there isn't a stencil for a motorbike . . .' But I might as well have saved my breath.

After a zillion centuries we managed to produce what I supposed might very loosely be described as a picture, though it looked more like a nuclear explosion to me. Madeline was never one to do things by halves, and blowing down a blow-pen tube was no exception. Her picture was a menacing blend of black, red and blue, blasted onto the paper with explosive force from point-blank range. The colours dispersed outwards in a radiating starburst, the black centre blending to purplish-grey streaked with violent slashes of crimson, and finally to a hazy blue, spattered with a faint spray of spit.

I looked from the demo picture to Madeline's masterpiece and back again. I felt like that guy in the Bible who lived to be nine hundred and something years old.

'Mopabite,' said Madeline smugly.

'Yeah, way to go, Picasso. C'mon, let's go and give it to Nick.'

I hefted her onto my hip and picked up the picture with my free hand, praying she wouldn't insist on the motorbike coming too. Down the passage we went, past Mum and Dad's closed door — I caught the rumble of Dad's voice as we passed, with a pause for Mum's quieter reply — to Nick's room. I'd already drawn a breath to holler at him through the open door — it was months since I'd actually ventured in through all the clutter.

45

But Nick's door wasn't open.

I reached out to knock, but with my mind on not smearing the still-wet paint, I didn't quite get round to it. Instead — not really expecting him to be in there — I thumped once with my elbow, then opened the door a crack and stuck my head round.

Nick was perched on his desk-chair with his back to the door, fiddling with something. 'Nick?' I said.

He jumped as if he'd been shot. His head whipped round; his hands, arms, eyes — everything — flying up and out in an exaggerated fright reflex like a cartoon. Something scattered and fell; then Nick was yelling *'GET OUT OF MY ROOM!'* I stumbled back as if I'd been slapped, feeling stupid tears jump into my eyes. Madeline was wailing, wriggling fit to bust, kicking her feet and squirming to get down; the top corner of the picture had flopped over onto the wet paint and stuck there.

Then I was outside the closed door, as if time had rewound itself and those few seconds had never happened.

Except they had. The picture was wrecked. Madeline was bouncing off the walls like a bumblebee as she stumbled down the passage to Mum. And I was standing there staring at Nick's closed door while the slowly developing after-image of the expression on his face took shape in my mind.

Nick, the same as ever, yet somehow not the same . . . and looming behind him, Horace, the same — and yet for that instant, not the same. Just for that second, poised in dark silhouette above my brother's head, Nick's trophy had shed its cosy familiarity and reverted to what it really was: the severed head of a wild animal, eyes staring, nostrils flared. Had Madeline seen what I had, or was it Nick's reaction that had frightened her?

46

I took a half-breath, a half-step forward to shove the door open and demand to know what the heck he'd yelled like that for; to give him the picture we'd made him, wrecked or not, and tell him I was sorry about his soccer, his present, everything.

But then I gave myself a mental shake. I had nothing to be sorry for. Nick had snapped at me. No big deal: I should have knocked. I'd get over it and so would he. I'd leave him to stew.

Anyhow, I had homework to do.

It was only as I was turning away, shrugging and trying to pretend I didn't care, that I realised the weirdest thing of all.

Nick's room had been completely tidy.

The Highlands team

The first place I headed when I arrived at the Igloo on Tuesday was to the notice board, and sure enough there it was: a classic Rob news-flash, cutting straight to the mustard.

HIGHLANDS SQUAD — U16
Fraser Reid, Beattie Burgess, Phil McLeod (Capt.),
Sasha Kendrick, Lee Powell, Gabriel Chambers
Coach: Rob Gale
Training: Igloo, Thursdays 5 p.m.
Camp: 10–13 March

I couldn't believe it. I was captain — Captain of the Highlands team! And Beattie had made the team as well. Before, that'd have been cause for wild celebration; now I felt a confusing mix of emotions, the strongest of which was gloom. The National Cup Series took place over five competitions throughout the year, each in a different town, which meant the makeup of the teams was vital. If there was anyone you didn't get along with it spelled misery all round. Fraser and Beattie were both Igloo club climbers like me; Fraser was a good mate, but Beattie? I'd heard of Gabriel Chambers: he climbed at the YMCA, and had won last year's Under 14 Regional Champs hands-down. The other names were vaguely familiar, but I couldn't place them. Beattie would know — she'd climbed with most of the juniors, and anyhow, Beattie knew everything.

And the camp — what was that all about? It was scheduled for the long weekend less than a month away. Beattie would know. . .

It all came back to Beattie.

I turned away from the board, my heart — which should have been bouncing along near the ceiling — squelching miserably in the bottoms of my trainers . . . and there she was, surrounded by a gaggle of kids, her face lit up and laughing — the old Beattie, same as she'd always been. My face cracked into a grin and I hurried over. 'Hey, Beat,' I blurted, 'well done on making the team! We —'

The look of polite enquiry on her face made the words stick in my throat like a cork. 'Oh, hello, Phil,' she said, as if she was answering the door to a used-toothbrush salesman. 'Thank you. Well done to you too. I'm sure you'll make an excellent captain.'

She gave the last word an ironic twist, somehow man-aging to make it seem like she was saying 'toilet cleaner'. Gave me a businesslike smile, then turned, walked purposefully across to the nearest wall and started examining the holds like some kind of safety inspector.

It should have been easy to follow her and swing her round, look her in the eyes and say, 'Beattie, lighten up. I'm sorry. For whatever I did — or didn't do.' But I still hadn't figured out exactly what Rob meant, and for some reason the thought gave me a hot, prickly feeling as if I might be about to blush. Uncertainty — and the new void yawning between us — made what should have been easy impossible.

So instead I plastered a big smile on my face and chattered away to the others as if everything was completely normal, hoping Mum's great saying about time healing everything was true.

A flash of something in Beattie's eyes before she turned away had made me worry about being dumped again when she was belaying me — from a dizzy height, this time. I needn't have worried. All afternoon Beattie behaved like a perfectly programmed climbing robot. At first I tried to go along with her pretence that nothing was wrong — even threw pride to the winds and started what I hoped would turn into a conversation. 'So, Beattie,' I said, in tones that even to me sounded unnaturally hearty, 'what's the goss on the rest of the team?'

But it was useless. 'Goss?' she repeated, as if I was talking Outer Mongolian. 'Team?' She stared at me as if I was transforming into some kind of fascinating but repulsive lower life-form, then turned away with a microscopic shrug.

It wasn't me who was transforming, I thought as I made my way up the Undertaker, it was Beattie. I'd always regarded her as one of the guys, open and straightforward, not one of those girls like Katie who seemed to belong to a separate species and kept you looking, feeling and acting like an idiot.

All this time I'd thought Beattie was different, but it looked as if I'd been wrong.

But nothing could stop the rush of excitement as I swung into the gym on Thursday and saw my new team-mates standing in a loose cluster round Rob and his assistant, Cam. Round their feet was an untidy pile of brand-new nylon kit bags, deep forest-green, emblazoned with the words HIGHLANDS CLIMBING TEAM.

Cam was the polar opposite of Rob — dark where he was blond, short where he was tall, chatty and clownish where Rob was still and self-contained. Cam reminded me of a pixie from one of Muddle's story books, with his sooty mop of lambswool hair, snip of a beard and wire-rimmed glasses. Just after Cam joined the Igloo a bunch of us had tried to figure out his accent and ended up asking him. 'I don't have an accent,' he told us. '*You* do. I'm from all over: your original patchwork quilt. Give me a month or two and I'll be sounding just like you guys. Chameleon-man, that's me.' He climbed like a chameleon, too — steady and unstoppable, with a reach that went on forever and hands that gripped rock-solid onto the holds. That's where the nickname had come from — and soon we'd all forgotten what his real name was, if we'd ever known.

'OK, guys, listen up,' Rob was saying. 'I don't want to waste time talking, and I'm sure you don't either. Do we all know each other? I'm Rob, this here's Cam; Phil's captain . . .' I glanced from face to face. They'd be watching to see if I lived up to the position, but I had no worries: I could climb any 15-year-old under the table. A dark, willowy girl in a tight black T-shirt with the horned goat's-head of the Ibexes gave me a faint smile; beside her a boy who must be Lee was glaring back at me, chin lifted and eyes narrowed, his mouth a tight line. He was a chunky-looking redhead, bigger than the rest of us, wearing track pants and a crumpled school gym shirt. I didn't need the badge on the pocket to recognise it: everyone knew the distinctive purple of Churchill Boys' High. I glanced over at Beattie, looking to catch her eye and exchange an unspoken appraisal: *The girl lean and stringy, a steely look in her eyes I liked; the guy not built for climbing, but muscular and strong, with arms like a Neanderthal. And an attitude to match* . . . My thoughts bounced off Beattie's averted head and clunked to the floor.

'And last but not least, Gabriel from the Y.' There were

51

a couple of grins. The YMCA climbers were nicknamed 'The Y-fronts', though of course Cam didn't mention that. Gabriel's eyes, half-hidden under a tangle of brown hair, drifted round the group without much apparent interest, as if he was thinking of something else. Then he turned away to resume his scrutiny of the climbing walls, his eyes travelling smoothly from one hold to the next, his hands unconsciously making those weightless, swimming-under-water movements that meant he was climbing the wall in his mind. I didn't grin like the others. I felt a click of recognition: Gabriel was a born climber, and I didn't need to see him lift one toe off the floor to know it.

'As far as the camp goes, these consent forms,' — Cam waved a sheaf of papers — 'are for your parents to sign, and include indemnities so we're not liable if you fall off a cliff. It's a four-day field trip, Friday to Monday, staying over in luxury at the Rickety Bridge Huts. The Climbing Federation's footing the bill — that's why you're staying in huts instead of the Hazard Hilton.' There was a scatter of laughter. There was no Hazard Hilton — the Hazard Range was a good three hours' drive away, in the middle of nowhere. 'Any questions?'

'What's the climbing like?' Gabriel's eyes had sharpened and focused.

'The emphasis will be on team-building rather than climbing,' Cam said, adding wryly, 'though it would be too much to expect rock spiders like you to go anywhere there's vertical rock and not try to get to the top. Any of you done much trad before?'

'Trad' was short for traditional climbing — the outdoor stuff many hard-core climbers regarded as the real thing, and there was an extra spark in Cam's eyes that made me wonder if he was one of them. Gabriel half-raised one hand

52

in a gesture that could have meant anything, but Lee spoke up, loud and assertive. 'I have. I've done heaps of sport climbing and trad top-roping; also some lead climbing up north. You kids don't know what you're missing. That's what it's all about — when you're first on the rope with only the rock above you. Real rock, not gunite crap.'

Rob and Cam exchanged a glance. 'We're planning to rig a top-rope and give you all a feel for it,' said Rob neutrally, 'but mostly we're just there to have fun and get to know each other better, with a couple of surprises thrown in.

'And now, let's wrap up the chat and see you guys climb. Oh, and there's some stuff for you all — a bag, some bits and pieces of gear . . .' But his words were drowned in the thunder of feet as we dove on the kit like a bunch of crocs in a feeding frenzy.

Then my bag was open and it was there. For a moment I hesitated, then drew it out. It was a moment so huge it was almost holy. Here it was at last, creased with newness, starchy and fresh. The colours were brighter, more vivid than I'd ever imagined. The green of the forest; the purple of the peaks. I could have been alone in the gym . . . could have been in a crowd of people. Nothing else existed. I turned it over so I could read the legend on the back — one word, white as snow against the royal purple: HIGHLANDS. It was mine. Mine to hold, touch, try on, wear . . . get so used to wearing I wouldn't even realise I had it on, or care if I spilled ketchup all down the front.

My Highlands track top.

A breaking wave

'I don't know what Lee's problem is,' I told Mike as we wove our way through the changeover crush to English the following day. 'But one thing's for sure: he's got one. A major one.'

'Maybe not. Could be he's just up himself. Or shy and over-compensating.'

I thought of the look in Lee's eyes; the belligerent set of his jaw; the way he'd searched me out from the top of Spaceboy and given me another dose of that hard stare before signalling Sasha to lower him back to the deck. 'Nah,' I said, 'there's more to it than that.' Deep in my gut I knew exactly what was bugging Lee Powell. He was one of those alpha types who has to be top dog. You see them all the time, everywhere — Dad moans about them on the highway, overtaking in crazy places just because they can't bear to have another car in front. Then Dad catches them up at the lights and gives them the finger.

Lee thought he should be captain of the Highlands team. And I had a sinking feeling he was going to make an issue of it, every step of the way.

'Today,' announced Mrs Holland, 'I want to discuss a subject close to my heart: poetry.' A good-natured groan went up from the class. Everyone liked Mrs Holland. She looked all ruddy-cheeked and ramshackle, but according to Mum she was 'one of those rare teachers with a gift of communicating her passion to her students'. That wasn't quite how I'd have put it, but the bottom line was that we all hurried to English, even last thing on a Friday when we were brain-dead and hanging out for the bell.

'Who would like to tell us what poetry is?'

There was an awkward silence while everyone stared at their desks and hoped they wouldn't get picked to answer.

'Come on, come on, I know it's Friday. Poetry, people: *poetry!* We've studied the various poetic forms, we've read it, we've analysed it, we've loved it . . .'

'We've hated it . . .' came from Shaun Wilson at the back of the class, to a ripple of laughter from the rest of us. But Mrs Holland was delighted.

'Yes! We've hated it! Though hopefully not all of it, Shaun. Come now, ladies and gentlemen: do you really have absolutely no idea at all?'

Shaun again, in his self-appointed role of class wise-guy, his voice cracking into ironic falsetto: 'Sentences that rhyme?'

'Always . . . or sometimes?' Now hands were going up everywhere, like one of those fast-track movies of bean sprouts germinating, and we were off.

After forty minutes of heated discussion we'd realised that agreeing on a single definition was impossible, and the bell was about to ring. The whiteboard was crammed with scrawled suggestions, from Shaun's 'rhyming sentences' to Katie's 'writing that sings'; from the official dictionary definition to Georgia's hesitant 'something that gives you a sort of religious feeling', to the one that reduced the whole class to hysterics, shouted by Shaun from on top of his desk: 'prose in drag!'

Mrs Holland clapped her hands for silence, but I had one last question. 'Mrs Holland, do you have a definition?'

She hesitated. 'Not a ready-made one, I'm afraid. But let

me think . . .' We all watched her expectantly. The bell rang, and no-one so much as twitched. 'Yes, this might do — today, at any rate. I suspect my definition might change according to my mood, and the weather, and what particular bird happens to be singing outside the window.' We rolled our eyes and grinned: vintage Mrs Holland. 'Poetry is a way of making the truths in our hearts accessible to other people.

'And now, before you all rush off, I have some exciting news. The school magazine is running a poetry section this year, and they're inviting contributions. I shall be expecting a poem from each of you: a long-term project, leaving plenty of time for the muse to visit. Start thinking and planning early,' her eyes were sparkling with amusement at our horror-struck faces, 'and don't panic: as we've agreed, poetry doesn't have to rhyme, or have any set form.

'Pretty much anything goes, as long as it's from the heart.'

Straight after school was photography club — the one-hour meeting that prepared us for our field trip on Saturday morning. This Friday we were doing composition for the third week running, which I was secretly thankful for — as latecomers to the course, me and my clunky old Nikon were struggling to keep up.

I was painfully aware that my battle-scarred war-horse was in a totally different league from the sleek thoroughbreds most of the other kids had. I'd been over the moon when Mum unearthed it from the junk trunk, but somehow the glow evaporated between home and the first meeting, where it looked battered and apologetic. The fact that Mr Greer fell on it with cries of amazement as if it was a relic from the ark made matters worse. But the worst thing of all was how stingy I had to be about taking shots. While

Mike with his digital Canon clicked away non-stop and then deleted ninety-nine per cent of what he'd taken, I agonised for hours over every shot, and then had to wait till the film was developed before I saw how they'd turned out.

After photography club I shot home to fit in some homework before the milk run. Like Nick, I had a desk in my room, but I preferred working at the kitchen table. Plus Mum baked on a Friday, and there'd be the chance of some quality control.

Not today. The kitchen was deserted and I flicked through my homework notebook in peace. I had a geography test and a history essay, though most urgent was the plan for my cookery practical on Monday. But Mrs Holland's poem niggled at my mind like a stone in my shoe, stopping me from concentrating on anything else: the 'truth from the heart' that was somehow going to have to find its way into my brain — which felt as creative as a cauliflower — and from there onto paper.

I dug out my pad of foolscap and stared at the page. My mind, like the page, was a total blank. Worse, because it didn't even have lines on it. What should I write about? I chewed the end of the pen and tried to think. What had Mrs Holland said? That we needed to discover some kind of truth in our hearts, and then use the poem to reveal it.

There was a crash that meant Dad was gearing up for the milk run and would soon be on the hunt for me, and I hadn't done a thing. But then, looking down at the pad, I was surprised to see I *had* done something: an elaborate doodle of a climber dangling from a cliff-top by a rope, an awesome overhang suspended above him like a breaking wave.

I'd write about climbing.

'Pip! What the hell are you doing? I need you here *now!*

We should have left ten minutes ago!'

'Coming!' I yelled back. 'I hate that damn milk run,' I grumbled as I piled my books into my bag. 'I'd give anything for it just to disappear.'

It was only when I made for the door that I realised Mum had come in, light-footed as ever, with Madeline on her hip. She was standing in the doorway looking at me with a strange expression. 'Be careful what you wish for, Pip,' she said softly.

Though her words were accompanied by a tired smile, they hit me with a force that brought with it all the closed doors and silences of the weeks before, as if the wave of rock I'd drawn had turned to ice water and broken over my head.

Hoof Hearted

When I was little I'd thought how cool it was to be a milky. The big kids hopping on and off the back of the trucks and sprinting down the driveways had seemed like heroes. Not any more. Now I knew there was nothing remotely cool about it. Stop start, stop start, rain or shine, too hot or too cold but never just right, like the three bears' porridge. The jingle the milk truck played had a horrible habit of getting stuck in my brain and sometimes I caught myself humming it on the way to class. And as for the sonic *moo* that reverberated through the neighbourhood every time Dad pressed the red button . . .

But worst of all was the expression on Dad's face these days when he *did* press the button. The crinkly-eyed twinkle there'd been the very first time was long gone. Now, without seeing them, I knew his lips under his bristling moustache were grim and rigid, and the crinkles round his eyes had changed to lines as deep and harsh as knife-cuts.

Usually the run took forever, but today it seemed over in a flash. We'd missed a couple of houses, I realised — they must be on holiday. Except it wasn't holiday time. I took a breath to say something to Dad, but the closed look on his face as he wrenched the truck into gear and the sick, sinking feeling I'd had in my gut since those few words of Mum's stopped me.

It was only ten to eight when we pulled up outside the Igloo. I was expecting Dad to slam right out of the truck and stomp on in, but he surprised me. He opened the door, then hesitated. Gave a furtive little glance over his shoulder, reached up and adjusted the rear view mirror, then squinted up and ran a hand through his shock of hair, smoothing his moustache with the back of his thumb. It was something Mum would do, sprucing herself up before heading out to face the world, but never Dad. Not once, in all the time I'd known him.

Then he heaved himself out onto the tarmac and forced a smile. 'Come on then, Son. We should just about catch the second half.'

Just being inside the Igloo, amid all the noise and activity, seemed to cheer Dad up. His shoulders straightened and his stride quickened as he led the way to Nick's court, pausing to exchange a word with a grey-haired geezer in an Igloo blazer. I went ahead and found a corner of a bench to perch on. There were more people watching the game than last week, most of them girls, squashed together at the far side of the court, whispering and giggling. They didn't seem to be watching the game, but that didn't fool me. Or Nick and his team-mates.

This week they were playing a totally different game. Last Friday it had been indoor soccer; today it was Impress the Girls. And it was instantly, horribly obvious that what they thought would impress the girls most was goofing around. Gone was the hard-out physical urgency, the tough tackles, the dazzling ball skills and slick teamwork. As I watched, a pass came through to Nick, unmarked and in line for goal; laughing, he twirled and back-heeled it, bouncing it off the back netting way off target and straight into the path of one of the opposition players. And he was playing for real, girls or no girls. He sliced through Hoof Hearted's sloppy defence like a laser, cutting the ball cleanly across to the striker, perfectly positioned to shoot. The ball whizzed past the goalie and smacked into the back of the net.

Smirking, sliding sidelong glances at their audience, Nick and his friends swaggered back into position for the kick-off, their body language saying more loudly than words: 'We're too cool to care!' . . . and at that moment Dad strode up beside me. Flinching inwardly, I glanced at the electronic scoreboard: 12-3, with six minutes to go. As I watched, the first number flicked to a 13. My heart gave a queasy twist.

'Aha,' said Dad cosily, 'missed a goal, did I?'

I didn't say anything. He'd find out soon enough. But then I had a sudden ghastly premonition: Dad rampaging up and down outside the netting like a tiger in a cage, ranting at the team, yelling encouragement that would soon turn to abuse . . .

Oblivious to our presence, his entire attention focused on the opposite side of the court, Nick was having the time of his life.

'Dad,' I whispered, moving over so I was squashed tight against the fat lady beside me to make room, 'sit down!' To my astonishment he sat, meek as a lamb.

I pulled myself inwards, silent and small as a snail in its shell, and waited.

But what I was waiting for didn't happen.

The run of the game didn't change. Nick and his mates hooned around, gave away goals, wasted opportunities, made idiots of themselves. The other team took ruthless advantage, slotting in goal after goal, to shrugs and laughter and rueful grins. With every goal, the opposition supporters exploded into jubilant cheers. And Dad . . . Dad stayed right where he was beside me, as if he'd been nailed to the bench. As each goal was scored, he clapped. Once, when the opposition's star player slotted a goal from over the halfway line, I even heard him mutter, 'Good goal', though admittedly it was through clenched teeth.

At last I dared to move my head and risk a glance at him. Not to see the expression on his face — which was like thunder, polite applause or not — but to check it really was my Dad.

But back in the car it was a different story.

On the way across the carpark Nick was still on a complete high, jabbering away as if he couldn't see the tension radiating from Dad's back view, or read his ominous silence. 'Man, what a creaming!' he crowed. 'Annihilation City! Didja see Dazzer trying to keep goal in his skate shoes? What a moron! Didn't move off his line once the whole entire game! And how's about old Curly, Pip — the dude with the Mohawk — too scared to head the ball in case he messed up his hairdo! How whack is that? And Stoner, still so wasted from last night it's a miracle he could find his way onto the court! What a bunch of losers! And when —'

'Nick,' I hissed, 'shut up!'

'Huh? What? Didja see when Tommo's cellphone fell out his pocket and Stoner stood on it? And then Stoner goes: *What's that?*, as if it'd beamed down from Mars or somewhere . . . Man, that guy's random. And didja catch my backheel flick? Hey Dad,' — he clambered into the front seat beside me and slammed the door with a crash that made the windows rattle — 'I hafta have a cellphone. Things've changed since the olden days when you were young and communicated by carrier pigeon. I . . . I . . .' At last — too late — Nick was waking up to the signs that had been flashing ten metres high the whole time he was rattling on — signs that made me want to run and hide.

'You what?' Dad's voice was low and dangerous.

Squished up close beside Dad I could feel the waves of anger pulsing off him like heat. Scrunching myself small, wishing I was invisible, I snuck a glance at Nick. He was slouched in his seat, mouth hanging open as if he'd been sandbagged. 'Nothing,' he mumbled sulkily.

Dad rammed the key into the keyhole. His bullet head was facing front, eyes boring into nowhere. He was mad as I'd ever seen him — madder, maybe. I wished he wouldn't drive. But the engine turned, caught, gunned to rattling life. I did my seatbelt up and huddled low. 'Nicholas,' said Dad, his voice sounding as if it was bound up tight with prickly twine, 'I have never seen such a humiliating display in my life.'

'Huh?'

'I am surprised at you. Ashamed of you. To think that a son of mine —'

'*Wot.*' My heart gave a sickening lurch of horror. That single word was a dead giveaway with Nick — said in that flat monotone, it meant one thing: Nick was losing his rag. I'd had Nick's temper directed against me often enough, and though he was my brother it reduced me to tears every time. He wasn't Dad's son for nothing. But he'd never dared get angry with Dad.

'To think a son of mine could give such a pathetic account of himself on a sports field! Pip I could understand, but *you!* I would expect you to have more pride — to have something to prove, after . . .'

'After?'

'*After being rejected by the Highlands Squad!*' Dad ground the words out like glass. 'Do you know what the exhibition you put on tonight proves, Nicholas?'

Silence.

'It proves they were right. You haven't got what it takes — the maturity, the bottle.'

'Dad,' I heard myself saying, my voice wobbling in a way it hadn't for years, 'it's only a game.'

'*Only a game?* That's the problem with you boys. It's all *only a game* to you, isn't it? Well, let me tell you both something. Nothing's *only a game*. In life, just like in sport, it's *all* for real, no second chances — and it's the people who realise that who get somewhere. You know what happens to the rest? They end up the way you will — *losers!*'

We were home, thank God. Dad swung the truck into the driveway so fast Nick's head cracked against the window, and rocked to a halt millimetres from the garage door.

Turning his head to Nick for the first time, he gave him a narrow-eyed, baleful stare. 'Do you know what you are, Nicholas?' he growled. 'A *disappointment*.' He glared at him for one last, long moment, then slowly shook his head. Opened the door and heaved himself out as if he'd aged ten years and shambled stiffly inside, closing the front door with a snick of finality behind him.

I sat there, stuck with Nick between me and the passenger door, not daring to look at him.

For a long time the only sound was the ticking of the cooling engine in the evening air.

Then, just as I was taking a breath to ask him to move, to say something — anything — to break the silence, he did: with just the tiniest hiccup I thought at first, impossibly, might be laughter, like the week before.

I turned my head and my heart froze. Nick's face was contorted, eyes squeezed shut, mouth in an exaggerated upside-down banana-shape, tears pouring down his face.

Without a word I slid across to the driver's door and away into the house.

Inside cycle

'Now, boys and girls, may I have your attention, please.'

We were lined up in a straggling crocodile outside the Domestic Science lab, our bags shoved against the corridor wall, lunch boxes, pencil cases and sweatshirts spilling out where desperate would-be chefs had ransacked them for aprons, recipe books and the vital master-plan that was the key to our Practical Planning Post-test. I glanced down at mine for reassurance: the tidily ruled template painstakingly completed in what started as orderly columns and had ended late Sunday night as a panic-stricken scrawl.

'Philip,' purred the Carling, 'please pay me the compliment of listening to my instructions. As I recall, your course mark currently rests on forty-three per cent. A modest pass in today's test would lift your average above the fifty per cent mark, an outcome I should strive for in your position.

'Today I shall be evaluating your ability to prepare and serve a simple three-course meal within a set time, working from a pre-arranged plan. Do you all have your plans with you?'

'Yes, Miss Carling.' A ragged chorus, anything but enthusiastic.

'Philip, Kathryn: do *you* both have *your* plans?' Since the ill-fated Katie-Pip cookery coalition had fallen by the wayside things had gone much more smoothly in Domestic Science, but as far as the Carling was concerned we were just as lethal individually as we'd ever been in partnership.

'Yes, Miss Carling,' I muttered, flapping my sheet of paper in the air for inspection. Glancing down the line at Katie, I saw she was favouring the Carling with nothing more than a haughty stare.

'I would remind you all that speaking to one another, for any reason whatsoever, will result in your immediate failure. Before we begin, does anyone have any questions?' Her frog-like gaze rested on me for a moment, her thin lips twitching in a chilly smile. But it didn't fool me. The Carling hated my guts, and everyone knew it. In spite of what she'd just said, she'd be over the moon if I failed Domestic Science — Katie and me both. She'd chalk it down as a personal triumph and celebrate for days, in whatever way werewolves like her celebrated. A banquet of broken bottles and battery acid, probably.

I felt a twinge of nerves as I tramped into the lab and took up my position at my usual table. Up front, Carling was going on about her beloved Theory of Planning for the zillionth time: 'The essential discipline of time management will enable you all — or *most* of you — to attain a high level of skill in planning, preparing and presenting food, which will stand you in good stead . . .'

I ran my eye down my plan. Even though it got a bit ramshackle towards the end, it was the right stuff. I'd cunningly chosen dishes either I'd made before — for cookery practical last year, in the case of beef stroganoff — or that were completely bombproof, like green salad. The starter was avocado ritz with home-made dressing, and dessert was jelly trifle.

Putting it all together was the problem. We had three hours to complete everything, the key to success being what the Carling called 'inside cycle'. This meant that while one thing was on autopilot in the background — the jelly

66

setting in the fridge, for instance — you'd be getting on with some other labour-intensive task.

I eyed my master-plan proudly. I was using every second to the max. It was all down there, in columns of diminishing tidiness, starting with Point Number One: *Boil kettle for jelly while collecting ingredients*.

My head jerked up. Ahead of me, to left and right, kids in aprons were measuring, chopping, beating, stirring. At her desk, the Carling was watching me over her reading glasses. My eyes shot to the clock and I leapt into action, cursing myself. A critical two minutes gone while I stood there dreaming!

Four and a half minutes later my strawberry jelly was made and nestling in the fridge beside Melissa's pancake batter.

Dusting my hands on the seat of my shorts, I turned my attention to the next item: the beef stroganoff. I half-wished the Carling was watching, because this piece of planning was a true master-stroke. I headed for my trusty little electric stove, saucepan in hand — and stopped dead in my tracks. There stood Shaun, poking dubiously at the contents of a skillet with an oversized wooden spoon. 'Shaun,' I hissed, 'butt out! That's *my* stove!'

He gestured me away frantically, keeping his mouth firmly shut and rolling his eyes in the direction of the front desk. Then he turned his back and stuck his nose back into the pot. What now?

Then I noticed Mike was also at a different stove from usual, and so was Katie. There must have been a re-allocation for the test. I shuffled up to the front desk, trying to look as inoffensive as possible. 'Excuse me, Miss Carling,' I said meekly, 'could you tell me which stove I'm supposed to use?'

'You should have been paying attention when the list was read out. Please retain the information this time, if at all possible. You are to use Stove Number Eight.'

'Thank you, Miss Carling.' I hurried over — and once again, stopped short. Stove Number Eight was a gas stove, and I'd never used one before. Leaden-footed, I retraced my steps to the front. 'Excuse me, Miss Carling.'

'What is it *this* time?'

'Number Eight's a gas stove, and I've never used one before.'

'For heaven's sake! Show some initiative! Operating a gas stove is so simple a child of . . .' She stared at me for a long moment. 'On second thoughts, I'll come and do it for you.'

'Will you take marks off?'

'No, Philip, not in this instance. Better safe than sorry.'

I trailed over to the stove and watched her light the burner, a tiny circular flame springing up obediently at her touch. She showed me how to adjust the heat and turn it off again once I was done, then left me to it.

I positioned the saucepan carefully and headed back to my table. Inside cycle decreed that while the hotplate was heating up and the fat in the pan slowly beginning to melt, I could use the time to chop the onion and the meat.

Back on track, feeling capable and in control, I found myself humming the MooZical Milk jingle under my breath as I settled to my next task.

I'd almost finished the chopping when there was a sound from behind me — a kind of watery swoosh, followed almost instantly by a collective gasp of horror. I froze in mid-hum, my heart leaping into my throat. Knowing with some deep instinct that I was about to be confronted by my downfall I whipped round, knife in hand and eyes staring like a crazed butcher.

Tall red-and-yellow flames were leaping merrily up from the depths of the shiny silver saucepan on Stove Number Eight. They were licking the ceiling and I could see a sooty patch beginning to form.

Without making any conscious decision to move I was running for the fire extinguisher on the back wall, wrenching it from its bracket and squinting desperately at the instructions on the side. I could hear Dad's voice yelling in my head: *The base of the flames, Son! A fireman always aims for the base of the flames!* But I couldn't get the damn extinguisher to work! *Break seal,* I managed to decipher. Seal? What seal? *Remove pin.* Pin?

I looked up, praying for help before the entire school burnt down . . . just in time to see Miss Carling marching towards the fire, a tin plate in her hand. In one precise, economical movement she snapped the plate down on top of the saucepan like a lid.

The effect was instant. Goodbye fire. I stood there cradling the fire extinguisher, reading my fate in the Carling's small, satisfied smile.

And then, over by the window, I noticed Katie. She was grinning at me — the old, sparkly-eyed Katie grin. And when she caught my eye, impossibly but unmistakably, she gave me the tiniest flicker of a wink.

Monkeys in my head

The phone call came just as we were sitting down to dinner the next day. Enchiladas — Nick's favourite. 'Get that, would you, Son,' Dad growled, his first forkful halfway to his mouth. 'Tell them we've already got one, and not to bother people when they're eating.'

I hopped up and sidled round Dad's chair to the phone. 'Pip McLeod speaking.'

'This is Mr Gilroy,' said a clipped-sounding voice. 'Could I speak with one of your parents, please?'

'Mr . . . Mr . . . Guh!' It was old Killjoy, the school principal — which meant that as far as I was concerned it might as well have been the Grim Reaper. I was dead meat. The Carling had dobbed me in. She'd ratted to Killjoy about how I'd nearly burned the school down, and now I was going to be expelled and Mum and Dad lumbered with the bill for rebuilding the entire Domestic Science block — or at least repainting the ceiling.

What could I do? Tell him we were in the middle of dinner? Pretend he was an insurance salesman? Say Mum and Dad weren't here?

'Ahhhh . . .' I heard myself say, as if I was at the doctor's and he'd told me to open wide.

'Philip!' The word sliced down the line, lethal as a guillotine. 'Your father — *now!*'

I'd blown it. My one chance would have been to hand him to Mum while the going was good, but now . . .

'Mum's right here . . .' I heard myself bleat.

But Dad's hand was out, reaching for the phone.

I passed it over and slunk back to my chair, my heart bouncing in my chest like a basketball. 'Mine!' Muddle was demanding, fingers clutching. She loved talking on the phone and would babble nonsense to any poor sucker who called. 'Me talk on pone, Daddy!'

'McLeod!' Dad rapped.

I glanced at Nick, knowing he'd catch my eye and mouth '*Who is it?*' But he didn't. He was slouched in his place staring dull-eyed at his plate, pushing a bit of chicken around with his fork.

I pronged a tendril of melted cheese and nibbled it, wondering how it could taste so different from how it had thirty seconds before.

'Mr *Who*?' Dad barked suspiciously. 'Greendale *what*? Oh. Yes. Well?'

There was a long pause. The phone made a faint chirruping sound that seemed to go on and on. I'd given up all pretence of eating. Madeline was trying to rub out scribble marks on her high chair with a piece of cheese; Mum was assembling forkfuls of enchilada and salad, oblivious to the fact that the world was about to come crashing down on her head. Nick was just sitting.

'I see,' said Dad.

'When was this?' said Dad.

'His attitude?' said Dad.

'Can't continue?' said Dad. 'Absolutely not. I agree. Certainly. Well, I'm disappointed . . . yes, disappointed, but not surprised. No, not entirely surprised. These things happen, eh? Boys will be boys, especially at his age.'

A tiny flutter of hope stirred deep inside. I'd flunked cookery and nearly burned the school down, and Dad was

71

saying it was because boys would be boys! That was the kind of get-out usually reserved for Nick.

I risked a glance at Dad, but he'd turned round so all I could see was the back of his head. 'Absolutely. You can rely on me to deal with this. Thank you for contacting me.' *Crash!* Down went the phone in mid-chirp. I had a flash of old Killjoy staring in perplexity at the dead receiver, wondering where Dad had gone. He wasn't to know that Dad hardly ever let anyone finish what they were saying, school principal or not.

Then reality surfaced again like a glob in a lava lamp, and I put my fork down and lifted my head to face the music.

'Who was that, Jim?' Mum asked. Dad was lumbering slowly round, that slightly baffled expression on his face that meant he was processing information — and once he'd finished, anything might happen. He looked at Mum, then at Nick. This was bad. If he didn't even want to look at me . . .

'Dad,' I gulped, 'I'm sorry.'

Dad glanced at me as if he'd forgotten I was there. 'So am I. Nicholas . . .' He sat down stiffly, his stiff leg stretched sideways. It always hurt worse when bad things happened. 'That was your headmaster. Says your grades have dropped, you failed three tests in the last two weeks and something about *unexplained absences* . . .'

A dam wall of relief burst inside me. I opened my mouth to say 'Didn't he say anything about . . .' Then I looked across at Nick. He was staring at his plate, the oddest look on his face. Not guilty or defensive; just a weird kind of blankness.

'Jim,' Mum was saying quietly, 'we need to talk to Nick about this alone. Pip, please read to Madeline in the lounge.' Mum was watching Nick too — looking at him with the special Mum X-ray gaze that saw right through you as if you were made of glass, and always made me squirm. But Nick didn't even seem to notice.

It was only as I was heading for the door with Madeline that I realised what the expression on Nick's face was, though I didn't begin to understand it.

Relief.

That night I couldn't sleep. There was too much happening in my brain — what Dad used to call 'monkeys in my head' when we were little. I'd imagined shrunk-down vervet monkeys with impish faces swinging on a jungle-gym that had magically sprouted in the space between Dad's ears. But the ones in my head tonight were big, hairy chimpanzees, baring their teeth and snapping branches and creating all kinds of bedlam.

At last I got up and padded through to the kitchen for a drink. The lounge light was still on, and through the partly open door I could hear the comforting sound of Mum and Dad's voices. I refilled the glass and took it back to my room, slid into bed and snuggled down — and then realised I'd forgotten to close my door. It didn't matter: the passage light was off, and the crack of light spilling through from the lounge wasn't enough to keep me awake.

I closed my eyes and tried Mum's old trick of giving the monkeys names. 'Once you've named a worry, you're halfway to taming it,' she always said.

My first monkey was a scraggy, moth-eaten female with protruding eyes and a wart on its chin. Carling-Monkey. Last night it had been the ringleader, but now it was sitting hunched under a bush, sulking. Its bluff had been well and truly called.

The second monkey had prickly red fur and long arms with knuckles that dragged on the ground. He was spending most of his time shambling round at ground level, occasionally shoving his face right up close to the Pip-Monkey that was me and baring his teeth in what looked like a grin, but wasn't. Between-times, he'd beat his chest with a hollow, booming sound. You wouldn't think he was much of a climber, but you'd be wrong. What Lee-Monkey lacked in agility and natural balance, he made up for with brute strength and aggression that had him up in the treetops raising merry hell before you could say 'banana'. Yeah, Lee could climb all right. But it was the aggression that worried me. I didn't dare take my eyes off old Lee for a second.

But there was another monkey causing more problems tonight than all the rest put together. It was a slim, silky monkey that wasn't creating much ruckus, so it should have been easy to ignore. A monkey that almost made me forget about little Beattie-Monkey sitting quietly in the shade, watching me with unreadable eyes: a graceful little monkey with a haunting face and slender monkey-limbs. Katie-Monkey.

Like a dork, I'd gone up to her after cookery, once I'd escaped the Carling's clutches. I had as much chance of staying away as an iron filing from a magnet after that look, that wink. I puffed up behind her on the way to gym, tripping over my own feet in my efforts to make it seem like I just happened to be passing. Mr Cool, that was me. 'Uh, Katie . . .' I began, then realised I had no clue what to say next. 'Hi,' I mumbled, already wishing I'd left her alone.

The two friends she was walking with exchanged a glance and tittered. But Katie didn't. She didn't say hi back — not Katie — but she actually looked at me, for the second time in months. A cool, searching, Snow Queen look, as if she was seeing me properly for the first time in a long while.

Then she half-smiled and turned away, but her eyes sort of clung for longer . . . and where they'd touched me they seemed to leave the softest dusting of Katie-gold, like pollen on my skin.

It was no use: sleep was a million miles away. I rolled over onto my back, staring up at the ceiling. Mum's and Dad's voices came clearly through the crack in the door; I was surprised I hadn't been aware of them before.

'It's just high jinks. Nick's no Einstein, we've always known that. He's a sportsman like his Dad.'

'High jinks are one thing, Jim, getting in trouble is another. Bunking school — failing *three* tests. If he hasn't been at school, where *has* he been? And what Mr Gilroy said about an *attitude problem* . . .'

'You're making too much of this. Boys like Nick need to sow their wild oats. I'd be more worried if he was a nancy boy, top of the class and in all the teachers' good books. I've given him a rollicking; he'll pull his socks up.'

'Mothers worry. That talk I went to the other day — she said this is the age they're most at risk, apart from when they're first learning to toddle and explore the world. It's the same process, but the dangers are different. Bigger . . . worse in so many ways.'

'He'll survive. I did — and I won't tell you some of the nonsense I got up to.'

Then Mum said something that really surprised me — sat me bolt upright in bed, sleep further away than ever. 'I wish he was more like Pip.'

'*Pip?*'

'You think Nick's the strong one, but you're wrong. Pip knows exactly who he is and where he's going. I'm not

75

worried about him. But Nick . . .'

Dad's voice took on the gentle note it only ever got with Mum when she was winding herself up about something. There was nothing Dad hated as much as seeing Mum cry. 'Nick's a chip off the old block. Dry those eyes now. You may be their mother, but it takes a father to know his own son. Stop worrying and come to bed.'

My room flooded with light as the lounge door swung open. Quick as a flash I whipped over on my side and shut my eyes. Lay still as a plank, heart thudding. The carpet masked the sound of their feet, but I caught a whiff of Mum's flowery scent and felt her gentle hand on my hair. Then the door snicked quietly shut and the room was in darkness.

My monkeys were settling down for the night, making leafy hammocks, yawning and rubbing their eyes. I had a yawn and a stretch too, then curled up into a comfortable position for sleep.

It was only when I was drifting into that twilight zone where thoughts blend into dreams that I realised there was another dark shape huddled among the other monkeys — a dark-eyed, silent one that hadn't been there before.

Nick-Monkey.

But almost before I realised he was there, I was asleep.

Rickety Bridge

The days rattled past like an express train and suddenly it was Friday afternoon and Dad was dropping me off at the Igloo with my shiny new kit bag, grouching away about having to do the milk run on his own. 'I'll be back for Monday's run,' I reminded him. 'Pick-up's at six — we can go straight there. Thanks for the ride.'

Dad's glower turned crinkle-eyed and he pulled me into a hug that just about busted my ribs. 'Have fun, Son,' he growled. Seems I wasn't too big to hug after all — and Dad had chosen the worst possible moment to prove it. No-one's dad hugged them goodbye any more.

I lugged my stuff over to the side door of the Igloo — the service entrance I'd snuck through a lifetime ago, before I'd known climbing existed. A minibus with the Igloo logo on the side was pulled up beside it, Rob and Cam loading it with supermarket boxes, climbing paraphernalia and their weather-stained backpacks and sleeping bags.

'Ah, Phil,' said Rob, turning with a box in his arms and catching sight of me. 'Just the man I was hoping to see. Do us a favour, mate . . .' And within seconds I was flat-out fetching, carrying, sorting and loading, so busy I didn't even notice the others arrive.

Taking the last bag from Beattie and heaving it on top of the pile I couldn't help giving her a grin, and thought I saw the corners of her mouth twitch before she scowled and turned abruptly away. Then in we all clambered, scrambling over one another for the window seats, and we were off.

We swooshed along the highway in slanting afternoon sunlight, talking climbing, swapping stories about the colourful personalities who seemed to inhabit the climbing world. Fraser and Beattie were both in fine form, exaggerating wildly in their attempts to outdo Sasha, and even Lee thawed enough to tell a couple of stories about his adventures on his zillion climbing trips, all starring him as hero. But at least he was talking, and friendly.

Gabriel was quietest, gazing out of the window. He'd answer any direct question with vague detachment, then go back to whatever was going on inside his head.

Then the afternoon had become evening and we were deep in the mountains. I realised we'd been climbing for a while: the sing-song hum of the engine had changed to a grumbling whine as the road began to wind, sharply and more sharply still, twisting in an endless series of bends. One minute we'd be in the deep shadow of the mountains, stone-cold and purplish-blue; then we'd round a corner and a dazzle of light would blind us before the road turned and plunged us back into dusk.

Rob flicked on the headlights and settled his hands more firmly on the steering wheel; Cam opened a map and peered down at it. The people who'd brought iPods plugged into them and disappeared into their music. The darkness thickened. Beside me Gabriel was asleep, his head jolting against the window, then lolling onto my shoulder as the van swung round the bends.

After a long while the headlights caught a brief flash of a sign, gone before I could read it. Rob changed gear, the tired engine heaving what sounded like a sigh of relief as a line of lights spun out on either side of the road, the familiar red and yellow of a petrol station beckoning among a scatter of shops.

'Last outpost of civilisation,' said Cam. 'Who's for fish and chips?'

The last leg of the journey was bumping over an unsealed road that seemed to go on forever, but finally the engine took on that distinctive homecoming note and we slowed, jouncing downhill over a series of bone-jarring humps and over a bridge. Rob drove so cautiously we were almost tip-toeing across; I could feel the planks sag and wobble and hear them creak. We bumped onto solid ground again; the headlights caught a gleam of water, two blocky shapes too small and squat to be huts . . . then we slowed to a final, merciful stop and Rob turned off the engine.

Utter silence and darkness thicker than paint descended. We clambered out, stiff-legged, our breath condensing in the icy air. Looking up, I saw a black bowl of sky spangled with a zillion stars.

'Welcome to Rickety Bridge,' said Rob: 'home sweet home for the next three days.'

Rock

I was jerked from sleep by Cam banging a tin plate right next to my ear. My heart did a handspring, my eyes flew open, and I was sitting up and staring blearily round the little room as heads popped out of sleeping bags all round, groans issuing from some, answering grins from others.

The huts were tiny, and once we'd fumbled all the gear into the smaller one the previous night there'd been hardly any room left. A quick count of bodies told me we'd all opted for hut number two — with the exception of Cam and Rob, who must have excavated themselves a corner somewhere among the gear.

We'd all slept in our clothes, so all we had to do was gobble down a bowl of gluey baked beans and gulp a mug of black coffee — Cam and Rob each blamed the other for forgetting the milk powder. I wasn't much of a coffee drinker; till then my only experience of it had been Mum's kids' version, pale khaki, lukewarm and syrupy sweet. This had a caffeine kick that blew the top of my head off and made my ears ring: I felt super-cool and grown up, and even though I didn't actually like it I knew from the first sip it was how I'd be drinking coffee from here on in.

I'd brought my camera, and snapped off a couple of quick pics of the others, hunched up like gnomes over their coffee mugs, hoods on and faces wreathed in steam.

'OK, rock spiders,' Cam was saying, 'while you were sending up Zs Rob and I rigged a top-rope on one of the easier climbs. Five minutes and we're off. Sort yourselves some lunch from the stuff over there and grab a sweatshirt in case the weather changes.'

'Beattie and Phil, you're on kitchen roster tonight,' said Rob. 'Know how to make spaghetti and heat cans of sauce?'

Beattie shot me a look that sliced to the bone, clambered to her feet and said, 'But can't . . .'

'Can't what?' said Rob innocently.

Something in his eyes made me wonder . . . Beattie opened and closed her mouth a couple of times like a fish, then muttered, 'Nothing.'

A fifteen-minute bump over a barely visible track brought us to a grassy glade surrounded by trees. A boondocks parking lot, I guessed, though there wasn't a tyre-track in sight. Once Rob turned off the engine the only sounds were the sighing of the wind in the trees and the trill of two birds calling to each other across the valley.

'This is the middle of nowhere,' grumbled Lee. 'All the camps up north have the huts right on site and there's no time wasted — or effort.'

'These huts weren't built for climbers,' said Rob neutrally, sharing out the gear. 'They're deer-hunting huts. In the old days this area was overpopulated to the point where the natural vegetation was almost destroyed. There was culling on a massive scale, bunches of carcasses carted out by helicopter . . . butchery, not sport — if you call hunting sport. All justified in environmental terms, of course. Look at it now: a drop of rain and it'll be paradise.' He was right: the surrounding bush was dense but a closer look revealed a parched, brittle pallor, as if the slightest spark would turn it all to tinder.

'Are there any deer left?' I asked, half-expecting to see a Horace-like head peering at me through the leaves.

'You see them now and again away on the hillside, and this time of year you can sometimes hear the stags roar. And here we are.'

We'd been filing along the path, and now the trees opened up to reveal a broken cliff face buttressing away to either side, a double length of multicoloured rope snaking down from way above. Automatically I scaled the face with my eyes, assessing the route, the holds, the cruxes. It wasn't a difficult climb, but it would be good for starters. Maybe ten degrees or so off the vertical, notched with sharp edges, pockets, ridges and one jagged almost vertical crack my fingers itched to wedge themselves into . . .

Listening to Rob run through the safety routines, I flopped down on the stony ground and yanked off my trainers, peeling off my smelly socks and shoving them deep inside. Like most seasoned climbers, I opted for bare feet under my climbing shoes — the Regional Champs last year had been the last time I'd worn socks to climb. Pros did without, and for good reason. A climbing shoe fits tight as a glove, and it's sticky-soled, so you can use the soles of your feet, your toes and heels and every other bit of equipment nature gave you to suction up sheer rock like a fly. Sensitivity is the key — the less between you and the rock, the better.

I fastened my last shoe and bounced up as if I had springs in my legs. Something told me I was about to discover the meaning of life.

I was right. I loved indoor — nothing would ever change that. It wasn't 'gunite crap' to me, and never would be. But climbing in the outdoors . . . that had a magic nothing could equal.

We have talks about addiction and stuff at school — about alcohol and tobacco and drugs, and how though they give you a high at the time they're really just paving stones on the road to ruin. You can get drugs at school; everyone knows where, and you can spot the druggies a mile off. We do these role-plays — how to say 'no', even if your friends are hassling you. Mike and I have talked about drugs and sworn blind we'd never touch them. You'd have to be an idiot.

But midway through that morning, spread-eagled against the cliff face with nothing around me but fresh air and freedom, I knew for certain. All the kicks I'd ever need were there on the end of a rope, and right then I knew what I'd say if anyone ever pushed me to try.

'I don't do chemicals,' I'd say. 'I get my high from climbing.'

The sun was long gone over the lip of the cliff by the time Rob and Cam finished stringing the last line of the day and grinned down at the bedraggled little group sprawled at their feet. Everyone looked the way I felt: sun-drenched, filthy and completely clapped-out. My legs and arms had turned to jelly, any energy I'd once had invisibly pasted somewhere up there on the cliff face. I had a suck of water from my bottle, wishing it was high-octane energy drink. It'd take rocket fuel to get me up there now.

'So,' said Rob, 'anyone got the voltage to give it a last go?'

'Not me,' said Beattie. 'Look at my hands — mincemeat from jamming in the cracks.'

'Aw, poor Beattie,' teased Fraser. 'No excuses for me — I'm just dead *beat*, if you'll excuse the pun.'

Gabriel, lying flat on his back in the tussock watching

two swallows spinning way high in the blue, just smiled and shook his head, and Sasha groaned, 'I don't think I ever want to see a rock bigger than a pebble again in my life.'

But Lee clambered to his feet. 'I'll do it,' he said. For the first time that day he looked directly at me — a flat stare that said more than words ever could. 'How's about you, *Captain*?'

Suddenly it seemed everyone was watching me. I opened my mouth to say, 'Nah. I've had it for the day,' but somehow the words got scrambled inside my brain and came out as 'Yeah, I'll give it a go.'

'After you,' says Lee, quick as a flash. Walked right into that one, Piphead, I told myself as I roped up. In climbing, going first is no advantage . . . but this isn't a competition, I told myself sternly. This is fun — isn't it?

Above me the cliff reared up, grim and forbidding in the dusk. Behind me, the group was silent, watching. Only Cam, belaying me, seemed oblivious. 'Belay on,' he told me. 'In your own time, Phil.'

I chalked up, took a deep breath and started up the wall. Before I'd reached head-height my arms were shaking; my fingers felt like rubber, and there was a tremble in my left knee. I dug deep, trawling for the reserves of strength, the elusive rhythm I knew were in there somewhere. Holding focus, keeping my weight over my legs and off my arms as much as possible, I climbed on.

I reached a bulge in the rock that had worried me from below: a convex potbelly with a couple of meagre handholds. I paused, resting, panning the crux with my eyes as I chalked up and assessed my options. There weren't any. Fancy footwork and all the balance in the world wouldn't help me now. There was nothing for it: I'd have to go for broke — rely on the handholds to pull my way through. But even as I hung there I could feel my remaining strength draining away, and I knew it was useless. I was done.

I gulped a deep breath and charged the bulge, arms cracking with strain, feet smearing for ripples in the rock that didn't exist. But like butter in a microwave, the remaining grunt in my arms melted to nothing. 'Falling!' I yelled, and dropped off the wall like a tick.

Cam lowered me down. 'Good try, champ,' said Rob. 'More juice in the tank, and you'd cruise that crux, no worries. What say we pack up and head for camp?'

'No.' There were two spots of colour high on Lee's cheeks. 'I want my go.'

'You sure?' said Cam. 'I know it's tempting to go for that final burn, but I'd hate you guys to overdo it.'

'I'm not a gumbo on rock,' said Lee bluntly, giving me a dismissive glance that stung like a slap. 'I know my limits.'

Rob had been stashing rope, but now he straightened. 'OK,' he said. 'Come on, Cam. I'll spot, you belay.'

We all watched in silence as Rob positioned himself behind Lee, hands outspread to safeguard him for the most dangerous part of a top-rope climb: the beginning, when there's enough stretch in the rope for you to hit the ground if you fall. Lee stood rubbing his hands and eyeballing the route, psyching himself up.

More than anything, I hoped he'd fall.

But if he was tired, it didn't show. He attacked the first section of the climb like a charging rhino, and when he came to the crux he powered right through it as if it wasn't there. Reaching with one long arm for the first pocket he gripped, heaved and was suddenly within reach of the next, using willpower and sheer strength to claw his way to the next and the next and the next . . . then the bulge was behind him and he was kicking for the final foothold that'd take him on and up over the last easy sloping slab, then home.

But he couldn't resist one triumphant glance down to where I sat in the dirt, staring glumly upwards . . . his foot sheared off the hold, his balance tipped and I saw him grab for a jug and miss, then drop into space with a disbelieving squawk.

Cam lowered him, spinning gently, to the ground. His face like thunder, Lee kicked the foot of the cliff viciously and said nothing.

Back at camp Cam handed out apples and lemon Reflex which we gulped down thirstily. 'There's a waterhole just upriver,' said Rob idly. 'The rock's good for bouldering and the water's deep enough to swim, but I don't suppose . . .'

The others were on their feet in a flash. Rather more reluctantly, Rob and Cam heaved themselves up to follow. 'You two'll be OK on your own, won't you? We won't be long.'

'Make sure you have dinner ready and the table laid!' laughed Sasha, flicking Beattie with her towel. But Beattie didn't smile back.

As for me, my heart settled dismally into my sneakers as I watched the chattering crocodile disappear round the bend in the river.

Fun and games, I thought bitterly. *Not.*

Pasta disaster

Stony-faced, moving like a robot, Beattie crossed to the row of cardboard boxes, hunkered down and rummaged inside. Out came more packets of Reflex, toilet rolls, about ten cans of baked beans in tomato sauce, a packet of rice, two packs of chocolate biscuits . . .

At least we won't starve, I thought grimly.

I wondered whether it was possible to make an entire meal with someone without exchanging a single word.

Looking down at Beattie, so hell-bent on ignoring me, I marvelled again at how fragile friendships are. Like the gossamer threads of cobwebs criss-crossing a path, one moment they're there, intact and perfect; the next, all that's left are a few broken strands drifting on the air. I wondered if it would be possible for a photograph to capture the hostility in her rigid back, the weight of words so determinedly not being spoken between us. Knowing it would make her madder than ever, I crossed to my pack, found my camera, and snapped.

Beattie whipped round, her face scrunched with irritation. Backing off, hands raised in surrender, I thought bitterly that I'd been right to compare her to a beetle. She looked exactly like one: a cross little stag beetle.

'I can do this on my own,' she said coldly. 'Opening a can isn't rocket science. Why don't you go and join the others?' There were four tins of Bolognese sauce on the floor beside her, and two packs of spaghetti.

Part of me wanted to answer her just as distantly; to say in that same matter-of-fact tone: 'OK, have it your way. Do it on your own. I'll leave you to burn the whole camp down if you want.'

But there was another part of me that was too stubborn to take the easy way out. If Beattie wanted to play games, fine: I'd play too. My conscience was clear, and it would stay that way. Beattie could be as offish as she liked, but I'd do my best to keep things ticking along on an even keel, even if we both knew it was just a big act.

Plus — more importantly — I remembered her once saying she couldn't boil water without burning it, while here I was, a fully fledged member of the Carling Academy of Haute Cuisine. I knew I could heat ready-made sauce and cook spaghetti, though I'd never done it before; having watched the Carling, I could even light the gas burner. As she was so fond of saying, I'd assimilated the basic principles of domestic science, and now they'd stand me in good stead. And I was starving — way too hungry to let Beattie loose on those precious tins.

'We're on kitchen roster together, so we'll do it together,' I said pleasantly. 'Pass the matches.'

Ten minutes later the double burner was lit and so was the fire, bathing the campsite in a cosy glow. Bruise-coloured dusk was deepening around us; birds racketed away in the trees, and further off in the bush I could sense a deeper, watchful stillness, as if night was some wild creature creeping stealthily closer.

I crossed the few steps to the river to fill the larger of the two saucepans. Behind me I could hear Beattie muttering as she opened the tins; it sounded like she was making heavy weather if it. Just as well I'd stayed, I thought righteously: darn girl couldn't even open a can.

'Tough job, Beattie? Need a hand?' I asked innocently.

'No, I don't,' she snapped. 'Leave me alone!' To my surprise she sounded close to tears. I shot her a glance, but a wing of dark hair had fallen forward over her face and all I could see was the tip of her nose. Nah, she couldn't be — not Beattie. Anyhow, what did she have to cry about?

'What's important,' I informed the tip of her nose in my most Carling-like tone, 'is not to put pans on the gas with nothing in them — or worse still, anything flammable.' With a flourish I positioned my pan of cold water on the left-hand burner, ripped open the two packs of spaghetti with my teeth and bunged the contents in. The spaghetti stuck jauntily up like some kind of modern flower arrangement. 'Quite clearly,' I continued, 'the spaghetti will take a long time to cook. See how hard it is? Take rice, for example. Takes ten minutes or so from when it comes to the boil; big sticks of rock-hard spaghetti will take at least three times as long.'

'How will the top cook if it's sticking out like that?' said Beattie critically. I'd been wondering the same thing myself. Maybe I should have snapped it in half beforehand?

'You'll see,' I told her mysteriously.

And we did. Once the sauce was sorted I turned my attention back to the spaghetti, and to my amazement a culinary miracle had taken place. The sticks that had been poking skywards were now coiled obediently in the saucepan, like the Indian rope trick in reverse. 'See?' I said. 'Told you.' Frowning, I poked the gleaming multi-stranded coil with a fork. It was doing well, little bubbles rising round it in a most satisfactory way. 'What we do now is turn the heat down and put the lid on tight. Another half hour or so and it'll be ready. Cooking is simple,' I informed Beattie's unresponsive back, 'once you know how.'

'I hope the others won't be too much longer,' I fretted. 'Generally with cooking, the longer you do it the better. But . . .' For the zillionth time I crossed to the stove and peered into the pots. Beattie, sitting on a log engrossed in a climbing manual, ignored me — though how she could see in the deepening darkness was a mystery.

Dinner had been simmering away for a good while now, and every instinct told me it was done. The sauce was thick and gloopy, bubbling like lava in a volcano and showing a worrying tendency to stick to the bottom of the pot. But it was the spaghetti that was the real problem. The water had practically disappeared, and I was sure it must be ready. What should we do? Put more cold water in? Or take it off the heat and hope the others arrived back soon?

I cast an irritated glance over at Beattie's bent head. Women! Useless — worse than useless!

Time for an executive decision. We'd drain the spaghetti and put the lid back on to keep it warm. I pulled the sleeves of my sweatshirt over my hands like oven gloves and carefully took the saucepan off the heat, then turned the burner off. Safety in the kitchen — the Carling would be proud. Crossed to a bare patch of earth and cautiously poured the milky remains of the water out, using the lid to stop the slippery strands of spaghetti slithering out. It was easier than I'd expected. I righted the saucepan, lifted the lid and peered inside. Gave it a tentative shake — and felt my insides disappear as abruptly as if they'd been extracted with an ice-cream scoop.

'Beattie,' I croaked, 'come here.'

Something in my voice must have told her we had problems — big problems. She was beside me in a flash. 'What is it? What have you done?'

'Look.' She looked. I looked. We both looked, staring at

90

the contents of the pan in disbelief. Instead of individual strands of spaghetti, the bottom of the pot was plugged with a single, immovable wedge.

'What's happened?' Beattie's voice was an awestruck whisper. 'Where's the spaghetti?'

'Beattie,' I said, 'this *is* the spaghetti.'

A long time passed while we stood in the gathering gloom staring at the disaster. We said nothing, because there was nothing to say. Steam was still gently curling up from the gelatinous mass when at last Beattie reached out a finger and gave it an exploratory poke. 'Do you think . . .' she said slowly, 'do you think we could maybe . . . untangle it?'

When it was cool enough to touch we prised it out of the pot. It was tough as rubber, and bouncy. Now Beattie took charge. Carefully, with delicate fingers, she tried to tease an individual strand free, but it was hopeless. The spaghetti was welded together. As the Carling would say, it had undergone a chemical change during the cooking process, and nothing short of a miracle was going to change it back again.

Now, far from looking anxiously along the river hoping for the others' return, we were dreading the sound of their happy, hungry voices. 'Phil,' whispered Beattie, 'what are we going to do?'

'Maybe we can rip it up,' I suggested. 'Kind of . . . tear it into smaller bits?'

Beattie took hold of one side, me the other, and we began to pull — a nightmarish tug-of-war with the spaghetti showing an elasticity that would have amazed even the Carling. At last a gluey hunk tore away in Beattie's hand, taking me totally by surprise; I staggered back towards the river, throwing my arms out for balance — and to my horror the pot-shaped plug of pasta flew out of my grip and away over the water like a Frisbee.

For something nature had never intended to fly, it seemed to hang in the air for an impossibly long time before it finally landed in the water with a dispirited *plop*.

Beattie and I stared at each other. Then her lips twitched and her eyes began to sparkle . . . she made a muffled choking sound, and started to laugh. We laughed till our sides ached, and then we laughed some more. At long, long last, hardly able to talk at all, Beattie gasped: 'This is all that's left, Phil. Who for — Lee, d'you think?' Tears on her cheeks, she held it out for my inspection. I peered at it in the darkness: a pale blob like a dumpling in her hand. Her hand . . .

Without thinking, I reached out and took it in both of mine, staring down. 'Beattie, your skin . . .'

'I know.' Her voice was prickly and defensive, but she didn't pull away. 'I told you all — my hands are wrecked. That rock was like sandpaper.'

'You should've said.'

'I did.'

Light dawned. 'Opening those cans . . .'

Beattie shrugged. I reached down and took her other hand, stood there, very close, holding her two hands in mine. Looked from her hands to her face, and back again.

I didn't want to let go.

And then, quite suddenly, Rob's words came back into my mind, and now they made sense. *Maybe it wasn't what you did, but what you didn't do* . . . Slowly, watching her eyes, I lifted one hand to my lips, turned it over, and gently, so softly I couldn't tell if it was my lips or my breath touching her skin, I kissed her palm. It smelled of sweat and rock-dust and apple. Beattie's eyes were fathoms-deep, secret and unreadable, but at the touch of my mouth something deep inside them seemed to shift and dissolve, and her lips parted the tiniest bit.

I don't know which of us it was that took the step that brought us together, but suddenly we were touching. One of my hands was on the curve of her back pulling her close, the other buried deep in the silk of her hair. It felt lustrous, alive, impossibly warm from the heat of her body. Her hands were on my shoulders, then on my neck, her skin burning with an electric tingle that turned the marrow of my bones to a deep, delicious ache.

Beattie? I thought — and then our lips touched and I didn't think anything.

The challenge

By the time the others finally arrived back, wet and bedraggled, we were sitting demurely side by side on a log. Rob gave us a quizzical look that made me wonder what he knew, or guessed, but all he said was, 'Hello, you two. Sorry we were so long.' Why *had* they been so long, I wondered... then gave a mental shrug and let it go. With Rob, anything was possible.

'I'm afraid the spaghetti got a bit overcooked,' I confessed, not daring to look at Beattie.

'Our fault for being late. Where is it?'

Beattie and I exchanged a guilty glance that bubbled with secret laughter. 'Well, actually... I'm afraid it's... in the river.'

'The *river*?' It wasn't like Rob to ask awkward questions, and true to form he went on, deadpan, 'Lucky pasta's biodegradable.' It had seemed about as biodegradable as India-rubber, but I wasn't about to say so. I was betting there'd be plenty of fish with indigestion that night — hopefully they wouldn't end up floating on the surface belly-up.

If they did, none of us were awake to see it. After dinner — rice Bolognese, followed by bananas and chocolate biscuits — we crawled straight into our sleeping bags, the soft chords of Cam's guitar harmonising with the wind in the trees. I'd been looking forward to some quiet time alone with my thoughts, but it didn't happen. No sooner did my head touch the pillow than I was asleep.

The next day was too full of action to leave any room for thinking. A ridge walk in the morning left the afternoon free for a basic session on trad lead climbing, translating the knowledge we'd gleaned over hours in the indoor gym into the different environment of the outdoors.

If it hadn't been for Lee it would have been the highlight of the trip. But he made it clear from the start there was only one person who knew anything about lead climbing, and no prizes for guessing who that was. Every sentence began with, 'When I was leading this climb up north . . .' or 'You'll find it's easier if you rack your shoulder-sling as a quickdraw by tripling the loops . . .' or 'I'd slot a nut there if I were you . . .' Soon the others were rolling their eyes the moment he opened his mouth, except for Gabriel, who just went quietly ahead doing things his way. For once I was sorry Rob was so laid-back; I longed for him to growl: 'Shut your mouth, Lee! Who asked you anyway?'

Lee was acting out some kind of warped leadership fantasy when the leader was supposed to be me. At every turn he was rubbing my nose in the fact that he had more experience than I did. But I wasn't playing his game; I wouldn't compete. My instinctive response was to back off — let him get on with it, if it was what floated his boat. I'd begun to wish they'd picked Lee as captain instead of me. It was all so childish and pathetic — but even though I knew it, even though I could tell Lee's behaviour was getting the others' backs up, it left me feeling more inadequate with every hour that passed.

Things can't go on like this, I thought grimly. Something's going to have to give — and maybe it should be me.

Things came to a head that evening. By now we'd all had a turn at kitchen duty and Cam and Rob had volunteered to make the final evening meal: Rob's world-famous chilli, followed by Cam's top-secret Rocky Road. 'The only camp-fire version known to mankind,' Cam bragged, brandishing marshmallows and slabs of chocolate he'd managed to keep hidden among the rest of the provisions. 'Wait till you taste it — this baby disappears faster than greased lightning. Hands off those marshmallows, Fraser! You vultures head on upriver and I'll join you once I'm done; the Chilli King can hold the fort.' Rob glanced at his watch and nodded, he and Cam exchanging a sidelong smile I didn't understand. But I didn't waste any thought on it — my dry, dusty skin was crying out for a dip in the river, though I knew it would be freezing.

The others headed off eagerly down the path, Beattie and me following more slowly behind. 'Lee's really getting on my wick,' grumbled Beattie. 'You should tell him to get out of your face. Everyone hates him. Who does he think he is?'

'Let it ride,' I told her. 'Things will settle down — they're bound to. Just as long as he doesn't make the National team . . .'

'And we do,' she said with a grin, picking up the threads of a discussion we'd begun the previous night. 'Why d'you think Rob's being so cagey about the trials? With only four places and one non-travelling reserve our chances can't be great, and the competition'll be deadly. But imagine if we both made the team! First step, the Regionals; second step the World Climbing Champs, Ratho, Scotland . . .'

We rounded a bend and for the first time I saw the waterhole the others had been raving about. The river gorge narrowed to a bottleneck, bush-clad slopes rising up on either side. Here and there the vegetation gave way to bare rock, head-height in some places, sky-high in others: a natural bouldering playground of rough, knobbly rock that cried out to be climbed.

Where we were standing the river was ankle-deep, clear water flowing swiftly over a bed of russet and grey pebbles. A stone's throw away it darkened and deepened, widening to a circular pool surrounded by a tangle of bush. On the far side a bare expanse of rock reared up a good twelve metres, the twisted flume of a waterfall cascading down the centre to plunge into the deep water below.

Lee was blocking the path, facing me with arms folded. Fraser and Sasha hovered behind him; further on Gabriel was sitting on a flat rock with his back to us, pulling off his trainers.

'OK, Phil, here's the deal,' Lee said bluntly. 'Having you as Captain of the Highlands team is a joke. You're not a captain's arsehole. You don't have the leadership skills to take a group of toddlers to the playground. You've been climbing less than a year and your competition experience is a laugh: one lucky break in the Regionals. The only reason Rob picked you is because you climb at the Igloo and you're one of his pets. The captain's job should be down to skill and experience, so I'm challenging you — winner takes all. Here's how it's going down. Done any free climbing before?' He pointed to the rock-face beside him. My eyes followed his gesture, my mind racing. The wall was pocked with hollows and protruding globs of rock as if someone had chucked lumps of molten lava at the cliff face and they'd stuck and hardened; it'd be a dream to climb. Already I could see the route I'd take . . .

'Free climbing?' Beattie squawked, in the same tone as she might have said *Space-walking?* 'Are you completely

97

out of your tree? Only two sorts of people free climb: world-class pros with a death-wish, and total idiots who don't know any better.'

Beattie was right. All the true free solo climber brings to the rock is a pair of shoes, a chalk bag and sheer skill — along with a streak of insanity. Free climbing is climbing without a rope — and on any wall higher than you can safely jump off, that's a high-wire act above infinity, with a fall meaning anything from serious injury to a death certificate.

I pulled my gaze away from the wall and looked Lee straight in the eye. 'No way,' I said flatly. 'If the captaincy means that much to you, take it. It's no big deal. I'm sure Rob wouldn't bother with a captain at all if he didn't need one for the team registration. We're all equal as far as I'm concerned.'

Lee's mouth twisted. 'So you're chicken. Surprise, surprise.'

I glanced at the cliff-face again. I knew I could do it, and part of me longed to try. Over the past two days I'd got hooked on the adrenaline high that comes from mastering a route set by nature with nothing but a thin line to safeguard you. How much more intense the rush, how much greater the thrill of knowing there was nothing . . . nothing other than guts and skill between you and eternity?

The climb was easy — well within my limits. And if it proved too tough I could always come down again.

Sasha's eyes were wide and anxious. 'Don't do it, guys,' she said. 'Remember Rob's ground-rules? If they catch you up there . . .'

'What ground-rules?'

'Rob said we mustn't boulder above head-height, unless it was over the water and we fancied a dunking.'

I looked across to the rock-pool, where the twisted

thread of the waterfall cascaded downwards, bisecting a wide expanse of rock similar to the one beside us. Two sides, two routes . . . a race for the top, with a slither back down via the overgrown path over on the left . . . it was made to measure. Ten minutes max and it would be over, things between me and Lee settled for good.

'How deep's the pool?'

Fraser goggled at me, a grin of delighted disbelief dawning on his face. 'Way deep. We couldn't touch the bottom yesterday, not even diving down with the longest stick we could find. But . . .'

'But what? If we fall, we get wet. We're not doing anything Rob's told us we can't. There's your deal, Lee: a straight race up, first to top out is captain — for what that's worth — and no arguments afterwards. Shake on it?'

A flicker in Lee's eyes and a sullen set to his mouth told me he didn't like my compromise, for the simple reason he hadn't thought of it himself — but it was all he'd get, and he knew it. 'I get to pick which side I climb,' he said sulkily, which was fine by me — the fewer excuses he was able to make afterwards the better.

He engulfed my hand in a freckled gorilla-fist before turning to pick his way along the overgrown path to the rocks at the foot of the falls. Wiping my hand on my cargo shorts I found myself hoping we'd make it to the top and down again before Cam appeared round the corner. Whatever Rob had said the evening before, low-level bouldering round the foot of the cliffs was a far cry from climbing to the top without protection, water or no water, and I had a hunch he wouldn't like it — not one tiny bit.

Face-off

Lee chose the right-hand pitch. That showed two things, neither of which came as a surprise: he was a good judge of a climb, and he was serious about winning. Though both routes looked relatively simple, Lee's had more hollows and pockets — not just little ripples and dimples, but good handholds and generous stirrups you could practically fit your whole foot into, as well as a couple of ledges higher up that looked almost wide enough to picnic on.

It wasn't a technically difficult climb any way you looked at it. But in places spray from the waterfall had made the rock dark and slimy-looking, with mosses, lichen and even ferns clinging to the cracks — a dead giveaway that in places the surface would be slippery and treacherous.

There was one major crux that stretched the whole width of the cliff. Just over halfway up the rock-face shelved outwards: a jutting overhang that on Lee's side held to an angle of about 45 degrees, but on mine came close to horizontal, so I'd be hanging upside-down right out over the water like a sloth. Here the water went into free fall, a drifting curtain of spray that would drench either of us in moments if the wind came up.

'OK, guys: seconds out!' announced Fraser, in a high good humour at the prospect of a face-off. By now we were all in position: me and Lee balanced precariously on the narrow ridge under the climb, the others on Gabriel's flat rock, the ideal vantage point to watch the race. We were both wearing our climbing shoes, which Lee had produced with a smirk from the bag we'd assumed held his swimming gear.

'The slimy rodent had this planned all along!' snarled Beattie. 'You're crazy to go along with it.'

Shoes on, chalked up, ready . . . breathing deep, psyching myself for the off. There was a prickling sensation between my shoulder blades, part nerves, part excitement, that told me this was one race I desperately wanted to win. Not to be captain, but because of Lee.

'Here's the deal,' continued the compere. 'First to top out's the winner. I'm judge, and my decision is final: no arguments or excuses — or sulks afterwards, Lee. In the event of a tie —'

'Shut up and get on with it!' said Sasha. 'Cam will be here any minute.'

'OK, OK,' said Fraser hurriedly. 'Climbers ready? On your marks, get set . . . *GO!*'

And I was off, powering up the cliff like a monkey up a tree. It was bouldering taken to the ultimate extreme — all the buzz of free climbing with none of the restrictions of having to manage a rope — and I was climbing like I'd never climbed in my life. On good days, rhythm and flow work together to send you floating up the rock like a dancer, as if every move, every hold has been preordained. This climb wasn't like that. There was no mysticism about it — only an insatiable hunger I'd never felt before, propelling me upwards as ravenously as if my body was a python gulping that cliff-face down.

Every instinct screamed at me to check on Lee, though I knew there was no way he could be close. But I didn't dare; didn't have a second to spare. I kept my eyes on the rock ahead, scanning my route for the bombproof holds and sure-fire shortcuts that wouldn't leave me stranded with nowhere to go, no option other than a downclimb that'd cost me the race.

Suddenly icy water flicked in my face. I jerked back, feeling my left hand slip on a hold that'd looked rock-solid but was greasy as soap, my body twist and corkscrew, balance slewing helplessly as I peeled off the wall. Roped up, I'd have been calling and gone. But the knowledge that a fall would be just that — a plunge into the unknown — gave me reserves I never dreamed I had. From a single toehold I powered upward in a leaping dyno that brought me in reach of the jug-handle at the foot of the overhang. My hand latched on and I swung, feet kicking, spray blinding me, then stabilised, hugging the wall. It smelled of wet rock and algae, but to me it was heaven. My heart hammering hard enough to knock me off into space again I gulped air, willing myself to settle down.

I had to be more careful. Glancing down, I saw Lee a good three metres below me on his side of the wall, pulling upwards with that unhurried rhythm I knew could go on forever. Underestimating him would be fatal. I didn't have this won — not by a long shot.

A breeze had sprung up from nowhere and was twisting the waterfall towards me like a veil blowing in the wind. My skin was misted with water, the rock glistening . . . but Lee's side would be dry.

I had no time to waste.

Tipping my head back I scanned the overhang. It was a classic jug haul — the kind of crux that made you wish you were a spider or a fly with suction pads on your hands and feet. But at least on the underside the rock was dry. Keeping my arms straight to conserve energy I walked them out into nothingness, using a drop knee and undercling to maximise reach. A foot jam took the weight off my arms, a high heel hook freeing my right arm to move upwards. Dangling upside-down I caught a fish-silver glint of water way below, a circle of white faces small as snowflakes gawking upwards. Back to the rock . . . I could see my route clear, but I was wrong-footed; to right myself I'd have to drop to vertical and monkey-bar my way round 180, then ratchet up again. Already my arms were screaming and my left leg had the shakes . . . and that brief glimpse downward had reminded me how high I was.

Sucking oxygen, I readied myself and swung. A quick one-two, my legs kicking in space, then I was swinging in a controlled arc back up to the rock. A toe-hook, a twist and a wriggle, and I was over and up. The home straight was above me. And no sign of Lee.

This section of the climb had been obscured by the overhang, and now my heart sank. It was the sheerest pitch by far: six metres or so of slick granite bisected by a meandering diagonal crack. Far above was a wide ledge that'd give me a chance to rest and shake out if I could reach it; then an easy haul to the top. But the pitch on Lee's side was kindergarten stuff: pocked and dimpled like Swiss cheese, a gift to a climber of his calibre. Once he was over his crux he'd be swarming up and topping out before I could say 'Spiderman'.

I'd never climbed anything like this before. For the first time I felt exposed and vulnerable. I was way high. I wished I had my harness, a rope as a lifeline between me and a fall.

As I hesitated, clinging to my meagre handhold, a movement below caught my eye. A hand hove into view and jammed itself into a horizontal crack; then another, followed by an effortful grunt and a thatch of orange hair.

I didn't have time to think. Crimping my fingers into the

edge of the crack I heaved with my hands and pushed with my feet, walking my hands upwards, feeling my T-shirt snag on the rock as I side-wound my way up like a snake. One minute my feet were pressing against the crack's far edge, the next they were searching out friction points the slick rock never knew it had, dreamed up out of desperation and the counter-pressure created by my jack-knifing body. Arched like a bow, every sinew twanging, I laybacked agonisingly on and up, every labouring squeeze of my heart inching me higher up the cliff face.

Fuzzy black splodges of effort were floating across my vision, but in spite of them — in spite of the sweat oozing into my eyes, in spite of my desperate focus on the crack, the wall, the elusive goal of that way-distant ledge — still I saw him. Like a clockwork toy, arms and legs moving in remorseless harmony, clawing his way closer, closer . . .

Now I could hear him breathing: husky pants like wood being sawed. His head came level with mine. He was breathing hard, but he was moving easy. He looked across and met my eyes, winked and gave a death's-head grin. His cushy crux and soft final pitch had given him the slack to catch me. He had the race in the bag and he knew it.

Then the vertical rock vanished under my hand and my fingers were hooking over the edge of the ledge. I gripped, turned, wedged one toe into the crack; hung my other hand on the lip and heaved with everything I had, hauling myself up like a kid clambering onto a windowsill.

Where there should have been bare rock my fingers slid on something thin and shiny that slipped and rolled . . . *spaghetti*? As my head came level with the ledge I realised. *Not spaghetti — straw. STRAW!* screamed my brain — just before the world exploded.

A thunderbolt of burning eyes and erupting feathers flew

at me, beak lunging for my eyes, talons like meat-hooks stabbing into my hair, pinions beating my face with a noise like sails snapping in the wind.

My brain shut down.

I pushed off from the bluff like a skydiver exiting a plane, hollering wordlessly, eyes staring, hands flailing helplessly to keep the monster off me. And still it came, erupting into the air with a screech like a train-whistle, wings slapping at me like paddles hitting water, a welter of talons, gleaming feathers and burning eyes.

I fell.

Inside my head was a vast silence, though the outside world was full of noise: the trailing shriek of my own terror, the echoing scream of the bird and the gliding whoosh of its flight as it wheeled towards me and away, dwindling to the size of a crow, a sparrow, a pinprick . . . then lost forever in the endless blue.

Consequences

Instinct took over, and instinct said: *you're dead*.

The fall seemed to take an eternity, and for most of that time my whole being was empty, numb, accepting. I didn't even feel afraid.

But my brain never stays quiet for long. Into it popped a question: *shouldn't my whole life be playing out in my mind like a movie?* That thought was instantly followed by another, crystal-clear and in brilliant Technicolor: the time Nick dared me to jump off the 5-metre board at the swimming pool. He'd bribed me with the penknife from the Cornflakes packet and was up top egging me on. 'A pin-drop, Pipsqueak — do a pin-drop, feet-first, or you'll splat like a ripe tomato. And shut your eyes tight, else the pressure'll pop them out.' With Nick, you never knew what to believe.

'But you said it was safe,' I quavered.

'Oh, it is!' Nick assured me breezily. 'Everyone knows you can't hurt yourself falling into water. But do a pin-drop just the same.'

Eventually I jumped. I'd done a pin-drop, but Nick hadn't warned me to keep my arms close by my sides. Some instinct prompted me to flap them on the way down — to try and slow my fall, or even fly. And when I hit the water, so did they, flat as flippers. The tender underside stung for a week, and that night I'd cried myself to sleep, muffling my sobs in the pillow so Mum wouldn't hear, clutching the penknife for comfort.

Now my brain was yelling at me: *Do a pin-drop! Keep your arms by your sides and your eyes tight shut or they'll pop out!* And another piece of wisdom from who-knew-where: *And keep your legs crossed or you'll split right up the middle when you hit!*

There was hardly any time left. I'd been falling spread-eagled like a skydiver, facing up instead of down. Windmilling my arms and lifting my torso, I felt myself swivel upright, the cliff face rushing past with horrifying speed. I had a second to be glad I'd pushed off so hard; another second to rotate my arms one final time for balance and pull them in tight to my sides, take a single massive breath, cross my legs and shut my eyes so tight my head sang.

One last thought popped into my brain: a story-thought that took a millisecond. Mum's favourite about this old-time dude who led a life of wickedness — a highwayman or something — and then got killed falling off his horse. Should've gone straight to hell, but: *Betwixt the stirrup and the ground / Mercy I asked, mercy I found.* Shows it's never too late to mend your ways. That last thought was as close to a prayer as I got.

I hit the water.

Thought splintered to mindless shock, cold, rushing deceleration, a churning maelstrom of bubbles. I must have opened my eyes: a galaxy of swirling effervescence boiled around me, my body braking through translucent aquamarine to swirling blackness, my eardrums bulging, my heartbeat suspended in an endless moment of plummeting dread, legs curled like a foetus, waiting for the crunch as I hit bottom.

Then I was kicking up again, green-black lightening to turquoise blue and bursting out to spluttering, sparkling sunshine.

I thrashed to the side and heaved myself out onto the warm rock, shivering and gasping. Lay there, sodden and panting, my brain repeating over and over again, *I'm alive; I'm alive; I'm alive.*

'You don't deserve to be.' The voice was deep and angry. My heart stopped for the second time in a minute. I cranked my head up and gawked at the sombre group surrounding me, the other kids hanging back, white-faced. Closer in, Rob, grim as I'd never seen him; Cam, eyes magnified to solemn hugeness behind his wire-rimmed specs. And another guy — the one who'd spoken.

This must be what that look had meant, I thought stupidly, between Rob and Cam at camp. This must be the 'surprise' they'd refused to elaborate on. They must have come to introduce him to us, whoever he was; come round the corner and seen me way up there . . . seen me falling . . .

I gulped, tasting river water, and scrambled to my feet.

'I'm sorry,' I said, my voice sounding very small.

Rob looked at me, and for once there was no warmth in his eyes.

'This is Phil?' asked the stranger. 'The one you told me about?'

'Yes,' said Rob. 'It is.'

'We'd better get him back to camp,' said Cam. 'Give him a towel, someone. Are you OK, Phil?'

'He doesn't deserve to be,' said the stranger again.

Cam wrapped a towel round me and, shivering so much I could hardly walk, I headed back with the others to camp.

Lee had joined the silent group at the waterfall, slithering shamefaced down the path. He didn't meet my eyes, and Rob didn't speak to him, just gave him a single glance, tight-lipped.

'Go and change into dry clothes,' Rob told me when we got back. I hated that he didn't use my name or look at me. It told me he was way mad. 'Then I want to talk to all of you.'

I went into the hut, stripped and towelled off. My skin looked like a dead chicken's, and I'd've traded places with one in an instant. I couldn't believe how stupid I'd been. Feet dragging, I joined the others round the campfire. There was no sign of Cam and the stranger — they must have gone off so Rob could talk to us alone.

Beattie had saved a place for me beside her on a log. Rob was standing in the centre with his hands shoved deep in the pockets of his faded fleece jacket. A smell of burnt marshmallow hung in the air, and that, more than anything, made me want to cry. I sat down and stared at the ground.

I expected Rob to start talking; to yell at me and Lee. Me especially. But he didn't. For a long time he didn't say anything at all. Eventually, reluctantly, I looked up to find him watching me and I couldn't look away.

'I don't know what to say to you,' he said. 'What happened today was my responsibility. That's the bottom line. Cam and I — we both realised the captaincy had become an issue, but we thought you had the maturity to sort it out yourselves. We were wrong.'

I opened my mouth to argue, to say it hadn't been his fault. It was mine.

'What you boys did today . . . do you have any idea what the consequences could have been?'

'But we were over the water,' mumbled Lee.

'Falling into water from that height is like falling onto concrete. The surface tension makes it solid. See this?' He pointed to a pale scar at the corner of his eye. 'I used to do high-diving when I was a kid. One time I joined some cliff jumpers; thought I'd try a dive from higher than I'd ever done before. It went fine, except some guy had thrown a match into the water. This is what that match did, floating on water, hitting it from that height. I almost lost my eye.'

'But cliff jumpers . . .'

'Cliff jumping is for idiots. Know its other name? Tombstoning. We could have pulled you out of that water dead.

'There are two issues we need to deal with. The first is the captaincy. Sasha, I'd like you to take over.'

Sasha's eyes flew wide. 'But —' she said.

Rob looked at her.

'OK,' she said.

'The second issue isn't so simple, but I want to make my position very clear. This is a team, and there is no place for animosity. If I see negative rivalry again, the person responsible will be dropped with no further warning. Understood?' We nodded. 'Phil and Lee, shake hands — and mean it.'

We clambered to our feet, crossed the fire-lit circle and shook. For the first time, meeting Lee's eyes, I saw a kid there, frightened and insecure. 'I'm sorry, Lee,' I muttered, though I wasn't sure what I was apologising for.

'Me too,' he said.

'We'll leave it at that,' Rob said. 'I hope you've all learned from what happened today. I know I have.'

Still, I wanted to try and fix things — make them how they were before. I waited till Rob was on his own and then went over to him. 'Rob, I'm sorry. I really, really am.'

'I know you are. You let me down today big-time. Worse, you let yourself down, in ways you can't begin to understand. We talked about second chances once. Remember?' I nodded. I remembered. 'Sometimes there are no second chances. Up there on the cliff could have been one of those times.' He put his arm round my shoulder and gave a brief hug.

'Come and have some chilli.'

Buzz Munro

That night I tossed and turned in my sleeping bag for hours listening to the others snore. Every time sleep almost sucked me under I'd flash back to the fall and jerk awake again, heart hammering, covered in cold sweat. Grim images and phrases kept marching through my brain: *split right up the middle when you hit the water . . . like falling onto concrete . . . splat like a ripe tomato . . . tombstoning . . .*

Finally I opened my eyes and turned on my back, watching ripples of moonlit water reflecting on the roof. I needed a mental change of subject, and I had the perfect one: Beattie.

Obediently my poor old brain ground into the new gear, stuttered . . . and stalled. What about Beattie? Things were OK again, that was clear — better than OK. That kiss . . . I closed my eyes, remembering. Then they popped open again. What did it mean? That she was my girlfriend? That we were going out? Or what?

What was it she'd said between the first, tentative kiss, and the second, not-so-tentative one? 'Phil, I need to know: that girl — the one you were ogling at the dance. Jordan Archer's girlfriend. Is she . . . are you . . .'

And I'd looked deep in her eyes and said, 'Beattie, she's just a girl I once knew. Past tense. History. I swear it.' And it was true. If it wasn't, I couldn't be feeling this way . . . could I?

A little dimple appeared in each corner of Beattie's mouth.

'I believe you, though thousands wouldn't . . .' And then we didn't talk any more.

But I wasn't a hundred per cent sure where I stood. She was still Beattie, just the same as she'd always been. There was no sudden transformation like when I fell in love with Katie centuries ago. No romantic code, no lingering looks, no 'accidental' touches of hands, no hidden messages.

Mind you, we hadn't been alone together. Maybe when we were, we'd talk. Maybe she'd lay on the line exactly what the situation was. But Beattie or not, she was definitely a girl, and somehow I didn't think so.

Maybe when we were alone together, there'd be another kiss.

Maybe . . .

Rob and Cam had introduced their friend the night before: a climbing mate from up north, name of Buzz Munro. He looked like a climber — a tanned face that needed a shave, with prickle-cut dark hair and eyes you could tell at a glance wouldn't miss much, a crooked grin and big, knuckly climber's hands. Like many of the climbing crowd he had a slight accent: Canadian, he said. He hadn't brought a tent and there was no room left in the huts; Rob and Cam offered to shift some gear into the van, but Buzz said he'd rather sleep under the stars. And in the morning when we emerged from our hut yawning and stretching, there he was, a curled-up purple caterpillar covered in dew.

As Rob had promised, the events of the previous day seemed forgotten, though part of me couldn't believe I'd gotten off so lightly. Everyone was cheerful, hurrying breakfast to leave more time for the final activity: trad lead climbing on a section of rock we hadn't seen before.

Rob and Cam loaded the van while the newcomer talked us through the morning's plans, showing an understated, quiet authority that made me wonder if he'd been a climbing coach himself. 'Most of us have done a bit of everything at one stage or another,' he said when Lee asked him, then changed the subject. 'You guys ever heard of redpointing?'

For once it was Gabriel who put up his hand. 'It's another name for on-sight, isn't it — topping out on a new climb, first attempt?'

'Close. It's lead climbing bottom to top in one go, no dogging, no falls. Unlike on-sight, prior knowledge and repeat attempts are allowed, so you get to watch and learn — from each other as well as your own mistakes. Sound good? I hope so, because it's what Rob and Cam have in store for you today.'

The morning flew by. Buzz didn't climb, but seemed content to spot, belay, organise gear and stand around chatting to Rob and Cam. 'Aren't you going up, Buzz?' Beattie asked him towards midday, with a cheeky grin.

'Me? Nah — I'm happy to watch you guys,' he said casually.

'Seems a waste of time coming all this way then,' muttered Lee, too quietly for him to hear; but it was fun having someone new to show off to, and Buzz was way cool.

But it wasn't Buzz I was trying to impress. I had a secret agenda. From the chance remark Buzz had made at the foot of the falls I knew Rob had mentioned me to him. I knew Rob thought highly of my climbing ability, and that knowledge meant heaps. I'd let him down the day before, but today I was going to make him proud.

And in spite of having one of the most technically difficult pitches thrown at me, I topped out on my first attempt — something none of the others did. I climbed the best

I'd ever done; I could feel it in my bones, and see it in the lift of Buzz's eyebrow as he lowered me down. 'Way to go, Cowboy,' was all he said.

Rob's body language as he turned away to stash the rope told me all I needed to know. The deep down part of me that had been cold and shrivelled since yesterday unfurled just the tiniest bit, because I knew if there was anyone who'd hand out free second chances, no questions asked, it would be Rob.

Welcome home

It was awesome to be home again. Even the milk run went well, with Dad in a cheery mood, singing as he drove. He wouldn't let me tell about anything. 'Save it for dinner, Son. It's a big occasion and your mother's planned something special. You know she'll demand every detail and you'll only end up having to tell it twice.'

Mum's face lit up when she saw me; she gave me a quick hug and then backed off hurriedly. 'Shower,' she said sternly. 'Plenty of soap, lots of deodorant and clean clothes, and then I'll give you a proper hug. The house hasn't been the same without you, Pippin.'

But Muddle didn't care how I smelled. Stinky or not, she dragged me into her tiny cupboard of a room to show off her latest treasure: a red plastic bucket. 'Looky, Biffin,' she said proudly, jamming it over her head so her eyes were completely covered like the Black Knight: 'Mopabite helnit!'

Dinner was my absolute favourite: lamb done Mum's special way, with roast veggies and loads of gravy. Mum can make a leg of lamb feed an army, or so Dad's always bragging, and though the leg looked small there was plenty left for seconds.

Truth was, I hadn't expected a welcome-home banquet or anyone except Mum to be interested in hearing about the trip, but to my amazement Dad listened closely to every

115

word. 'Rickety Bridge,' he repeated thoughtfully through a mouthful of potato. 'Now where have I heard that name before?'

And a few minutes later he slapped the table so hard the pepper grinder fell over. 'That's it!' he said. 'Deerhunting! Sarge mentioned the area a while back — had a job from some guys who'd been up that way and bagged themselves a stag.' Ron Sargeson was Dad's old firefighting and hunting buddy. He'd been injured in the same fire as Dad: the girder that fell on Dad's leg smashed Sarge's back and now he was a hero, though he had a face that looked like crinkled pink tinfoil and he'd never walk again. But that didn't stop Sarge. Now he was in charge of the rifle range, running what Dad called 'a tight, zero-risk facility to rival any you'd find in the world', plus he supplied reloaded rounds of ammo to other hunters and had taught himself taxidermy to earn a bit of extra money. That's stuffing dead animals — which was how old Horace got himself a facelift and up on Nick's wall for the knockdown price of nothing. Uncle Sarge was like a brother to Dad — that's what being almost killed together does, I guess.

As for the rifle range, it was a kind of paradise for Dad — 'a place he goes to play at being a boy again', as Mum put it. I'd never been there, though of course Nick had. But while Mum might look on it as a kind of Peter Pan Neverland, to Dad it was way different. 'It's man's territory, Son, and that's when I'll take you there. When you talk, think and act like a man — and not before.'

The sound of the doorbell interrupted my thoughts just as Mum was getting up to serve dessert. 'I'll get it,' she said; 'I'm up anyway.'

We heard the door open and Mum's voice drifting clearly across the hallway. 'Barney! We haven't seen you for weeks!

116

Come on in, stranger!' Barney was Nick's best friend from primary school; they both enrolled at Greendale High, and the friendship stuck. Ole Barn was like one of the family and had put Mum's 'feed an army' reputation to the test more times than I could count. From old habit I shifted my chair to make room for him and glanced at Nick, expecting to see his grin break out as he headed for the door.

But he just sat there chewing mechanically.

I tuned back in to Mum, still chirping away, but with a new note of uncertainty in her voice. 'You won't? Come now, don't be shy! We have apple pie for dessert . . .'

A sheepish mumble, in Barney's bass croak.

'Well, if you're sure . . . thank you for returning the book. And remember, we're always happy to see you.'

Mum came slowly in, holding Nick's battered copy of the Highway Code. 'He said he wasn't hungry,' she said in the same kind of wondering way she might say, 'He's grown an extra head.'

Everyone looked at Nick, even Madeline. I felt like it was the first time I'd seen my brother for weeks — *really* seen him. Seemed he was always either at school, hanging out at the Igloo, or in his room with the door shut. He had this pale, unhealthy look like a grub under a log, and purplish smudges under his eyes. He swallowed his mouthful with a clicking sound, then looked up from under his eyebrows. 'What?'

'Don't you think you should have gone to the door, darling?' asked Mum gently. 'To thank him for returning the book, even if he couldn't come in?'

'He is your friend,' chipped in Dad, always quick to piggyback on Mum's little lectures. 'It's common courtesy, Nicholas.'

That's when I realised I hadn't seen Nick and Barney

together for an age. At school they'd always been together, in line for tuck shop, perched on a wall in the sun, chatting up girls, hurrying to class. But not lately. Now I was more likely to see Nick mooching along on his own, eyes to the ground, or on the fringes of a group I didn't know, a kaleidoscope of changing faces, sullen and hang-dog.

'It's high time you started studying for your driving test,' continued Dad. 'It costs good money, so you'd better pass first try.'

Nick's eyes flickered. 'If I pass, can I have a cellphone?'

'A cellphone?' parroted Dad. 'What would you want a *cellphone* for? There's a perfectly good telephone right here in the kitchen.'

Nick gave him a look. 'That's not the point.'

'Oh, really? Then what is the point?'

'You wouldn't understand,' said Nick witheringly.

'Try me,' smirked Dad, unwithered; 'though I dare say I wouldn't, being an intelligent adult. As for a reward, Nicholas, the only reward you can expect is free driving lessons and the chance to burn out the truck's clutch.'

'The truck?' repeated Nick with a hunted glance at Mum, family shorthand that meant: *Mum, please rescue me from being taught to drive by Dad!*

Dad bulldozed on, oblivious. He hadn't absorbed family shorthand by osmosis like the rest of us, and none of us had tried to teach him. 'Of course the truck!' he boomed. 'Your mother's car's an automatic, and men drive manuals. Every boy should be taught to drive by his father. You'll be a natural, just like I was at your age.'

'And now,' said Mum diplomatically, setting down the steaming pie in front of Dad, 'who's for apple pie?'

Normally, put a pie on the table and it'd be dished up and gone in seconds. So Nick and I both sat up and took notice when Dad gave the pie-dish a regretful glance and said: 'Later, Trish. I think it's time for our announcement, don't you?'

I had a sudden flashback to the last time Mum and Dad had an 'announcement', heralded by exactly this kind of secretive glance. That was almost three years ago, and it had been the news that Madeline was on the way. Nick had been grossed out, and I'd been too excited to think straight. Now, watching Madeline bang on her table with her spoon and grab air for the pie, my heart did a scary flip-flop. Surely . . . not?

Dad's news

Mum slipped into her chair and folded her hands on the table. Her eyes were smiling. 'Go on then, Jim,' she said. 'Tell them.'

Dad's chair creaked dangerously as he tipped back, folded his arms and stared round at us. His eyes, his moustache, his whole self was blazing with contained excitement, just the way Nick did when something huge had fired him up.

'Listen up then, Nick, Pip . . . Madeline.' Even little Muddle was staring at him, eyes like saucers, as if he was about to tell her a very grown-up story. *You ain't gonna like this if it's what I think it is, Princess,* I thought.

But I was wrong.

'You boys know your mother and I have been struggling to make ends meet lately,' said Dad. 'The milk run . . . it hasn't been easy. We've been losing customers to the supermarket hand over fist, and it's got worse instead of better. We've hung in there, tried to ride it through. I don't want you boys to think you just give up when times get tough. That's when you dig in and make it work. Remember that. You too, Madeline.' Dad glared round at us and we all stared back, wondering what was coming next. I had a queasy feeling in my gut. I wished Dad had told his news after the pie instead of before.

'We've tried everything. Changing delivery days, improving service, expanding our product range . . .' I remembered the banana custard Dad tried selling a while back. Nick said it tasted like cat puke, and he'd been right. He also said it'd sell like rat sandwiches, and he'd been right about that, too. My sick feeling was getting worse.

Dad cleared his throat. 'But in the end we had no choice. We put the franchise up for sale. Sometimes —'

We'd been taught never to interrupt Dad, but I couldn't help myself. 'The milk run? You're selling the milk run?'

Dad wasn't angry. All the puff had gone out of him and his moustache had a sorrowful droop as he nodded, saying nothing.

'You boys must understand the decision wasn't easy,' said Mum. 'And finding a buyer . . . well, that hasn't been easy either.'

'It's simple economics,' said Dad. 'Nick, you do Business Studies. You'll tell your brother that people don't just buy a business on trust; they want to see the balance sheet, profit and loss account, cash flow forecasts . . . if a franchise hasn't been performing for one person, it doesn't make for an attractive investment to someone else.'

Dad's news was going from bad to worse. There was a shred of lamb caught between my teeth; I could feel it with my tongue. Save it for later, chirped my brain. It's probably the last food you'll ever see. Already my tummy felt hollow. Nick, businessman-in-training, was staring at Dad as blankly as if he'd had his brain extracted.

'There's a guaranteed buy-back clause in the original contract,' Dad went on. 'You boys don't need to know the details, except that we'd have lost a lot of money.'

'You're scaring them, Jim,' said Mum gently. 'They don't need to know all this. Move on to the good news.'

There was good news?

Dad's moustache bristled to life again. 'Well,' he said, 'the upshot of it all is, we've found a buyer. Approved by

MooZical Milk and signed this week. The holder of the Borrowdale franchise wants to expand his territory; he's offered less than we paid, but there's a time to cut your losses and start over.'

Dad beamed round at us as if this was the best news ever.

'But . . .' I croaked, 'you won't have a job any more. Where will the money come from?'

'Your old Dad's thought of that. All this time I've been looking around, keeping my ears and eyes open. And just this week things have come together.'

'Dad's been offered a job,' said Mum, holding out her hand to him. Dad gave it a squeeze, then reached for the pie-slice and started to cut.

'Yup,' he said, 'I sure have. With a cast-iron salary and paid sick-leave to boot. And I bet neither of you boys can guess where.'

My mind was a blank. Dad — a proper job, like other people's dads? 'The supermarket?' I hazarded, a hazy vision of Dad in his MooZical Milk jacket behind the dairy counter swimming into my dazed brain.

'Nope,' said Dad, snapping off a piece of pie-crust and popping it in his mouth. 'The Igloo.'

The Igloo?

Dad beamed round at us. 'Yes,' he said proudly, 'you are looking at the newly appointed Fair Play Coordinator, starting next week.'

Nick had been listening, expressionless. But now he was on his feet, fists on the table, glaring at Dad. 'You?' he spat. 'Fair Play Coordinator? That's a joke!'

Dad flinched as if he'd been slapped.

'The Igloo —' Nick could hardly get the words out — 'the Igloo — it's *our* place, mine and Pip's! You shove your way in everywhere — into every tiny corner of my life! There's

nowhere I can go — nowhere I can just be myself! The *Igloo*
— you — ' His voice broke and his chair clattered to the
floor as he shoved it away and headed for the door.

But Dad was blocking his way. 'Sit down,' he growled. 'I
have something to say to you.'

They were inches apart, Nick's face livid, dark eyes
burning like coals; Dad's red and splotchy, jaw jutting.

'*Wot*,' said Nick, very low.

'You're not going anywhere until you've apologised to me.'

'*Get out of my face*,' hissed Nick.

Then it happened, as quickly as when two dogs are
circling stiff-legged and all it takes is one to snarl and snap.
Nick went to push past Dad, Dad gave him a shove in the
chest — and Nick swung at him. I saw tears on my brother's
face, but all there was on Dad's was a kind of furious
desperation as he shoved Nick again, then again, sending
him staggering back across the kitchen. Nick had his hands
up like a boxer now, sobbing, trying to dance with feet that
seemed sticky, glued to the floor. 'Try and stop me,' he was
sobbing; 'just try and stop me . . .'

Then Mum was up, fierce as a little cockatoo between
them. 'Don't you dare touch him again,' she snapped at Dad.
'Nicholas, go to your room. You should both be ashamed.'

Madeline was utterly silent, staring from Dad to Nick
and back again like someone at a tennis match. Her mouth
was a square shape, the way it goes before she cries, but
her face was frozen still.

It was me who started to cry — great, gulping sobs that
tore out of me as if someone was ripping up my heart.

I pushed past them all and ran to my room, buried my
head under my pillow and cried as if my heart was broken
forever — broken in as many pieces as Mum's celebration
pie, going cold on the deserted table.

Birdsong

The next afternoon I was back in the kitchen again, staring at a blank piece of paper and trawling hopelessly up and down my blank brain for inspiration, or even the tiniest tiddler of an idea. Yup: Mrs Holland's poem.

The sun was shining, the birds were singing, I had the kitchen to myself — what more could a budding poet want? Digging in my bag for my notes on poetic form, I bent my brain reluctantly to the task ahead.

Problem was, I couldn't seem to keep my mind on it. Niggling away on the back burner was a memory of last night. I didn't want to think about it, but it was there, just under the threshold of my consciousness. Nick . . . Dad . . . Nick. That kind of thing didn't happen in our home. We were this perfect family, considerate, polite to Mum and Dad, respectful . . . it was how we'd been brought up, and how we always were. Dad made sure of that.

What happened last night . . . it was like combing your hair before the school photo and feeling pretty pleased with yourself, then suddenly noticing a spot the size of a volcano on your nose. It can't be happening, but it is. And once you know it's there you can't forget it.

Nick, I thought. What's going on with Nick? He's never home, and when he is, he's . . . different. Shut away in his room, music on, door closed. Should I talk to Mum about it? But I knew what she'd say: 'He's growing up, Pippin. It happens. You will too, you know.'

I'd never thought growing up would be like this. Like living with a powder keg just waiting to blow itself sky high. *Sky high* . . . I printed the words on my sheet of refill and stared at them. That would be an awesome title for my poem. *Sky high* . . . *I get my high from climbing* . . . Yeah! Progress was being made.

I stretched and yawned. The sun on my back was making me sleepy, and the chirping of the bird outside was beginning to carve a serious groove in my brain.

It was a starling. I'd know that call anywhere. It was one of the few I recognised and could mimic to perfection. Long ago, back in the mists of time when I was a little kid and life was simple, that was the secret signal Katie and I . . .

That was the secret signal Katie and I used to call each other to the fence to talk.

Here it came again. Was it a starling? Or was it . . .

Now the only sound was the distant thump-thump-thump of bass from Nick's room, and the flicking dentist's drill of a fly against the window.

It came again. Clear, musical, just once; then silence.

I was on my feet, cheek squished against the window pane, trying to see past the angle of the house to the gap in the hedge.

I had to go outside. But suddenly going outside seemed an impossible thing to do at twenty to four on a Tuesday afternoon, weird and unnatural, something only someone completely unhinged would even consider.

Why would I go outside?

I could go outside to check for the milk . . . except Dad was still the milkman, and we didn't do deliveries on Tuesday. I knew that — and Katie knew I knew. If it was Katie.

I could go outside to check the weather. Except I could do that through the window. I could go outside to play ball with Madeline — her new Swingball, rusting in the back garden. Except Madeline was out shopping with Mum. I could go outside to help bring in the shopping. Except they weren't home yet.

I could go outside . . . I could go outside to fetch the mail!

I raced to the front door, terrified she'd be gone by the time I got there . . . if it was her. How long had she been calling? How long had I been sitting there, wasting time?

I flung open the door and sucked in a huge breath . . . then sauntered oh-so-casually down the driveway, bent and peered into the letterbox. There was stuff in there. Numb-fingered, I pulled it out and flicked through it, trying to stop my eyes from skipping away in the direction of the fence. There was a community newspaper, a bank statement, a couple of bills in brown envelopes. I heaved a 'been there, done that' kind of sigh and allowed myself to turn and amble slowly back towards the house. My head was dead straight like a soldier on parade, but my eyes swivelled straight to the fence as if they were ball bearings and it was a magnet.

There she was.

Katie.

Roses are red . . .

Katie, sitting cross-legged in faded jeans in her old place, watching me with a little smile that told me she saw straight through me like a pane of glass, same as she'd always done.

I pasted a look of surprise on my face and strolled over to the fence, all kinds of stuff churning round inside, all kinds of feelings, some I recognised, some I didn't.

'So,' I heard myself say, 'Jordan got sports training or what?'

It was as if I was hovering somewhere above myself like an astral body or something; I felt a momentary surprise at how the words came out, followed by a twinge of satisfaction. Cool, distant, offhand. Just the way I ought to feel. Who the hell did Katie think she was? She'd rejected me, broken my heart, ignored me for months, and now just when my life was coming right here she came, cool as a cucumber, calling me to the fence as if she knew I'd come running. Well, I wouldn't. She could whistle till she was hoarse. I had better fish to fry.

'Jordan?' she repeated, as if she'd never heard the name before. 'Oh, *him*. He's history.'

The word held an uncomfortable echo of my exchange with Beattie a few days ago, but I pushed the thought away. 'History?' I heard myself repeating. I didn't want to be having this conversation, but somehow I couldn't seem to leave. In fact, I'd shuffled closer.

Katie grinned up at me — the old Katie grin that had captured my heart way back when. Her eyes were blue as the sky, dancing with hidden laughter. '*Ancient* history. Since just after the Valentine's Ball.'

I made one last superhuman effort. 'Ditched you, did he?'

She gave me a quelling glance from under her eyelashes. 'He did *not*. It was the other way round.'

I'd known it all along, of course. Who'd ditch Katie? She'd lowered her voice, as if she had more to tell. Somehow I'd crouched down so I was half-kneeling, my face almost level with hers, separated only by the rusty chickenwire we used to pass lollies through, a few bedraggled leaves and a spiderweb. Now I lowered myself gingerly so I was sitting cross-legged, a mirror image of her.

'What happened?'

'I sent him a Valentine's card a week after the ball.'

Did I have it wrong? I wasn't an expert on romance, but I thought a Valentine's card was . . . 'It was rather romantic, really, but Jordan didn't seem to appreciate it:

Roses are red,
Violets are blue;
Rubbish is dumped
And so are you.

'And it was home-made.'

'Why did you dump him?' Any moment I expected the shutters to come down on those beautiful eyes, the hair to toss, the lips to pout; her to signal that I'd overstepped the mark I knew must be there somewhere, get up and flounce away from me forever.

But she didn't.

'Because,' she said. 'Because he was acting like he owned me. Because he expected . . .' the lashes lowered '. . . too much. Because his attitude stank —' her mischievous smile burst out like sunshine — 'and so did his feet. I don't know which was worse. There are jocks like you,' she said, giving me a glance that brushed my skin softly as a feather, so I felt myself flush, 'and there are jocks like him. Smelly jocks. Jordan made me feel like . . . like . . . *arm candy*!'

I blinked. Me, a jock? Did climbing count where jockdom was concerned? I guessed if it counted for Jordan, it must count for me.

'Anyhow,' she went on, 'what about you?'

'Me?'

'Well,' she said, a teasing note in her voice, 'what's going on in the world of Pip McLeod? I've been hearing all kinds of things about you.'

'What kind of things?' I asked guardedly, all too aware that girls are capable of knowing stuff about you that you don't even know yourself.

'Oh, just . . . things.' She was drawing with a little stick in the dirt, tracing some kind of a pattern. She was looking down at it. I badly wanted to see the look in her eyes, the shape of her mouth. I wanted her to look at me. Suddenly it seemed almost airless in the breezy little tunnel under the hedge.

'I've been busy,' I said. 'I've taken up climbing.'

'You've taken up climbing,' she mimicked. 'I *know* that, Pip, or should I say *Phil* now? Everyone knows that. Just like everyone knows you've been selected for the Highlands team . . . or weren't you going to tell me?'

I kept getting wrong-footed here. 'Why wouldn't I tell you?' I mumbled. 'It isn't a secret.'

'No,' said Katie, 'but you're so modest. Not like some people. I've known you a long time, don't forget — a *long* time. Long enough to keep calling you Pip if I want to. Long enough to know all your secrets.'

What secrets? I didn't dare ask. I was staring at the ground, watching Katie's stick. She was drawing tiny interlinked hearts.

She looked up at me — a shy glance that took me back to when she was a little girl. 'Though in some ways I wouldn't have recognised you.' Her voice was so quiet I had to lean forward to hear her.

I opened my mouth to ask why, but nothing came out.

'You've grown up. You've changed. You're not a little kid any more. You're . . .'

There was a silence. My heart was going *thock, thock, thock*; I wondered if she could hear it.

'So,' whispered Katie, 'how's the algebra?'

'Huh?'

'You know.' She wouldn't look at me. 'The As and the Bs.'

For a crazy moment I thought she'd said *the birds and the bees*. I blushed scarlet, my throat closing up so I couldn't breathe. Thank goodness she wasn't looking at me. And then I understood.

All that time ago, on the roundabout . . . I'd tried to talk to Katie about relationships. How I felt, how I wanted to try and change our friendship to something different, a 'B-type' relationship . . . now, remembering, I wanted to crawl away and hide. What had Katie said? *Relationships aren't algebra — and even if they were, some combinations just don't add up. As far as you and me are concerned, it's an 'A'-type relationship or nothing, Pip McLeod.*

But now she was watching me through her eyelashes. 'It was a beautiful way of putting it,' she said softly. 'I've never forgotten.'

Me neither. The whole episode was tattooed on my soul.

'I have tickets to Rock Quest next Saturday,' Katie said, still watching my face. 'Two tickets. I wondered . . .'

The world stopped.

'I wondered if you'd like to take me.'

Without meaning to, without even so much as suspecting the words were in my mind, I heard myself say them: 'OK. I'd like to.'

'Good,' said Katie. And with that she gave me a dimpled smile and scrambled to her feet in a sudden, graceful movement, and walked away.

Silver cellphone

That night I was booked to baby-sit Madeline. First dibs on baby-sitting jobs normally went to Nick, so I'd grabbed the chance — top dollar at five bucks an hour, COD. I guessed Nick was still in Dad's bad books, lying low till the dust died down. Mum and Dad were heading into town to celebrate Dad's new job with dinner, then a show. I still couldn't get my head around it. The thought of Dad — *Dad!* — Fair Play Coordinator of anything, let alone the entire Igloo, just didn't compute. But thinking about it cranked the Nick worry-jingle up again, and I quickly flicked to another mental station. I didn't want to go there.

I gave Madeline her dinner — French toast soldiers drizzled with maple syrup — and had my own two-minute noodles. We were playing a board game on the lounge floor when Mum and Dad came in to say goodnight, Dad stiff-backed in his best navy blazer, Mum all smiles in a shimmery top and lipstick. She kissed us both, issuing last-minute instructions while Dad rattled the car keys and checked his watch. 'She's to be in bed by seven at the latest. Nick will be home by then; make sure he locks the front door — he has his key. Finish your homework before you go to bed. Have fun, darlings. Remember your teeth . . .'

'Come on, Trish, come *on*!'

'. . . and take Madeline to the toilet before you tuck her in!' Mum called from the hallway. Finally the door banged, the key turned in the lock and they were gone.

We played the board game three times back-to-back — it was a race to assemble multicoloured sausage dogs using a colour-coded dice, and Muddle loved it. Then I read her *Are You My Mother?* twice, and it was time for bed. Easy money! I tucked her up and kissed her, then turned her light low, tiptoed to the kitchen and spent the next ten years on homework. The house had that echoey stillness it gets when you're alone, as if the air is somehow thinner: you feel kind of self-conscious, as if you're being secretly filmed for some weird reality TV show.

By nine o'clock I was cold to the bone and yawning. For the past hour I'd been watching the clock — Mum said Nick would be back around Madeline's bedtime, which meant eight at the latest. What should I do? Wait up for him?

But he was the big brother, and my feet were freezing.

I cleaned my teeth, changed into pyjamas and slid into bed. I'd listen for Nick and give him Mum's message the instant he came in. There was no way I'd fall asleep: there were too many worries racing round my head.

Sure enough, my brain started in on me the second my head touched the pillow.

You should never have said you'd go to Rock Quest with Katie, it told me accusingly.

'But I —'

You what? What about Beattie?

'What about her? We're not going out or anything.'

Yeah, right. So you're planning to tell her, then?

'Tell Beattie?'

Yup: tell Beattie you're taking Katie to Rock Quest.

'Well . . . not unless she asks.'

So unless Beattie says: 'Hey, Phil, are you by any chance taking Katie to Rock Quest?' you're not planning to tell her, right?

'Yeah . . . I guess.'

You should be pretty safe then, shouldn't you? Way to go, Pip.

There was an uncomfortable silence while I listened for Nick's key. My worry about the Katie/Beattie thing was mixing itself up with a new worry about Nick. Where was he? But at least my feet were warming up . . .

The sound of the truck's engine woke me. I knew from the density of the darkness that it was late, way late. Across the hallway a strip of light shone from under Nick's door — the same strip I'd noticed the second I'd snuggled down in bed. I'd thought about getting up and turning it off, then decided he could do it himself when he came home.

Why was the light still on in Nick's room?

Quick and quiet as a ferret I slipped out of bed and across the passage. Tapped softly on Nick's door. 'Nick?' I breathed. *'Nick!'* But I knew he wasn't there. I opened the door a crack and peeped in.

The room was tidy, the bed neatly made, the duvet cover smoothed flat with not a single crinkle. Only Nick's soccer bag in the corner to show my brother lived there.

Where was he? Mum and Dad would come and check on us, same as they always did. He'd be dead meat for sure. After last night . . .

There'd be another scene — an even worse one. Without thinking I crossed to the bed, took the top corner of the duvet and yanked it down, grabbed the pillow and shoved it down deep. Tugged the duvet back up, punching and scrunching it to make it look more like Nick was under there. It didn't. Frantically I scanned the room, hearing the rattle of the garage door opening over the faint vibration of the idling engine. The soccer bag! I grabbed it, hoisting it up onto the bed, then under the covers. Pulled the ball out and positioned it up top; pulled the duvet way high. Then I was over at the door, flicking off the light. As I eased it shut I caught a glimpse of the shadowy shape of Horace, his glass eye gleaming at me in the dark.

I dove back into bed and lay with my back to the door, praying Mum and Dad would do one quick check and head for bed. What if they came to kiss us like they sometimes did? What if Mum went to stroke Nick's hair and there was the soccer ball, all bald and stitched together like some kind of horror movie?

What if Nick was lying somewhere, run over by a car, or lost, or murdered? I should be meeting them at the door, telling them he hadn't come home . . .

'Fast asleep.' Mum's whisper, then a wordless rumble from Dad. Then Mum again, wrenching my gut with guilt: 'Bless them. They're good boys, Jim.'

Eyes scrunched shut I waited for the gentle touch of Mum's hand, for the world to implode when they went into Nick's room and discovered what I'd done. Waited with a hammering heart for what felt like an eternity . . . but it didn't happen. And at last I saw the wash of light from Mum and Dad's bedroom disappear into darkness as they closed the door.

It seemed hours later that I finally heard it: the stealthy scrape of metal on metal. Anger surfed in on a wave of relief. Where had he been?

He was taking his time about unlocking the door. How hard could it be to put in a key and turn it? At this rate he'd wake Mum and Dad — though Dad slept like the dead, and if Mum could hear anything over his snoring it'd be a miracle. I clambered out of bed for what felt like the millionth time that night and prowled into the hallway, ready to give him a piece of my mind, younger brother or not. At last I heard the tumblers turn, and slowly, with exaggerated caution, the handle inched down. I felt a sudden intense misgiving. Something was wrong.

Then the door barged open as if something had collapsed against it, banging against the wall with a thud that made me wince. And there was Nick leaning on the doorjamb, eyes blank as holes punched in paper. I stared at him, frozen, horrified. I'd been right. There'd been an accident. Nick stood there swaying slightly, hair everywhere, face white as chalk. Then he took a single, shuffling step towards me, stumbled and almost fell.

My first crazy thought was, 'He's been shot.'

Instinctively I grabbed for him, my eyes still locked on his face. His gash of a mouth split wide in a stupid grin. 'Well, hel-*lo*, baby bro,' he drawled, his voice stretching out like chewing-gum.

And in that instant I knew.

'Shhhh — you'll wake Mum and Dad!' I hissed. 'Nick, you're . . . you're . . .' I couldn't say it.

'I'm what, Pipsqueak? Just a teensy bit . . . pished?' He hiccupped and pushed past me on a waft of stale beer fumes and empty-ashtray smell.

He was heading for the kitchen, relentless as a robot with its circuits gone haywire. A vision of him fumbling and clanging around the pots and pans flashed through my head. I leapt after him, almost tripping over my pyjama pants, grabbed his arm and spun him round, as much as he was able to spin. 'Wha'?' he mumbled.

'Where are you going? Go to bed! If Dad catches you . . .'

'Lea' me alone. I'm hungry. Starved. Got da munchies bad . . .'

'Tough,' I growled. 'Go to bed.' I gave him a push that sent him stumbling back down the corridor. Any second I expected to see Mum and Dad's door open, Mum's sleep-smudged face, or — worse — Dad's bleary, stubbled one.

Nick reached his door and stopped, swayed, hiccupped again. But this hiccup was different — a cross between a hiccup and a burp. I glanced at his face. It was greenish-white, fluorescent in the darkness, black smudges like thumbprints under his eyes. 'Blug,' went Nick again, a fixed expression in his eyes.

I don't know how I knew. Without a word, I shoved him roughly on down to the toilet, and in.

Just in time. He thumped down on his knees, cradled the bowl in his arms and spewed. I hovered just outside the half-closed door, flinching away from the wrenching heaves and the chemical, boozy stink. One eye on the toilet door, one on Mum's and Dad's, one ear on Nick's spasms, one on Dad's rhythmic snores, I waited. Eventually there was silence. Furious, sickened, I approached the gap. 'Nick?' I whispered.

Silence.

I eased the door open and peered round, holding my breath. Nick was sprawled on the floor, legs all over, bent at weird angles like a string puppet. There was puke in his hair, his eyelashes; on the toilet seat, the floor. His head was lolling, eyes drooping, mouth hanging half-mast like an idiot. A string of vomit swung from his lip.

I couldn't leave him there for Mum to find in the morning.

Somehow I levered him up, one arm over my shoulder, and heaved him the few feet to his room. Lowered him none-too-gently onto the bed and yanked his shoes off, then his socks. Pulled his stained jacket off in one rough motion, the sleeves turning inside-out, something heavy dropping out of the pocket in a flash of silver.

Nick jerked out of his comatose state. He lurched forward in a blast of puke-acid breath, almost tipping off the bed in his attempt to catch whatever it was before it hit the floor. I shoved him back on the pillow and picked it up.

It was a cellphone — one of those ones that opens like a clam. Shiny, silver, brand new.

'Nick,' I said very slowly, 'whose is this?'

'Mine. It'sh mine. Gimme,' he mumbled, grabbing at the cellphone and missing.

I held it out of his reach. 'Did you . . .' anything would be possible on this nightmare night, but still I could hardly bring myself to whisper the words. 'Did you steal it?'

The puffy slits of my brother's eyes widened fractionally in an attempt to signal outraged innocence. 'Steal it? Why would I? I toldya, it's mine.'

'But how . . .'

A furtive look crept over his face. 'Mum and Dad aren't the only ones with something to shelebrate. I've been celebrating too. Passed my Learner's Licence today. Mum an' Dad won't care a damn. Dad won't buy me a shell phone, so I bought one myself. Wanna see?' Fingers clumsy with care, he opened it up. 'Top-of-the-range, shtate of the art. Check it out, baby bro. PXT, MP3 player, poly . . . poly . . . WAP-something . . .' His voice trailed off and he sat staring at the cellphone as if it was the Holy Grail.

'Nick, how much did this cost?'

He stared on, glassy-eyed.

'Where did the money come from?' Nick got paid for his work at the Igloo, but it went straight into a savings account for university, same as my milk money. We both got an allowance — when Dad remembered — but it'd be

138

nowhere near enough for this, not if Nick saved up for a million years.

Something in Nick's eyes was changing, very slowly, like a light being turned down on a dimmer switch. He sank back on the pillow as if he was being lowered by invisible strings, gave a single low groan and passed out.

I cleaned up the best I could and went to bed. I thought I'd never sleep, but I did — and dreamed all night of Mum going into the toilet to find the floor knee-deep in puke; Dad lifting the corner of Nick's duvet to find the soccer ball staring up at him, mud crusted like dried blood on its surface; Madeline digging in her toy box and pulling out a shiny silver cellphone.

At last it was morning.

I slunk into the toilet and checked it out; gave it a good spray with pine air freshener and opened the window an extra notch. Nick emerged from his room and shuffled through to the shower like an old man. At breakfast Mum and Dad told about their evening, the show, what they'd had for dinner.

Life went on.

Neverland

The truck bounced over the rutted track that led off the main road to Samson Gorge, if it could be called a main road. Though it was only twenty minutes out of town it could have been a different world — a place families would go for picnics if it wasn't for the risk of being mown down by hoons on off-road bikes and jet-boaters showing off their 4x4s and beer bellies.

The track was unmarked: the kind of turnoff you'd miss if you blinked, and even if you didn't. 'Why isn't it signposted, Dad?' I asked.

'Why d'you think? Keep out the riff-raff.' Dad changed down and swung into a stub of driveway, stopping with a jerk in front of a farm gate with a serious-looking chain and an economy-sized padlock round the business end. Beyond the gate the track veered right and vanished into eucalyptus scrub; on the fence a wooden sign with hand-painted lettering stated flatly: *Samson Rifle Range — Keep Out.*

For someone who was supposed to be talking, acting and thinking like a man, I was horribly nervous. Dad blipped three times on the horn, wound down his window and waited.

Wednesday evening we'd done the milk run for the final time. Thursday, a balding guy in MooZical Milk overalls came to the door asking for Dad. They stood on the front porch exchanging grunts while Mum and Madeline and I lay low in the kitchen trying to seem busy; I saw them shake hands before the guy hopped up into the milk truck, started up — second try, I noticed — and drove rather jerkily away.

There was a feeling in my throat like I'd swallowed a piece of glass. Mum was pummelling her bread extra-energetically, a determined little smile on her face. Madeline was posting shapes into her Tupperware ball, happily oblivious to it all. The guy must've pressed the red button, because as the familiar sound of the engine faded into the distance the old truck gave one final lonesome 'moo', as if it was saying goodbye.

Dad came in, his moustache very straight. 'Well,' he said, 'that's that.' He stood there for a moment with his hands kind of hanging by his sides, as if he didn't know what to do with them. Then Mum came, all over flour, and gave him a hug that left two white handprints on the back of his shirt, and a kiss under his moustache that lasted way longer than their kisses usually did.

And that was the end of Dad's milk run.

Dad's a high-energy kind of person and it wasn't two minutes before he started getting the jitters. He wasn't due to start work at the Igloo till Monday, so he paced round the house like a caged tiger, prowling from room to room muttering under his breath and making everyone feel edgy. And then he lit on me, doing my algebra at the kitchen table.

'So, Son,' he said, man-to-man: 'what say we head out to the range this Sunday? High time we started planning our hunting trip, eh? Look at you — almost as tall as your Dad.'

It was true. My voice had broken ages ago — the unspoken

yardstick of manhood in our family — and it was months since I'd cracked one of those embarrassing high ones. I'd known the traditional father-son hunting trip couldn't be far away, same as Dad had done with his own father, Grampsy; same as Nick had done with Dad the winter he turned fourteen.

Part of me was excited, part of me was proud — and part of me was just plain scared. Not of guns, or bullets, or the bush. Of letting Dad down.

Sarge powered to the gate in his wheelchair and gave Dad a salute, me a wink, unlocked and let us in.

We parked next to Sarge's old Landcruiser and climbed out. The whole place was lean and mean and shipshape like you'd expect from Sarge, the kind of place Dad would feel right at home. A dusty parking area leading across to a big open shed; a workbench kitted out with a scale, a funnel and some other random paraphernalia, and a guy with a beard fiddling about with some dismantled cartridges.

And over on the left, the range itself: a businesslike row of four firing bays like concrete block stables, roofed and walled, each with a platform at chest-height. Through the open backs I glimpsed the range itself, a long sweep of gravel bounded by high banks with targets set up in the distance.

Wherever I looked were printed notices, red on white, saying 'Warning: unauthorised use of range prohibited,' 'Danger — Keep Out', 'Never leave a firearm unattended', and stuff like that.

Sarge grinned, holding out his hand. 'Gidday, Pip. Safety's number one here, as you can see.' He nodded at a makeshift red flag hanging limply above the firing station. 'That means *firing in progress.* My first job when I arrive is to unlock the shed and log in; then I hoist that to tell folks: *If you get your butt shot off, it's your own damn fault!'*

I'd noticed a burly guy in camo pants in the far booth; now the air was punched by a shot that made me do a kind of leaping pirouette, though neither Dad nor Sarge so much as twitched. Dad gave me a sidelong glance that gleamed with amusement, and Sarge, deadpan, handed me a pair of earmuffs. 'Might want these, Pip.' Hurriedly I put them on. Dad might think it was funny once, but he wouldn't like it if I kept cavorting about like a ballet dancer every time a gun was fired.

I'd expected we'd load up and start blasting away pretty much immediately, but I'd reckoned without Dad and Sarge. The pace of life at the range was kinda leisurely — in reverse, more like. No wonder Dad spent so much time there. First I was introduced to the bearded guy, Jed, who gave me a long-winded explanation of reloading ammo; then the young guy who'd been firing shambled up and asked Sarge for advice on his scope, which had got itself out of whack.

But at last Dad crossed to the truck and lifted out the green gun bag with his rifle in. At home it was kept in the locked cabinet in the back of Dad's wardrobe; I'd seen it often, even been allowed to hold it and — once — help clean it. But I'd never come close to firing it before.

Dad had owned the rifle ever since I could remember, and growing up in a house where a firearm was a fact of life meant there were some things I felt I'd been born knowing. Only a shotgun was a gun; a rifle was a rifle. In Dad's case, a Winchester 70 .223. It had a telescopic sight all wrapped round with masking tape — to protect it, not to stop it falling to bits — and it was old. But as Dad liked to say, his rifle would kill as dead as a brand new one if you knew how to use it.

I concentrated hard on Dad's detailed explanation of how the Winchester worked, slightly muffled by the earmuffs and punctuated by dull *whumps* from the range. I wasn't surprised that most of what he said revolved round safety — how you never have a round in the chamber till you're ready to shoot; how you must always make one hundred and ten per cent certain of your target; and most important of all, how you never, ever leave a firearm unattended.

'There's a lot of rubbish talked about firearms,' Dad said sternly, 'and most of it comes from ignorance. Gun safety is simple common sense — the rules are there for a reason, and they're unbreakable.'

At last we were ready to shoot. Dad showed me how, holding the rifle tight against his shoulder, supported on the bench rest. He worked the bolt to load it, then squeezed the trigger. WHUMP! I jumped, but this time I didn't care; my heart was thudding with excitement and I couldn't wait to have a go. Dad handed the Winchester over. 'You're left-handed, so it will be a bit more awkward for you. Pull the stock tight in to your shoulder so there's less of a kick. Look down the scope: see the target?' I did — way closer-looking than I expected. Just like in the movies, there were fine cross-hairs; I adjusted the position of the barrel so they rested exactly on the bull's-eye. 'When you're ready, Son . . . squeeze, don't pull . . .'

Time held its breath. Gently, carefully, keeping the rifle still, I tightened my finger. *WHUMP!* The rifle bucked in my hands; the butt whacked me in the shoulder. I was shaking. 'Did I get it?' I was asking. 'Did I get the target?'

'Well now, let's see.' Dad took the rifle and sighted down the scope. His moustache was smiling. 'Humph. Looks like you've doubled my shot, just twelve o'clock of the bull. Not bad for a first time. Now, what you're aiming to do is group your shots in a tight formation . . .'

The last thing I'd expected was that I'd fall in love with shooting. But there was something addictive about it: about lining up the cross-hairs on the target; about that endless, frozen moment when I focused my whole being on that single spot 100 metres away, close enough to reach out and touch through the magic of the scope; about the instant my finger reached that critical pressure and the rifle suddenly leapt to life in my hands. About the whiff of hot, burnt-rock smell that drifted back at me after each shot, that some deep part of me recognised instantly even though I'd never smelt it before: gunpowder.

I shot with the rifle on the bench rest at first, but soon Dad got me firing off my elbows, resting my forehand on an old cushion from Nick's room. 'Likely as not that's how you'll shoot in the field,' he told me as we unloaded the rifle and lowered the metal plates that showed we were heading forward of the firing station. 'Most times you'll be in cover, with a branch to rest your barrel on.'

We crunched to the end of the range and inspected the target. There were a couple of tidy holes punched near the edges, and close to the bull one big, ragged gap where the paper had been completely shot away. I looked at Dad, but his face wasn't giving a thing away. 'That's what we mean by grouping,' was all he said, taking the A4 sheet down with more than his usual care. 'You might want to keep this, Son.'

We walked back to where the other men were waiting, me matching Dad stride for stride. 'Let's have a look then,' said Sarge, holding out his hand. He whistled, then handed the target to Jed. 'Pity the deer that gets in your sights.'

I stared down at the big, ragged hole. I'd forgotten it

was a deer I'd be shooting at, not a paper target. But that jagged gap had been made by more than twenty bullets smacking into the same place. 'How can such a small hole kill something?' I wondered.

The men grinned.

'It's not so much the bullet that does the damage,' said Jed; 'it's the hydraulic shock the bullet causes.'

'Yeah,' chipped in the young hunter, 'and the bullets, they have these exposed lead points, see? They mushroom out when they hit the deer, leaving behind this, like, tunnel of destruction — pretty much blow 'em to bits.'

Sarge glanced at my face. 'It's quick,' he said. 'Shock, adrenaline . . . then bleeds to death internally in seconds. Never knows what's hit it.'

'Yeah, but,' said the young hunter, 'I've seen deer shot in the hindquarters pull themselves along fast as an express train for kilometres. That's why you go for a front shot, kid — in the eye if it's close enough, the brain, under the chin — lungs are good, eh? Even if you don't get a clean kill, the animal's hit, runs, ploughs into the ground stone dead. Nailed one-time.'

'That's what shooting's all about,' agreed Dad: 'delivering lethal energy to a target. You want to drop your deer where it stands, Son, right where it stands.'

The young guy drained the 2-litre Coke bottle he'd been swigging from while we talked. 'Here,' he said, tossing it to me, 'fill that with water — tap's right there. I'll show you something.'

I filled it like he said, screwing the top on tight, then we walked back down the range and propped it on the bank of shredded rubber behind the targets. Dad was waiting for me in our bay. 'Here you go,' he said, handing me the rifle. 'One shot this time.'

146

I worked the bolt to put the single round in the chamber and drew a careful bead on the bottle. Steadied myself, took a slow breath, and squeezed. *WHUMP!* As the sight jerked up I caught a flash of the Coke bottle cartwheeling, water exploding everywhere.

I went down on my own to pick it up while the men stood smoking and talking hunting. At first I didn't see what the big deal was. There was a splash of water all round the gravel, but the lid was still on the bottle, a single grey-rimmed hole punched through the transparent plastic, dead centre.

Then I turned the bottle over.

The whole back had been blasted out, the edges peeled open and gaping. And the bottom, where the plastic was thickest, didn't exist any more.

We'd arrive just after lunch; now the sun was low in the sky and it was cold. We crossed to the car and I reached down to shake Sarge's hand before thanking him and clambering in. Dad stood outside for a few minutes more chatting, everything about him telling me clearer than words that he was pleased. His window was still open a crack from when we'd arrived, and a few words drifted in on the chilly air.

'Nick did good,' said Sarge, 'but Pip's a natural. Coulda told you from the way he held that rifle.'

'We'll see,' was all Dad said.

The king of all bogeys

On the way home we set the date for our trip: two weeks'
time, spending Saturday night in the bush. Already I felt
different, more grown-up, closer to Dad, and I pushed my
doubts down deep. I hadn't thought I'd take to shooting,
yet look how well I'd done. Maybe thousands of years of
evolution had made a hunter out of every man, the way Dad
said.

Dad went to lock the rifle away in the safe and I headed
for the bathroom, planning on a shower before dinner. I'd
show my target, explain to Mum why the big hole in the
paper was good. Hopefully Nick'd be there . . .

My arms were full of clutter: the day pack, my fleece
jacket, Nick's cushion, complete with coffee-stains. I rapped
twice on his door and elbowed my way in. The room was
empty, tidy. I threw the cushion on Nick's chair and turned
to head out, then paused and looked at old Horace. In the
grey half-light he had a mournful, placid expression, like a
donkey with its head over the stable door.

I wondered where the bullet had hit. I'd never asked;
never wanted to know. In the eye, the brain, the neck?
There was no bullet-hole I could see. Had Horace been shot
in the lungs, the heart . . . or in the hindquarters, dragging
himself half-crippled through the bush in a desperate effort
to outrun the agony exploding through him?

I'd never touched him. It was as much as my life was
worth. But now I reached out a hand, a quick glance at the

door confirming that Nick was nowhere near and would never know. Horace's coat was nut-brown and shaggy, coarse as coconut matting, but the end of his nose was plush velvet, soft-looking and pearly-grey. I rested the palm of my hand for a moment on the hard bone of his muzzle and stroked gently downwards. He felt inert, unyielding, inanimate as a piece of furniture, but I couldn't shake the notion that he wasn't dead at all, that suddenly his head might turn, his great yellow teeth snap . . .

It wasn't fear of Nick that had stopped me touching him all this time.

His glass eyes stared past me as if I wasn't there — and suddenly I felt something shift under my hand. I jerked away, my heart pinballing. Stared, cold sweat prickling my skin. There was something bulging out of Horace's right nostril: something that hadn't been there before.

It was hard to see in the gathering dusk, but I didn't dare put on the light. I peered down, not wanting to get too close. It was dark and bulbous, like a tumour or a gigantic bogey . . . the king of all bogeys.

I'd thought it was Horace who'd moved. Still, I half-expected him to snort out the glob like a snot-rocket, shake his head with a clash of antlers, then settle back to being dead again.

I stood motionless, watching him. He hung from the wall still as a hat-rack, glass eyes fixed and distant, as if he didn't give a damn that an enormous bogey was dangling from his nose.

As my heartbeat steadied my mind began working again. So much for Sarge's skill as a taxidermist. It was stuffing: Horace's stuffing was falling out. Nick would see, guess I'd been in there touching his precious trophy, and slaughter me. I was going to have to fix it, shove it back. I'd better be quick. Nick didn't like me hanging about in his room at the best of times, and just lately I was guessing he'd like it less than ever.

I put my stuff down on the floor. It was dumb, but suddenly I didn't like the thought of touching him. *Stupid*, I told myself. *Baby*. My brain listened and said nothing.

I took Horace's nose warily in one hand and went to grab the bogey with the other, but couldn't help cringing away. *It's not a bogey*, I told myself. *It's stuffing.*

As I touched it, brushing it with squeamish fingers, it fell. Plopped onto the carpet and lay there. Now it didn't look like a bogey, it looked like a turd. A fat round horse apple.

A door banged somewhere and I jumped guiltily. I didn't have time for this. Nick could come in any moment. Quickly I bent and picked it up, not caring what it looked like, not caring what it was, only wanting to jam it back where it came from and get out of there. But something about the way it felt stopped me.

It wasn't wadding. It was stuff in a plastic bag, the kind of flimsy plastic bag you put vegetables in at the supermarket. The size of a cricket ball, squashy and yielding.

I held it up close and peered at it. What was it? In the gloom it was impossible to tell. It looked grey, greenish-grey, dry and flaky, like the oregano Mum bought in bulk because it was cheaper . . .

I knew what it was.

It wasn't oregano, and it wasn't stuffing.

It was something else.

Nick had hidden it.

And I knew why.

Telling

'Hey, Phil, know what I was thinking?' said Beattie, pulling off her climbing shoes and tossing them in her kit bag.

'No. What?' I said, only half-listening, half-registering her odd, almost shy little smile.

'Maybe we should try to get tickets to Rock Quest.'

'*What?*'

'Rock Quest: you know, that awesome concert they have in the —'

'No!'

'No, you don't know, or no, you don't think we should try? My sister says there are still —'

'No, I don't want to go! I hate that kind of music. Plus Mum and Dad . . . they've planned something for that night . . . it's Nick's birthday.'

The lies spilled out, stumbling over each other faster than I could talk. Beattie sat cross-legged on the floor looking up at me, a puzzled, slightly hurt look on her face.

I felt like lower than a worm, but at least my brain was mercifully silent.

What could it say?

It was marijuana. A stash of marijuana big enough to sink a battleship.

The knowledge had blown my mind apart like a bullet, shock waves rippling out and leaving me numb and trembling with disbelief, cold with certainty.

Nick was on drugs.

One second I didn't know, didn't even suspect; the next I did. In that split second the knowledge became part of me, a toxic chemical in my blood. I carried it everywhere. All day Sunday, all day Monday, all day Tuesday it was there, pulsing through me with every beat of my heart.

Nick. My brother. On drugs.

I didn't know what to do.

Part of me knew. I should tell Mum and Dad. That's what I'd have told anyone else to do — Beattie, if it was her sister; Mike, if it was his brother. But it wasn't. It was mine.

I could imagine doing it. Going into the living room where Mum and Dad sat reading by the fire and saying: 'Mum and Dad, we need to talk', or 'Mum and Dad, I've got something to tell you', even 'Mum and Dad, I have some bad news.' But however I planned to start, it always ended up the same: 'It's about Nick.' And the words that would have to come next — be said out loud — were unthinkable.

Time after time I planned the scene out in my mind, rehearsed exactly what I'd say and how I'd say it. Imagined the look on their faces. It would blow their world apart, but it wouldn't change anything. Everything was already changed. Nick had changed it.

The year I was six Mum let us help decorate the Christmas tree. We'd done it before, but always with decorations made of paper, pine cones and painted putty that were practically indestructible. This time was different: for the first time we'd be using the glass ornaments handed down from Dad's Grandma; irreplaceable family heirlooms.

Nick and I were allowed to choose one special ornament to be our very own, for every Christmas to come. Nick chose a brass trumpet; I chose a glass ball the dark electric blue of a peacock feather. It was frosted with gold glitter, the most beautiful thing I'd ever seen. 'Be gentle with it, Pippin,' Mum said as I went to hang it on the tree. 'It's very delicate. If you squeeze too tightly it will break and you'll cut your fingers.' It hadn't been my fingers I'd been scared of hurting; it had been the fragile eggshell ball. I'd held it gently, so gently it slipped onto the hearth and smashed into a million pieces.

Small as I was, I knew instantly there was no way it could ever be mended. That glass ball taught me, once and forever, that time can never be rewound.

A cold, hard fist of anger clenched in my chest: anger at Nick. He deserved me to tell on him. Dad would kill him; he'd break Mum's heart. But he deserved it all. He was an idiot, a selfish moron.

But he was Nick. My brother.

The more time passed the harder it became, the more unthinkable. There was no-one I could share it with, no-one I could go to for advice, no-one I could trust with my terrible secret. *I didn't know what to do.*

Then it was Tuesday, and climbing, and as I rode my bike to the Igloo with my thoughts churning round my mind like dirty washing, I remembered.

There was Rob.

Eventually Beattie left, with a reproachful backward glance that would have made me feel worse than I already did, if that had been possible. I was glad to see her go.

Rob had been making some adjustments to one of the climbs using the hydraulic scissor lift; as he lowered himself I hovered, my guts in a knot, wondering how I'd begin.

I needn't have worried. As soon as he turned and saw me standing there the words came tumbling out. 'Rob, I need to speak to you. About something . . . personal.'

'I've been wanting to have a chat to you too, Phil. Let's go somewhere we won't be disturbed.'

'It's my brother — my brother Nick,' I gabbled before the door of the isolation room swung closed behind us. 'He's on drugs, I saw them — there was a truckload — I'm scared he's selling it. He's got this new cellphone that must've cost a bomb — he threw up everywhere and he's never home — I know I have to tell Mum and Dad but — but he's my brother and I can't —'

'Steady on, Phil.' Rob didn't sound shocked. He didn't even sound surprised. 'Take a deep breath, now.'

I sucked air into my lungs like a deep-sea diver. The huge weight I'd been carrying had lifted. It must have shifted onto Rob, but he didn't seem changed. 'Tell me slowly,' he said; 'everything, from the beginning.'

So I told him, trying to remember it all: the letter from Highlands Soccer, the fight with Dad about Hoof Hearted, how different Nick seemed, the scuffle in the kitchen, how Nick was never home, Nick drunk, the silver cellphone, Horace . . . hearing it out loud made it all fit together like an ugly jigsaw puzzle.

'And now I don't know what to do,' I finished. 'If I tell Mum and Dad — tell on Nick — he'll never forgive me. And if I don't . . .'

'If you don't?'

'I'll never forgive myself. If something happens . . .'

'It's an unwritten law, isn't it?' said Rob. 'The twelfth commandment, second only to *Thou shalt not get found out. Thou shalt not tell on.*'

I nodded miserably.

'You're right to be worried about him,' said Rob, 'but that doesn't make it any easier. You're between a rock and a hard place, kid. The right thing can be the hardest to do.' He thought for a moment. 'A lot of kids fool around with pot out of curiosity and a bit of rebellion, and that's as far as it ever goes. But sometimes, if you're unhappy, drugs can be a symptom of that unhappiness, an escape . . . or so you think. If that's the case with Nick, you need to sort what he's so unhappy about, or there'll be trouble. Know what I believe?' I looked at him hopefully. If anyone had the answers it would be Rob, though how he knew all this was a mystery. 'There's a big difference between telling *on* someone, and just plain telling.'

The glimmer of hope flickered and died. He was wrong. They were the same — he'd just said so.

'*Telling on* is telling to get someone in trouble. But *telling:* telling is something you do to get a person *out* of trouble — to save them from a situation that could be dangerous for them. If you tell your parents about your brother, you'll be telling them because you care about him; he's in trouble and you want to help him. It's an important distinction, and one I'm sure Nick would appreciate — if not right now, then certainly down the track when he's thinking more clearly.'

Rob had told me exactly what I didn't want to hear. 'So I guess that means I have to tell them,' I said, knowing the answer.

'Probably, in the end. But I'd suggest something else first. Your first concern is your brother, and your first loyalty lies with him. Find a time when you can talk to him alone. Tell him what you found and what you think it means. Be open with him and give him a chance to explain. Sometimes things aren't as clear-cut they seem.

'Most important of all, let him know you love him.'

That was it, then. The prospect of telling Mum and Dad had been replaced by a new one, just as daunting, even more of an unknown: talking to Nick. But Rob was right: it had to be done.

'Hang on a moment, Phil. I needed to talk to you too, remember? It's about the National trials.'

I stared at him blankly. National trials? 'Oh, yeah,' I said, trying to remember how it felt to care. 'When are they?'

'That's what I wanted to tell you. They've already been.'

Suddenly I did care, desperately. I'd been wrong; Rob hadn't given me a second chance. This was it: my punishment for the crazy stunt I'd pulled on camp. It had come back to bite me in the bum. The trials had been and gone, and Rob hadn't even told me.

'But . . .' I stammered, 'but . . . why didn't you tell me? I wanted to try out . . . I'd've given anything to be there.'

Rob gave me a peculiar sidelong look I didn't understand.

'You were,' he said.

The Name of the Tree

I stared at him as if he'd gone crazy. 'No, I wasn't.'

'Remember I told you the National trials were going to be different— more low-key, less formal?' Rob was saying. I nodded. 'Well, they were. Remember Rickety Bridge?'

Rickety Bridge? Of course I remembered it. What was Rob on about?

'Remember Buzz Munro?'

I remembered him. The tomahawk face, the shrewd eyes that didn't miss a trick, how he'd taken control without seeming to, watched us, saying little, seeing everything.

At last I understood.

'Those were the trials,' I said slowly. 'That day — the redpointing. Buzz is . . .'

'The National Climbing Selector,' said Rob expressionlessly. 'Yeah.'

And then I remembered the rest.

The way Buzz had looked down at me lying gasping on the wet rock like a fish on a slab; the dismissal in his voice when he told me I deserved to have died. The way he'd looked over at Rob and said *This is Phil? The one you told me about?* I knew what Rob would have said about me, how he rated me. It hadn't occurred to me to wonder why he'd mentioned me to Buzz. Now I knew.

Worst of all, I remembered Rob's words at the campfire. *You let me down today, big-time. Worse, you let yourself down, in ways you can't begin to understand right now.*

He'd been right, I hadn't understood. But now I did.

The next day, at the trial we hadn't known was a trial, I'd climbed better than I ever had in my life to make up to Rob for my stupid behaviour the day before. I hadn't cared what Buzz thought, though I could tell he'd been impressed. But that didn't matter, because I'd already blown any chance I had of making the National team as high as the sky.

'It takes a lot to make a top-class international climber,' Rob was saying, 'and a lot of the qualities are ones you have. You know that. But Buzz was looking for more. He was looking for responsibility, maturity, good judgement.' He shrugged. 'The ability to work as a team. Leadership. All those things.'

Blown it.

'But Buzz and I go way back,' Rob continued, watching my face, 'and I told him you had those qualities, all of them, in spades. We all make mistakes. It's how we learn. Buzz knows that as well as anyone. He phoned me this morning to tell me.' He held out his hand. 'You've made the National team, Phil. You'll be going to Ratho in six weeks' time with Buzz Munro, you and Gabriel and a couple of climbers from up north. Lee is non-travelling reserve.

'Congratulations, kid. You've earned it.'

I barged through the front door. Mum, Dad . . . I couldn't wait to find them and blurt out my awesome news. Hearing myself tell it out loud might make it easier to believe. And Beattie . . . I must phone her . . . she'd be so excited she'd forget all about stupid Rock Quest . . .

'Mum?' I called. 'Dad?' My voice echoed back at me in the way it only ever does in an empty house, silent except for a rhythmic bass thumping, a vibration rather than a noise, like the heart of the house slowly beating.

Where was everyone?

Feeling stupidly let down I mooched into the kitchen and headed for the fridge, planning to take advantage of Mum's absence by raiding it before dinner. There was a note on the door in Mum's handwriting: *Book club tonight @ Lyn's*, then a phone number. *Lasagne & salad in fridge — 200° 30 mins. Love you! XXX* My stomach did a little icy skid. I'd been banking on the usual pre-dinner havoc as an excuse for . . . for not . . .

I felt sick. Where was Dad?

Dad didn't leave notes. He didn't need to. The absence of his special electrical charge in the air told me that wherever he was, it wasn't here. Then I remembered: he'd started his new job. He'd be at the Igloo till late.

The only person home was Nick.

I didn't feel hungry any more. *Find a time when you can talk to him alone*, Rob had said. I'd expected that to happen sometime in the distant future, but it hadn't. It had happened now.

Do it. Get it over. I walked down the passage and stopped outside Nick's door. Took a deep breath and knocked. *Tock-tock.* Waited. Knocked again, louder. *Tock-tock-tock. THUMP, THUMP, THUMP*, went the bass. *Thump, thump, thump*, went my heart.

Just as I was about to reach for the handle the door opened a crack. A slice of Nick's cheek and part of an eye appeared in the gap. 'What?'

I hadn't thought what to say. This was all happening way too fast.

'C-can I come in?' I asked, feeling about as welcome as a Jehovah's Witness.

'No. Piss off.' The door started to close.

'Nick, I know about the —' I hesitated just the tiniest

159

second, and in that second the door slammed shut.

I stood outside fuming, feeling like an idiot. I knocked on the door again, harder. 'Nick?'

Nothing. I hammered louder. 'Nick!'

Inside, I heard him rack up the volume another notch. I tried the handle. It was locked. I bent down and cupped my hands round the keyhole to make a megaphone. 'Nick?' I condensed my voice into a funnel shape I hoped would squeeze through the hole and into the room without being drowned by the music. 'Let me in. We need to talk.'

THUMP THUMP THUMP —

Frustration pumped through me in time with the music, building to anger. 'NICK!'

THUMP THUMP—

'*NICK, YOU DAMN DRUGGIE, LET ME IN!*' I yelled.

The door burst open and Nick grabbed my arm, yanked me in and slammed the door, then crossed to the console and snapped the music off.

The room went deadly quiet.

He turned slowly to face me. His hair was sticking up in prongs as if he'd just crawled out of bed and his eyes were like something out of a Dracula movie, wild and bloodshot. *'What did you say?'*

'I . . .' I gulped. 'I was in here putting your cushion away and a bag fell out of Horace's nose.'

We both glanced automatically over at the wall. Horace gazed loftily over our heads as if our discussion was of no concern to him, but I felt sure he was listening.

'Crap,' said Nick flatly. Crossed and jammed his fingers up Horace's right nostril like a doctor doing some kind of obscene examination. 'Nothing there, baby bro. See? You musta been dreaming.' I could almost see Nick's long fingers waggling about in the socket, demonstrating its emptiness.

'Nick, I'm not stupid. I know what I saw. I'm trying to help you.'

'Then leave me alone.'

For a moment I was tempted to do just that. There was a flatness to Nick's voice, a dullness in his eyes that made me feel like I was talking to a hostile stranger. Even his face seemed unfocused, as if someone had smudged an invisible hand over a bad portrait of him before it dried. He was moving weirdly, like a bad actor in a play, every gesture overdone, every action a fraction mistimed.

The window over his bed was open, the curtain billowing in an icy breeze. Nick's room was on the south side of the house; it was always buttoned up snug and tight this time on a winter evening, or it turned into an ice-box. But in spite of the draught there was a cloying, sickly smell in the air.

'Nick,' I said slowly, 'have you . . .'

'Have I what?' He grinned at me — not his familiar mischievous grin: a new grin, wide and fake and mocking. Thrown up between us like a firewall, stopping any communication from getting through. He was stoned. I should go away and come back some other time, a better time . . .

But I knew that once I went out that door I'd be gone for good. I'd never have the guts to do this again. I sat down on the bed to show I meant to stay till we were done. 'Nick,' I said, 'sit down and listen to me.'

Nick straddled the desk chair clumsily and pasted a caricature of a polite, enquiring expression on his face.

'Here's what I know. I know that on Sunday night you had a bag of marijuana here. A lot more than you could use. I think you're dealing. If you're taking drugs yourself that's bad enough, but if you're selling them it's way worse. Either way you're in trouble, big trouble. You have to stop.' The more I said, the more shuttered Nick's eyes became and the

161

more certain I was that I was right. But I said it anyway: 'If it's true.'

Silence hung in the air like smoke. The curtain flapped.

At last Nick spoke, but he didn't look at me. 'What do *you* know? You're just a kid. Weed never hurt anyone. It's not addictive, doesn't do you a scrap of harm. Tobacco's way worse, and everyone smokes. Hell, Dad used to smoke, remember? Go lecture him.'

'Wanting to believe something doesn't make it true. You're wrong, anyhow: the latest research shows it is addictive, and teenagers are three times more likely to get hooked than adults. It messes with your mind just like cocaine and heroin: screws up your short-term memory and your concentration span, and it causes cancer, chromosome damage, depression . . .' Nick's eyes were glazing over and I could tell I was losing him. 'A whole heap of other bad stuff too — and it does way more damage if you're young and your brain's still developing. Some professor at Oxford University studied the brains of heavy marijuana users and they were smooth as marbles — as stuffed as 90-year-olds'.'

'So what? I'll never get that old.'

'You're going to wreck your life, Nick.'

'It's already wrecked.'

'So you admit it?'

'What?'

'That you're smoking dope.'

'I never said that.'

'Look at you: close your eyes or you'll bleed to death. I can smell it. What if Mum comes in? Or Dad? You might as well hang a notice on the door saying *Pot-head*. And that cellphone — you could never afford it, not in a million years. You're dealing.'

'Grow up, Pipsqueak.' Months back I'd made a stand about Nick using that baby putdown. At the time it had been a big deal, but now I didn't care. He could call me what he liked. 'Ever heard of supply and demand? They demand, I supply. Top quality hash, rock bottom prices. That's business. As for the cellphone, it's a tax-deductible necessity.' He gave a high-pitched giggle that made the hair on the back of my neck stand on end. 'Heard of quality control, Pipsqueak? All simple economics; Dad would be proud.' Something flickered in his eyes, but he blinked it away and leered at me. 'Can't guarantee the goods unless I sample 'em.'

That was it then. Yes, Nick was smoking dope; yes, Nick was dealing. What now? 'You have to stop.' But even as I said the words I knew I was wasting my breath.

'Make me. Go play in the traffic, you little try-hard.'

'I'll tell Dad.'

It was my trump card, but if I'd expected Nick to fold, I was wrong. Something deep in his eyes flinched, then hardened. 'So tell him. Dad doesn't care about me. He says he does, but that's crap. All he cares about is the perfect son he'd like to have. He doesn't give a stuff about who I really am. So go on — tell him. Now get out.'

It seemed to me there was something I'd forgotten — some magic formula I should be using to make everything right. The feeling reminded me of the African folktale Mum used to tell us, *The Name of the Tree*. There was a terrible famine in the land and all the animals were starving, gathered under a magical tree loaded with fruit. Only problem was, the name of the tree had to be said out loud for the spell to be broken and the fruit to fall. One after another the animals travelled to a wise man and were told the name, and one after another they came all the way back again . . . and forgot it along the way. In the end it was the good old tortoise who remembered the name and saved the day.

In the story the name of the tree was some unpronounceable African word, impossible to remember, but I had a feeling the words I was searching for were simple, right there in front of me if only I could see them.

But I wasn't like the tortoise, and at last I got up and walked slowly to the door. I'd done my best, but it hadn't been good enough. Nick was wrong. Dad did care. He just showed it in all the wrong ways.

I turned back for a second on my way through the door. Light from the passage slanted in, a bright slice like sunshine cutting a swathe through the greyness of the room. It lit the desk with its pile of books and its neat array of pens and pencils, but it didn't light Nick's face. That was dark and unreadable, deep in the shadow of the severed head hanging over him.

It was only after I'd closed the door that I remembered what Rob had said. *Let him know you love him.* The moment it clicked into place in my brain, snug as a missing piece of jigsaw puzzle, I knew it was what had been eluding me as I hovered in the doorway.

The name of the tree was Love.

I'd been wrong: it wasn't a magic word with the power to make everything right again. It hadn't been important after all.

Waiting

The right time to talk to Nick had pounced on me when I least expected it, ambushing me way before I was ready. I was scared the same thing would happen with Mum and Dad: that the right time for telling them about Nick would sneak up on me in just the same way.

Nestled inside me alongside the dark tumour of the drugs was something else, something light and bright as a shimmering soap bubble: the incredible news of Ratho and the National team, still untold.

On Wednesday morning I stumbled into the kitchen early, still in my pyjamas and bleary-eyed with sleep, and there they were: Dad brushing toast crumbs from his moustache, Mum unloading the dishwasher and Muddle grinding a toast soldier into her boiled egg. My stomach did a loop-the-loop, the two things — the bad and the good — jostling for pole position on the starting grid. I opened my mouth, made a weird kind of bleating sound as they log-jammed together in my throat . . . and the news of Ratho burst out. *Better to tell them without Nick there*, my brain babbled in the background as I heard myself tell: *he'll have to know eventually, but you don't have to be the one to tell him.*

'Hey,' I blurted, 'you'll never guess what! Rob — at the Igloo, Dad —' Dad pricked up his ears like a dog when it hears the rattle of the biscuit-barrel, 'Rob told me yesterday I've been picked for the National team — the climbing team that's going to Scotland!'

The reaction was more than I could ever have hoped for. Mum dropped the plate she was holding and it clattered to the floor, miraculously not breaking; her hands flew to her cheeks and her eyes filled with tears. She held out her arms but Dad was already on his feet, swinging me round and giving me a hug that made my ribs creak. 'Scotland now, eh, Son?' he growled, his brows beetling and his eyes blazing. 'The National team? Well, *there's* one for the money! You wait till I tell 'em about *that* at work this morning!'

'Me!' chipped in old Muddle, never one to let someone else have the limelight. 'Me climb!' She threw her sucked toast on the floor and reached out an eggy hand to me. 'Dungle-dim *now*! Parky pease!'

It hardly seemed the moment to say, 'And something else . . . about Nick . . .'

After that, every time I biked up the driveway I found myself looking for the truck, praying it wouldn't be there; every time I walked into the kitchen I checked the table to see whether there was a place laid for Dad or he'd be eating alone, later, when I was in bed.

But even if he had been there — even if I'd blundered in to find him and Mum opposite each other in the lounge, Mum with her mending, Dad frowning over his newspaper — I still wouldn't have told them. Not yet. It was Dad's first week in his new job, and Mum had taken Nick and me aside and explained how stressful it was for him, how understanding we needed to be, how he needed our encouragement and support more than ever before. She hadn't looked at Nick when she said it, but she didn't have to. A dusky flush crawled up from under his collar and he jerked away, though she wasn't even touching him.

'Whatever,' he growled. 'Can I go now?'

Though what Mum was saying was aimed at Nick, I still felt she'd sent me a secret message without knowing it: *Now's the time to build Dad up, not kick his feet from under him.*

'It's all true,' I muttered to Rob on Thursday. 'About Nick. I talked to him.'

'And?'

'And . . .' I gulped, then said it. 'I'm going to tell Mum and Dad. When the moment's right.'

Rob gave me a glance that was shrewd and understanding. 'Good on you. But remember, things like that get harder the longer you wait.'

Now it was Friday and almost a whole week had gone by. The knowledge had solidified during that time, becoming denser, heavier, more a part of me. Put roots down, dug itself deep. Like Rob said, it was more difficult to imagine telling with each hour that passed.

Even when I wasn't thinking about it, it was constantly in my mind, clouding everything I did, every other thought I had, even Ratho.

After photography club on Friday I hung out at Mike's, then biked home to find the house full of the warm, chocolatey smell of baking and chocolate chip muffins on the cooling rack. There was no note, but we didn't need one: 'Don't be shy, boys,' Mum always said; 'they won't ever be this fresh again.'

I chose the one with most chocolate chips on top and took a massive bite, then grabbed another to keep it company and heaved my bulging book bag up onto the kitchen table. Dad would be at the Igloo till eight, when he'd be giving Nick a ride home from indoor soccer; Mum and Muddle would soon be home from the library and the kitchen would be full of the bustle of dinnertime. Much as I hated the thought, it was the perfect time to knock the worst of my homework on the head before the weekend. *The weekend* . . . a vision of Katie and the secretive, sidelong smile she'd slanted my way as she brushed past with a whispered 'See you Saturday' made my skin tingle.

As I sat down and opened my homework diary I thought I heard the engine of the truck, then moments later the front door banged back on its hinges in the way that could only be Dad. Automatically I glanced up at the clock and frowned: it was way too early for him to be home.

Uneven footsteps thumped down the passage and the kitchen door blasted open. 'Aha!' said Dad: 'Muffins!' Dad's the only person I know who can fit a whole muffin into his mouth without even trying.

'Can I have one too?' I asked, hoping he wouldn't see the telltale scatter of crumbs on the tablecloth. Why was he home so early? Could he have been fired? If he had he wouldn't be in such a good mood, wolfing down muffins like there was no tomorrow.

'No,' said Dad, reaching for another. 'You'll spoil your dinner. Hurry up or we'll be late.'

'Late?' Already I was pushing back my chair. 'Where are we going?'

'Igloo,' said Dad in a spray of muffin-crumbs. 'It's finals night, remember?' I didn't — didn't think it had ever been mentioned, even by Nick. But one of the spin-offs of Dad's new job was that every aspect of the running of the Igloo had become family property, just like the milk run. If Mum was the still eye of our family's hurricane then Dad was its swirling vortex, whisking us all up and carrying us helplessly along with him in whatever direction he was headed.

'But why . . .'

'Your brother's taken a few knocks lately,' Dad told me, eyeing the remaining muffins, 'or so your mother feels. She says we should front up as a family, show our support. You know his team, Hoof-whatsit, have made the finals? Up against the top squad from Churchill Boys', so it should be worth watching.'

A few knocks . . . was this it, the opportunity I'd been waiting for? But Dad was already halfway out the door and I was swept along in his slipstream like always, with just time to grab my sweatshirt as I followed him to the truck.

I couldn't help smiling at how Dad pulled himself up tall and straight in his special tracksuit and nodded to everyone we passed as he wound through the crowd to Wembley, where Nick's team would be playing. Mum was already there, perched uncomfortably on one of the Meccano-style benches with Madeline snuggled on her lap. I cast a wistful glance at the entrance to the climbing gym as I slid onto the seat beside her, giving her a grin and Muddle a friendly poke in the tummy.

Madeline regarded me in solemn silence. She'd regressed into Cabbage-Patch-doll mode, which always happened when we went out somewhere. At home she ruled the roost, but take her somewhere different and she battened down the hatches, two fingers plugged into her mouth and eyes the size of dinner plates. If a stranger tried to prise her away from Mum she'd cling like a leech with superhuman strength, not even giving vent to The Shriek. But if it was a member of our family she'd happily allow herself to be handed from person to person like Pass the Parcel, showing as much animation as a dumpling.

I turned my attention away from my stuffed-fish baby sister to the action on court. Nick's opposition had already arrived and were passing the ball to and fro with awesome skill — six tough, professional-looking guys in purple T-shirts with CHURCHILL BULLDOGS across the front and their surnames on the back. It fit with what Lee had told us about Churchill — big on discipline and tradition, deadly on the sportsfield: the kind of school where you called even your best friends by their surnames, and where you'd be scalped if your hair so much as brushed your collar. All the boys on court looked like skinheads or army conscripts, their short hair making them look way older than sixteen.

I risked a glance at Dad. He was standing, arms folded, looking on with undisguised approval. You could see him thinking that here was a team who knew what soccer was all about.

Over by the entrance to the court the members of Hoof Hearted were gradually assembling. You were supposed to wear the same colour shirts — each player who didn't cost their team a goal before the game even started. But it seemed that in Hoof Hearted's book same-colour shirts was way uncool, and so was warming up. The guy with the Mohawk was slouching against the netting wall, hair dyed red as a parrot's crest. It'd be interesting to see how he handled any headers that came his way. Up shuffled Dazzer in his skate shoes, as out-of-place as a clown's; then two other guys whose names I didn't know, one in aviator shades and the other with a camo cap worn back-to-front and a vacant grin. That made four; there were six in a team. Where was Nick? And the other guy, Stoner . . . My gut twisted as the implications of the name hit me. *Stoner* — where was he?

The muffins sat like lead under my ribs. On came the ref in his smart striped shirt, swinging his whistle and checking his watch; he slipped through the gap in the netting and strutted over to exchange a word with the captain of the

Bulldogs, then blew a single, sharp blast on his whistle.

Where was Nick? They didn't have a team — Hoof Hearted was beaten before they started. In their random assortment of T-shirts and hoodies they were four goals down before they'd even kicked the ball.

I wished I was at home writing my history essay.

And then there was Nick slouching in from the side door, hair awry. Frowning, the ref crossed to meet him at the corner, spoke to him through the netting . . . they'd know each other from reffing, but the guy didn't seem friendly. Nick was mumbling, shrugging, gesturing . . .

Then Dad was striding over, bluff and confident in his official role. 'Now, fellers,' I heard him say, watching Nick cringe, 'what seems to be the problem here?'

They were joined by the Bulldog captain, and there was a brief discussion, punctuated by more shrugs from Nick. The other Hoof Hearted players shuffled their feet and nudged one another and grinned; the Churchill squad stood in a silent semi-circle listening, stern-faced.

Dad turned and strode straight over to where Mum and I were sitting, Mum cheerful and expectant, me wishing I was anywhere but there. And things were about to get worse — a lot worse.

'Pip,' said Dad abruptly in a voice I hadn't heard him use before — his Fair Play Coordinator voice, I realised with a sinking heart, 'we have a problem. The Hoof-ahem team is short a player. Seems a boy's been taken ill unexpectedly. Be a damn shame if the final couldn't go ahead. The Bulldogs have agreed to waive the regulations and allow a stand-in.' Dad's teeth glinted briefly under his moustache, eyes glittering in a look I knew too well. I stared up at him, a metallic chill seeping into me even though I was sitting on my hands to keep my bum off the cold bench. 'What d'you

171

say, Son? Help your brother out, eh? In goal, that way your size won't be such an issue.' *Or your skill*, he didn't say.

Dad shepherded me towards the entrance to the court. 'But . . .' I said feebly, glancing back at Mum and Muddle for support. But Mum made an encouraging little face — of course I should help out, why wouldn't I? Even Muddle just sat and watched me go, eyes wide.

'Go hard — don't let them down!' Dad gave me a pat on the back, then drew himself up to address the teams. I didn't dare look at him, wincing at what he might say, but to my amazement the words that came out of his mouth in his Fair Play voice didn't sound like my Dad at all. 'Bulldogs, you've offered to waive the goal penalty for the shirts — that's true sportsmanship, and to be commended. Well done. Good luck to both teams — play fair and have fun.'

I squeezed through the tight gap in the net, the tough elastic snagging my foot and nearly sending me sprawling, and trailed dismally down to the goalmouth to take up my position.

The ref raised one hand and glanced at the opposition keeper, looming like Goliath in the far goal, then at me. I nodded my head woodenly.

His hand dropped and the whistle blew.

Keeper

Everyone expected a massacre.

I hadn't played indoor soccer for years — not since I'd signed up aged ten because Nick was doing it, suffering through one season before I quit. Even in those days the game had been hectic, but at high level indoor is relentless and brutal, all about speed, commitment and skill. I'd watched games often enough to know how hard-out physical they were, with crunching tackles and kicks hard enough to take your head off. As keeper, I'd be in the firing line.

But I barely touched the ball at first; just fielded a couple of back passes and caught it when it bounced in my direction — hardly a save at all. It was lighter than I remembered, furry-surfaced and harmless. Soon I was almost enjoying myself, and the reason was simple: if Hoof Hearted had been goofing round last time they played, this time was different. A bunch of ill-assorted dope-heads they might be, but they could play soccer — and they weren't too cool to want the miniature silver trophies waiting on the sideline.

Their savagery and skill took me, the spectators and especially the Bulldogs by surprise. Seconds after the whistle blew, Aviator Sunglasses — minus the shades at the insistence of the ref — flicked the ball round two opposition players, then passed it across court to where Mohawk was waiting, apparently half asleep; one foot scooped it out of the air, tapped it round the defender and then nonchalantly buried it in the top corner of the net.

There was a stunned silence, then some scattered applause from the spectators. Dad was motionless, staring bug-eyed. The Bulldogs exchanged sheepish glances and jogged back to their starting positions. The electronic scoreboard flicked to 1-0, the whistle blew and we were off again.

Three more goals followed in quick succession. While the Bulldogs had muscle and fitness on their side Hoof Hearted seemed to have a peculiar kind of magic — a sleight of foot that left the more physical Churchill players like stunned mullets in their wake. Only Nick seemed half-asleep, stumbling over his feet.

At 4-0 the Bulldogs had a whispered consultation, and I saw them exchange grins. By now I was starting to relax — with only a minute to go till half-time I was beginning to believe I might actually survive, though I couldn't quite get my head around the crazy chance that Hoof Hearted could win.

The players took up their positions for kick-off. One of the Bulldogs touched the ball, a tap on top with his toe; then a guy called Hutch — a bullet-headed powerhouse with a kick like a pile-driver — took a couple of running steps and drove the ball straight at me like a rocket, the full force of eighty kilos of angry muscle behind it. *Jump!* screamed my brain, but before I could wonder where or how, the yellow ball had thwacked into the net above my head. The automatic siren blasted to signal half-time. 'Hey man, you gotta watch for that, eh,' mumbled Dazzer as he shuffled past me to fetch his drink bottle.

A quick sip of water and we were off again. Adrenaline had kicked in now, and I was determined that if Hoof Hearted lost it wasn't going to be because of me. Two minutes later I took my first serious save — a low, driving shot I instinctively blocked with one foot. 'Choice, man,' goes old Dazzer, and I felt a surge of pride.

The next few minutes flew by in a ding-dong battle of wild shots from both sides. Then a back pass by Nick went wide and was intercepted by Mac — way the most skilful of the Bulldog players — who dribbled it through our defence; I was ready for the shot, hunched over like an orang-utan with my eyes glued to the ball . . . but what I wasn't ready for was a flick across the goal-face to the other striker, who booted it into the bottom corner while I dove desperately to save it, half a second too late.

The scoreboard read 4-2. My stomach felt like someone was winding it up too tight with an invisible key. 'Nuffin' you coulda done about that, dude,' Dazzer told me comfortingly, but I knew it wasn't true. I should've saved it — and next time, I would.

The game was nearly over and the superior fitness of the Bulldogs was starting to show. Hoof Hearted's greased-lightning moves were rusting up; more and more they were being muscled off the ball. The whistle blew for a foul from the Bulldogs; two minutes later Dazzer was hacked down from behind, to a stern warning from the ref. Dad's face on the sidelines was a thundercloud, but he said nothing. Nick took a feeble free kick and Hutch charged it down, bull-dozing the ball past Aviator and Camo Cap before switching it to the right wing. *Smack!* the ball came at me like a bullet; my hands flew up and warded it off, palms stinging. Hutch and Mac bracketed my goal, ghoulish grins in place as they hovered for the kill; Hutch passed to Mac and he shot, the ball arcing towards the top corner of the goal; I punched it away, but Hutch jumped like a dolphin and it met his shaved head sweet as a bell, bombed straight through my outstretched arms and into the opposite corner of the net.

'Tough luck, kid,' snarled Hutch with a wolfish grin.

Two minutes to go and 4-3.

All the spectators were on their feet now; the other games were over and it seemed like everyone in the entire Igloo had come to watch.

Nick moved back into defence, my mate Dazzer shuffling up into midfield. Nick was greenish-pale, sweat slicking his skin. He gave me a hunted glance that left no need for words. He'd had a shocker and he knew it. Dad would be ropeable.

The whistle blew and Hoof Hearted kicked off, slipping the ball smoothly upfield, left to right, dodging, back-pedalling, hunting for the opening that would clinch the game. And suddenly it came: a gap in the Bulldogs' defence. Mohawk was through it slick as a switchblade, the ball at his feet. A defender bore down on him; he ducked, hesitated, then Mac had snaffled the ball and was powering downfield, ducking past Dazzer, dodging past Aviator . . . now there was only Nick between him and the goal. Nick — and me. Mac hesitated, the ball at his feet; feinted left, then darted right in a lunging drive that blasted him past Nick and in line with the goal where I stood poised on the balls of my feet, hands outstretched to make the save.

Then Nick was steaming in from the side, one foot hooking the ball from under Mac's nose. A scuffle and a shove and he had it; then Mac shouldered him off, lashed out and connected with the ball; it ricocheted off Nick's foot and came zooming towards goal. But I had it in my sights, I was onto it, already scooping it to safety in my mind's eye.

Nick stumbled backwards, so close I could smell his sweat. With a desperate lurch he deflected the ball with his foot, sending it spinning away into the side netting. I caught a flash of his face, hair plastered to his forehead, eyes glaring . . . a flailing hand caught me on the side of the head as he windmilled for balance and staggered half-into the goal circle before overbalancing completely and landing on the deck on his bum.

The siren blew. The timer on the scoreboard read 0, the score 4-3 — the game was over. Or was it? The Bulldog players were clustered round the ref shouting and gesturing, the keeper jumping up and down in his box like a dog on a chain, punching his fist in the air and yelling, puce-faced.

I stood uncertainly in my goal. It was over, surely? But I knew in my heart it wasn't. Something was wrong.

'OK, guys, listen up, listen *up*!' the ref was yelling. 'Stepping in the goal-box — that's a penalty. Sorry, Nick. Rulebook states penalties are to be taken after full time if the infraction occurred prior . . . settle down please, lads; let's finish up here, let's finish *up*!'

A penalty from point-blank range. My neck was on the line. If the ball got past me the score would be levelled, and I knew what that meant. There'd be a shootout to decide the winner, and with me in goal that could only end one way. In moments the stadium was silent: a fragile, dangerous silence like the high-pitched hum a glass makes when you rub the rim. 'The kid in goal . . . ' Aviator had his shades on again, the crowd reflecting off them in miniature like coloured confetti. 'Can we sub?'

The ref glanced at Mac, the Bulldog captain. He shook his head. 'Nah. No substitutes. Sorry, guys — deal was, he played in goal. You can't change the rules every time it suits you.'

'It's all down to you then, dude,' droned Dazzer, expression-less as ever. 'No pressure, eh?'

Suddenly the goal seemed awful big. The ref came and set the ball down on the penalty spot. My mouth was dry.

I felt like the guy in *Honey I Shrunk the Kids* — ten times tinier than I was two minutes ago. I could almost hear the drum-roll as Hutch stepped slowly forward, eyes narrow. He positioned himself alongside the ball, one foot squarely planted. His eyes swivelled to one corner of the net, then the other.

'Keeper ready?' said the ref.

I didn't dare nod — didn't dare take my eyes off Hutch, the ball. Every atom of my being was focused on it. Every muscle, bone, tendon tensed. Ready. Waiting.

I saw Hutch draw back his foot, freeze-frame by freeze-frame, slowly, slowly — then his foot powered forward and connected with the ball with a *smack* that punched my brain to numbed silence and the ball was flying through the air like a comet and my body had taken over and was diving, arms outstretched — a freight train smashed into my hand — something buckled and fire shot up my arm and I was rolling over and over like someone in a car wreck and the Igloo was exploding round my ears and Nick and his druggie friends were mobbing me, boosting me to my feet and carrying me off court shoulder-high and I knew I'd done it: I'd saved the penalty and we'd won.

Screwed

It was way past Madeline's use-by date so Mum slipped out before the presentations, but as she sidled past me she must have seen something in my face. 'Are you OK, Sweetheart?'

'Of course,' I whispered back with a big, phoney grin. 'Never better.' But I wasn't. The middle finger of my right hand felt like it had been stomped on by an elephant. The skin had a bluish tinge, and already it was starting to swell.

Nick and I went home with Dad. From the look on his face I could see Nick was prepared for pretty much anything as he trailed behind us to the car . . . anything except what he actually got.

'I've seen you play better,' said Dad, clicking on his seatbelt, 'but it's a team sport after all, eh? It was a great game. Those mates of yours put on a damn fine show. Just goes to show, you can't judge a book by its cover, as your mother says. And as for you —' he reached over and ruffled my hair the way I hated — 'you showed more bottle than your big brother on the night, eh, Son?'

Nick's voice came from the dark rear seat, flat, expressionless. 'Here.'

I twisted round. He was holding out his trophy: a silver soccer player on a wooden pedestal.

'I've seen it,' I said. 'It's way cool.' But I reached and took it anyhow, so's not to hurt his feelings.

Nick's eyes widened. 'Jeez,' he said. 'What's with your finger?'

He stared, Dad stared. I didn't want to look. Seeing it would make it true — what I already knew, deep in my bones. 'Nothing. It got bent saving the penalty is all. I'll be fine.'

Dad reached and took my hand, turning it gingerly this way, then that. 'Can you bend it?' I tried. It felt like an overstuffed sausage, and hurt so bad I had to bite my lip to stop myself snivelling, but yeah, I could bend it . . . kind of. 'Humph,' Dad said. 'May take a day or two to come right — needs one of your mother's packs of frozen peas. That was a great save. Worth a sore finger, eh?'

'The trophy,' said Nick from the back. 'It's yours.'

'*Mine?*'

'You saved the penalty.'

'But . . .' I looked to see if he meant it. There he sat, slouched and boneless, face shuttered, eyes flat. It was impossible to say what was going on behind them. The old Nick would have been crowing away, gloating, ordering me to keep my sticky fingers off his trophy, reliving every second of the game, talking it up into a glorious single-handed victory that was entirely down to him.

The little trophy felt suddenly heavy. My finger was throbbing in time to my heartbeat, as if an invisible giant was bashing it with a mallet. It wasn't that I didn't want the trophy. I wanted Nick to want it. Wanted things to be like they used to be. It was as if Nick was somehow shuffling it off, pushing away something that should make him happy for reasons I couldn't understand.

'Hey, c'mon, Bro,' I said awkwardly. 'You played good. Like Dad says, it was a team effort.'

'I don't want it,' said Nick.

'Well, that's mighty big of you, Nicholas,' said Dad, giving me a glare. 'I'd say anyone'd be proud to have such a trophy.'

I looked at it. Dad was right. Anyone would want it. 'Nick, I . . .'

'Keep the damn trophy.'

We drove home in silence.

Mum took one look at my finger and said, 'I'm taking you straight to the hospital. Put this ice pack on your hand and keep it raised. I don't like the look of the swelling and discoloration — the sooner it's seen the better. Look at you: you're white as a sheet.'

Accident and Emergency on a Friday night was a real zoo — bearded, grimy drunks lurching against the water cooler and mumbling to themselves, a bunch of thugs in a morose huddle, one with a bloodstained pad clamped to his forehead, and across an invisible barrier us normal people: a pregnant woman with her husband hovering anxiously, a grey-faced lady with a blanketed shape cradled in her arms, a man in a business suit sucking in breaths as if his lungs had turned to pumice.

At last it was our turn. A nurse ushered us through to a tiny consulting room where we waited another ten years. The door blew open and in bustled a dapper little doctor with a stethoscope round his neck. 'Always like this on a Friday, I'm afraid,' he told Mum. 'Now, what can I do for you, young man?'

'Pip's hurt his finger playing indoor soccer,' said Mum while I was still wondering how to convince him it was a superficial thing a sticking plaster would fix. 'I think it may be broken.'

'Mum!'

'Let's have a look. Hop up on the bed here, young man.' Typical doctor, I grumbled to myself as I hitched my bum up on the hard bed. Always wanting you up on the bed even if it was your finger they were looking at; making you drop your boxers if you went to them with a sore throat.

The doctor took my hand and glanced at it briefly. 'Hmmm.' He crossed to the computer on the otherwise bare desk and started tapping away rapidly.

Mum and I looked at each other.

'Well?' said Mum at last, a slight edge to her voice. 'Is it a break? A sprain?'

'Oh!' said the doc, as if he'd forgotten we were there. 'A break, beyond doubt. I'm referring you to X-ray just down the corridor. The radiologist will let you know whether you need to make an appointment with an orthopaedic surgeon.'

'A what?' I croaked.

'An orthopaedic surgeon,' repeated the doctor testily. 'In someone of your age such injuries are always of concern — we need to be sure the fracture hasn't extended into the growth plates.' He gave me a harassed smile. 'Don't look so worried. At worst, you might be looking at the insertion of a wire or a screw to give stability while it heals . . . but that may all be completely unnecessary.'

I felt as if the sky was falling on my head like Chicken Licken. A wire? A screw? 'Are you sure it's broken?' I managed. 'I can bend it, look.'

'That means nothing,' he said, ignoring my finger, which was twitching reluctantly. 'That just shows the tendons are still operational. Fractures, young man, are about bones, not tendons.'

He scrawled something on his prescription pad and pushed it across to Mum. 'Now, if you'll excuse me . . .'

And he was gone.

The radiologist's name was Bruce and he was young and friendly, with all the time in the world. 'I have a kid brother your age,' he told me. 'He's into sailing. How about you?'

'Climbing,' I muttered. 'I'm into climbing.'

'Pip's been picked for the National team,' Mum bragged, but I wished she hadn't told. It seemed bad luck, somehow.

'Ah, rock climbing! Excellent!' Bruce enthused, twiddling his machine. 'Indoor? Excuse me a moment . . .' He left the room in a swirl of white coat and came back a short while later, looking sombre. He clipped my X-ray up on a flat pane of light and studied it for what seemed a long time. 'Climbing, eh?' he continued at last. 'You're not going to like this then. Come over here and let me show you.'

'Now,' he said, pointing, 'this is your finger. What we have in your case, Philip, is a minimally displaced spiral fracture of the middle phalanx of the middle finger. Quite a mouthful, eh?'

'Minimal?' I echoed. 'Does that mean it's not serious?'

'Well,' he said, looking uncomfortable, 'not as such. The good news is that it shouldn't require surgical intervention, though we'll get that confirmed tomorrow. The nature of the fracture means it's prone to further displacement, so it'll need strapping, possibly even a splint while it heals. So no more climbing for you for a while, I'm afraid.'

My voice came out in a feeble croak, like a tadpole with tonsillitis. 'How long?'

He pulled a sympathetic face. 'A fracture like this? You'd be looking at four to six weeks.'

Four weeks! Ratho was five weeks away. 'Four weeks till I'm climbing again!'

'No, Philip.' He looked very solemn. 'Four to *six* weeks till you're able to lose the splint and start using the finger again. You'll need to retrain to reduce the stiffness, have physio to get the movement back in the joint . . . you'll be given a regime of strength exercises, among other things.' He saw the look on my face and shrugged. 'You have to take the long view. If you go too hard too soon you'll overcompensate and open yourself up to further injury.'

'So?' It was all I could trust myself to say, but he knew what I was asking.

'So it will be ten weeks before you're back to climbing, Philip, and twelve minimum before your finger's back to one hundred per cent.

'I'm sorry, mate, but that's the way it is.'

The colour of dreams

I was back in the vinegar bottle. All it took were a couple of brief, matter-of-fact phone calls and Ratho was history, the Highlands team history, at least till my hand was healed.

I hung my green and purple track top on my cupboard door so I could see it from my bed. It was all I had to prove my dreams had once been real. I lay on the bed staring at it, my finger throbbing, playing those few moments of soccer over and over again in my mind.

It made no difference. The blue ornament was smashed, the fragments lying on the hearth. There was no going back, no doing things differently. The clock can only go forward. My own personal Good Fairy had got her boot in good. I wasn't to know that she hadn't finished yet.

All Saturday the phone kept ringing. In and out of my bedroom came Mum, bearing little messages I knew were supposed to comfort me, glasses of iced lime juice like she did when I was sick, tiny eggcups full of M&Ms. Beattie phoned. I didn't want to talk to her. Couldn't.

Mike phoned. Left a message saying he'd come round tomorrow; we'd do something together soon.

Gabriel phoned. Told Mum he was sorry, I was a great climber, he'd see me around.

Lee phoned. I felt a hot ball of resentment smouldering inside. This could only mean one thing for Lee: he'd be taking my place on the Ratho tour. I knew he wasn't phoning to gloat, but I also knew he wouldn't be able to believe his luck. He was human, after all. Well, so was I. I wouldn't speak to him.

Rob phoned. 'Tell him I'll phone him back,' I told Mum, feeling a ripple of shame deep down. Mum gave me a sorrowful little glance that told me she expected more from me but went out quietly, closing the door.

Five minutes later the phone shrilled again, and this time Mum brought the cordless into my bedroom. 'It's Buzz Munro,' she said. 'You need to speak to him, Pip.'

'Hello?' My voice sounded as if I hadn't talked for weeks.

'Sorry to hear about your injury, Phil,' said Buzz, faint and far away as if he was on top of Mount Everest. 'Tough news, for me as well as you.' The line crackled and his voice broke up, then came back stronger than before. 'We'll be looking out for you next year. These things happen. Look after yourself.'

Click, the phone went down. I could picture him crossing my name off the list, writing Lee's in, moving on.

I lay on my bed and stared at the track top. Green and purple . . . the colour of the mountains. The colour of dreams.

The one person I was expecting didn't come. Not to find out how I was, not to say he was sorry. Though I knew it wasn't his fault, there was a hard edge to my heart that blamed him. Everything was about him, always had been: Nick.

He hadn't cared about the soccer final, hadn't gone hard. I had. I'd put myself in the firing line for him and his team — and look where it got me. I'd even had to take his damn trophy. Now it was shoved deep in my bottom drawer under a load of underwear. I might have to have it, but I didn't have to like it.

I felt as if I was carrying the burden of my brother round my neck like a dead albatross, rotting, stinking, ruining my life. If he'd come, I don't know what I'd have said to him. But he didn't.

Dad did. Holding out the phone, his face expressionless. 'Katie,' he grunted, 'from next door.' He stood by with his arms folded like a jailer while I propped myself stiffly up on one elbow, clearing my throat.

'Katie?'

'Hel-lo, Pip McLeod.' I could hear the smile in her voice. 'A little starling told me you're the injured hero. Want me to come and soothe your fevered brow?'

I shot a glance at Dad, wishing he'd leave. She was flirting with me and I wasn't sure how to flirt back, or even if guys did. 'Nah. Well, yeah, maybe. I'm OK. Better every minute.' That was good. Tough but tender.

I couldn't believe Katie was actually phoning to find out how I was.

'So are we still on tonight, or are you in too much agony?'

'Tonight?' It was only then that I remembered Rock Quest. 'Tonight! Of course! It's nothing serious, just a minimally displaced spiral fracture of the middle phalanx.' Now I was glad Dad was there. 'Dad, can you drop us off? Katie and me, at that concert-thing in the park?'

Thirty seconds later our plans were made and I swung my legs off the bed, feeling as if maybe my life hadn't come to an end after all.

'That's what I like to see,' Dad said. 'I know this has been one below the belt, Son, but I want you to see it as a test of character, a challenge. We don't have control over all the

187

things that happen in life, but we sure as hell have control over our response to them. I want you to look back and feel proud of the way you handled this — and that means taking the disappointment on the chin like a man, not hiding in your room like a rabbit.'

It was a long speech for Dad, and I could tell he meant every word. His life had been tough in patches, I knew: his accident, having to leave the fire service and the career he loved, struggling to raise a family, make the milk run work . . .

And now, make a go of his new job as Fair Play Co-ordinator at the Igloo. A joke, like Nick had said, or a new beginning?

'Focus on the little things, and the big ones will take care of themselves,' Dad was saying. 'This date with Katie, eh? Our hunting trip next weekend.'

'Will we still go?'

'It's the "middle phalanx" of your *right* hand, South-Paw.' Dad's eyes crinkled at me. 'I'd say a crack shot like you will still be more than a match for an unsuspecting deer, broken finger or not.

'A date's a date, whether it's with your old man or the girl next door. And now you'd better go and get yourself spruced up. Women don't like to be kept waiting.'

Rock Quest

At seven sharp I was knocking on the Woods' front door, and twenty minutes later Dad dropped us a few blocks from the park. I couldn't wait till I was old enough to drive like Nick, though by now I'd been a reluctant passenger on enough lessons to know that with Dad teaching it wasn't all plain sailing.

But now Dad was on best behaviour: silent and ramrod-straight, eyes front like a taxi driver, only sneaking the occasional peek in the rear view mirror to check how far apart we were.

He needn't have worried. Katie had brought along a tartan picnic blanket and a Red Riding Hood basket that weighed a ton; they were on the seat between us, uncrossable as the Himalayas.

We thanked Dad and climbed out to join the stream of kids converging on Ashgrove Park, where open-air events were held throughout the year. Rock Quest was a competition between school bands; this was only the second year it'd been held, and the first time I'd been. If I'd been with my mates we'd have shoved our way deep into what Mike called the 'mosh pit' — the sardine-crush right at the front, where the amount of jumping up and down you did was limited only by how tightly packed the bodies around you were.

Katie had other ideas. We made our way to the fringes of the crowd, where a slight rise in the ground gave a good view of the stage and a line of trees gave shelter from the easterly breeze. 'This is as close as I want to be,' said Katie, spreading out the rug. She was wearing hipster jeans and a zip-front fleece the colour of grape Kool-Aid, with a low-cut T-shirt underneath. Everything stopped at belly-button level, revealing a curve of Milo-coloured skin and a glimpse of something that glinted gold deep in the secret hollow of her navel.

I couldn't take my eyes off that bare skin. It would be satin-smooth; cool to touch, or warm? I sat down hurriedly, trying to distract myself by wondering what might be inside the picnic basket.

Sitting demurely on her heels Katie unpacked the basket, producing each new offering like a rabbit out of a hat. Two cans of diet cola that could only have been chosen by Katie; neatly wrapped sandwiches that received a disdainful wrinkle of her nose and a dismissive: 'Mum made these, but we don't have to actually eat them.' Sausage rolls and fruit cake — end bits with icing on the side as well as the top. A jumbo bag of corn chips and a slab of cashew nut chocolate, with a flask of hot chocolate for later. 'If it gets cold,' Katie said, 'which it won't dare.'

The music began, the night darkened, the stars came out and the food disappeared — most of it my way, Katie's sandwiches as well as my own. They were chicken salad with mayo, but they might just as well have been sawdust for all I cared. When the time was right I planned to tell Katie the whole story of my shattered hopes and dreams, but for now I couldn't bring myself to spoil things: being with her at last, watching her sway to the music and smile into my eyes as if I was the only guy in the world.

But it did get colder — much colder. I could see Katie shivering, and my neck was starting to cramp from being tensed against the wind.

'Pip,' said Katie at last, 'I'm frozen.'

'Me too,' I said. What next? Part of me wanted to make some grand, romantic gesture, but part of me was still wary of her, warning me to keep my distance. Part of me couldn't see beyond Katie's waterfall hair, her softly parted lips, her eyes so wide and helpless. And part of me kept seeing Beattie, four-square and scowling, more than capable of dressing for an autumn night in the open air.

'There's always the rug,' I said, 'and the hot chocolate.'

'How dumb can you get?' said Katie. 'It's been right under our noses all this time. Of course the rug!' We'd packed the picnic stuff away; now she shifted the basket and lifted her side of the blanket up, brushing off bits of grass and twig.

I scrambled to my feet. 'Lean against the treetrunk,' I told her. Leaning back against the rough bark she smiled up at me, hugging herself for warmth, and the sight of her open face and trusting eyes melted away my last doubts. This was Katie, the girl I'd loved forever, vulnerable and innocent.

I tucked the tartan rug snugly round Katie's shoulders and down over her knees. 'What about you?' she said softly. 'You're cold too.'

I hesitated, then lifted the edge and wriggled under, Katie shifting slightly so there was room for me to lean against the tree beside her. The ridges of bark dug into my back, but that was the least of my worries. Katie was close, so close. The bass of the band was getting tangled up with my heartbeat; I'd almost forgotten about my broken finger, but now something was happening to my blood and it was back, throbbing and swelling. The splint felt small and tight. 'This tree wasn't designed for leaning against,' said Katie with a little wriggle that pressed some soft, hidden part of her against my arm.

I didn't trust myself to speak; didn't dare look at her. I

raised my arm and Katie curled forward to make room for it behind her, then leaned back against it, snuggled into the hollow of my shoulder. 'That's better.'

Under the blanket something touched my thigh, then settled to a warm, steady pressure. I could feel the hum of live electric current running between us, as if that slight contact was completing some vital circuit. My breathing felt tight, constricted. It was her hand. Did she realise it was there? Something else was happening under the blanket: I could feel a stirring, an uncurling like a live creature waking from sleep. Part of me wanted to shift and make room for it, but another part was too afraid.

'Pip?' I turned and looked at her. Her face was close — so close I could share her breath. It tasted of roses — that same dusky, musky softness as the dish of rose petals on the hall table at home. Her eyes gazed into mine, dreamy and unfocused. 'You never used to be so shy, Pip McLeod.' Her voice was the merest whisper.

'I'm not shy,' I started to say, then realised I didn't have to say anything.

'Guess what?' Katie whispered.

I couldn't guess anything — couldn't think. The blanket was tangled round our legs; my jeans had turned into a tourniquet, shutting off my entire circulation, cutting me in half. I was in agony, but I wanted it to last forever, or until whatever needed to happen to make it stop.

'What?' I croaked, burying my face in her neck.

'The music,' said Katie. She wiggled away, pushing herself up on one hand. I squinted up at her. Her hair was wild, her lips swollen-looking and smudged where I'd kissed her. She'd never looked so beautiful. 'It's stopped.'

She combed her fingers through her hair and tossed it

back into place. 'And I thought your brother was the bad boy of the family!'

Feet and legs were tramping past on the nearby path, blankets trailing. The spinning stars had settled to steady points of light again, and my breathing was slowly returning to normal.

A pair of denim-clad legs clumped to a stop, feet pointing straight at us. There was something about the scruffy hiking boots, the candy-cane laces . . . The face flew into focus and the dark dome of sky smashed into a thousand pieces.

Beattie.

She looked very slowly, very deliberately at Katie, sprawled gracefully beside me on the grass; then at me, in who knows what kind of state, still clutching the rug over myself and all at once ice-cold.

She didn't say a single word.

The next day was Sunday. Because every self-respecting teenager sleeps in till at least eleven at weekends, I waited till ten past to phone the Woods'.

'Hi, Mrs Wood, Pip here. Can I speak to Katie?'

There was a long pause before Katie came on the line, still blurry with sleep.

'Katie?' I said, pitching my voice deep and masculine. 'It's me. I was wondering, would you like to do something today? Catch a movie, maybe?' It felt good knowing where I stood. The brief episode with Beattie at Rickety Bridge had a dreamlike quality that left all kinds of question marks hanging in the air. What happened between Katie and me last night had been unfinished too, but in a way that left no doubt about how we both felt. For a moment I found myself wondering about her and Jordan, how far things had really gone, but then I pushed the thought away. This wasn't about Jordan or Beattie. It was about Katie and me. I pictured her cradling the receiver close, whispering into the mouthpiece. Imagined later, holding her hand in the darkened cinema . . .

'Oh, Pip.' There was a pause. 'After we dropped you off last night . . .'

My heart did one of those icy slithers. Mr Wood did transport home; had he noticed something, with a parent's freakish sixth sense? Said something?

Katie's voice sounded odd. 'My dad said what a shame it was, about you . . .'

'Me?'

'You and the National team.'

'Oh, that.' I felt a lurch of relief. Of course Katie would be upset for me. 'It's just one of those tough breaks. You can't control all the things that happen to you in life, I always say, but you sure as hell —'

'Why didn't you tell me this last night?'

I blinked. 'Well, I was going to. But one thing kind of led to another, and —'

'So,' said Katie, like someone figuring out one of those logic puzzles, 'let's get this straight. You aren't on the National team. You aren't even in the Highlands squad. Right?'

'Well, yes,' I said, a chill like cold water trickling down the back of my neck, 'but what difference does that make? What's important is us: you and me.'

'I'm sorry, Pip: there is no us. There's you, and there's me. You're a cute guy, and last night was fun. We'll always be friends. Neighbours, right? I'll see you around.'

There was a click and the line went dead.

Damage control

Almost my first thought — when I was able to think at all — was Beattie. But that was only after I'd finally managed to get my head around the knowledge that all Katie had wanted me for was some kind of trophy boyfriend. I had this crazy vision of my head sawn off and up on Katie's wall beside her Justin Timberlake poster, a bullet-hole between the eyes and my Highlands track top arrayed beneath, along with the National one I hadn't clapped eyes on and never would.

Beattie . . . the look on her face. And all for nothing.

Because that's what it was: nothing. I couldn't believe I'd been so stupid, talked myself into making so many dumb moves, one piled on the next. It all imploded in that single moment when my eyes met Beattie's and I saw the look in them. Contempt.

This time I'd taken things way too far. There'd be no magical moment by the campfire this time round. Beattie had given me my second chance and I'd blown it. From being Joe Cool with two girls in tow, now I had none. And the worst part was, I didn't even like myself.

There must be something I could do to make things better. Damage control. My knee-jerk reaction was to contact Beattie somehow, apologise, explain. But what could I say? The truth was, I lied — made up a million reasons why I couldn't go to Rock Quest when I was already going, with Katie. Now all I could do was admit I'd been a jerk and say I was sorry. Maybe that way we could still be friends.

Half a dozen times I went to the phone, then chickened out. Trouble was, I knew what would happen if I phoned. She'd hang up on me. I wouldn't blame her; I'd hang up on myself.

If I had a cellphone I could text her. You could do just about everything by text — asking people out, dumping them — whole relationships seemed to be conducted by phone, though after last night I could see drawbacks to that.

If it wasn't for my finger I could have talked to her at climbing. But if it wasn't for my finger I'd be going out with Katie, being sucked deeper and deeper into a relationship that was eggshell thin and on fast track to who knew where.

I could still have gone to the Igloo, intercepted her on Tuesday after training, but the Igloo had closed after the indoor soccer finals and the upgrade would soon be in full swing. Dad had a key; he'd be working flexitime on admin stuff up on the second floor for the next few weeks.

I could write her a letter. That way I'd be able to explain everything. I could use bullet points to make double sure I didn't leave anything out. Except I was almost certain she wouldn't read it. That left me with only one option, but it was Thursday before I summoned up enough courage.

After school I blitzed to Beattie's house and stationed myself out of sight behind a neighbour's wall. Checked my watch, my pulse pounding from the hectic dash across town, from nerves and dread and worry I'd missed her.

But the private schools finished later than we did, so it was a few minutes more before the first girls in the turquoise and grey of Oriole High started to drift past in ones and twos, kilts swishing, book bags swinging. Some freewheeled by on bikes, fragments of their conversations flicking past me in their wake; some rode in herds, chattering and laughing. There were guys too, in the purple blazers of neighbouring Churchill, swooping their bikes in show-off arcs, jumping them off the footpath, shouting and whooping and hooning around. A few boys and girls walked together, heads close, ignoring the rest.

Just as I was beginning to think I'd missed her, there she was rounding the corner. My heart skipped a beat, then somersaulted with horror. Someone was with her, walking beside her. As I watched their arms brushed, hands touching in a way that looked almost accidental. Then Beattie looked up at him, flashing her million-dollar grin, and I knew.

The someone was tall and broad shouldered, wearing a faded purple blazer that clashed horribly with his shock of red hair. The someone was Lee.

They reached Beattie's white-painted gate and stopped, still talking. Beattie half-turned away, then looked up at him and said something, a question in the tilt of her head. He looked at his watch, shrugged, nodded. Opened the gate and ushered her through before clicking it shut behind them. He followed her up the path and into the house.

I wanted to vault over the gate and kick the door down, to shout and scream and smash things up, starting with Lee. I wanted to rush inside and drag Beattie out and shake her and yell, 'Don't waste your time on him, Beattie! He's a loser — a complete and utter dickhead!'

But I knew what would happen if I did. She'd look me in the eye and say, 'Wrong, Phil. You're the dickhead.'

And she'd be right.

My own problems had pushed my worries about Nick onto the back burner, so when the knock came on my bedroom door that night I'd pretty much forgotten I had a brother.

'Come in,' I said, expecting Mum with a last pile of washing.

The door opened and in came Nick. I barely remembered his old jaunty walk, the cocksure lift of his chin, his devil-may-care grin. He mooched in, shoulders slumped like an old tramp. He was still in his school clothes, wearing his fluffy gorilla slippers.

This was the first time he'd bothered to come and ask how I was since the final on Friday. Since then — since the goal I'd saved for him and his druggie friends — my whole existence had turned into a train-smash. My climbing ambitions were history. My romantic dreams were in tatters. My life was a wasteland, and here stood Nick looking sorry for himself.

'I suppose you've come to apologise,' I said.

'Apologise?' Nick echoed, looking confused. 'What for?'

Something about the slippers, the goofy kid's design on his size eleven flippers, almost made me weaken. 'If you don't know,' I said coldly, 'I'm certainly not going to tell you.'

'Pip,' he said, 'I . . . I wanted to talk.'

'Well, I don't,' I said stonily. 'As far as I'm concerned, there's nothing to talk about. You're an idiot. You're hell-bent on wrecking your life, and you're not going to start on mine. I'm going to tell Dad about the drugs.' Suddenly I knew — it was clear as day. 'On our hunting trip this weekend, that's when I'll do it. Then you'll see whether he cares.'

Nick scuffed slowly backwards till he was touching the door. I'd have been running for the hills if I was him, but he still seemed half asleep. Stoned, I thought bitterly.

'That's what I wanted to talk about. If you don't get your deer . . .'

'My deer?' I couldn't see where this conversation — if you could call it that — was headed. Marijuana destroyed about a million brain cells a minute, our Health teacher said, and here was SuperZombie, living proof.

'Yeah, your deer . . . if you don't get him, you can have Horace.'

'Horace?'

'Yeah, Horace. I just came to tell you. I'll put it on the list . . .' He turned and fumbled for the doorknob, then made to shuffle out.

An alarm bell was ringing somewhere deep in my brain, but I ignored it. 'I don't want Horace,' I said. I didn't want any deer head on my wall, but I didn't tell him that. Why was Nick suddenly palming everything off onto me as if I was an op shop? I thought he was gone, but then he turned round and said, in a wondering, dazed kind of way, 'Pip . . . d'you think it hurt?'

It took me a second to figure out what he was on about. Horace again. A bit late to start worrying about that, with him stone dead, stuffed and mouldering on the wall. 'Sarge says not,' I said, 'but I reckon it'd have to. Where d'ya hit him?'

'In the butt,' said Nick. 'He . . . he dragged himself . . .'

'Well,' I said, 'that'd have to hurt. A bullet in the butt, huh, Nick?' I meant it as a joke, hoped to see him brighten, even laugh, but he didn't.

'Yeah,' he said. 'I guess it would hurt pretty bad. If I'd only got him in the head, like Sarge said . . .'

It was the next day when I was packing for the trip that I came across the paper.

Not the list of stuff Nick was planning to offload on me — if it even existed, which I sure hoped it didn't — but the pad of foolscap with the poem. And it put a whole new slant on the way he was moping about.

I'd gone into his room to find my polypropylene top, the heavyweight one Dad said I should take in case the forecast cold front came through. I was betting it'd found its way into Nick's cupboard, and I was right.

I was heading for the door when something made me stop and eyeball old Horace. He was staring at the opposite wall like always, deadpan. I remembered what Nick said, about how he had run . . . looking at him now there was no sign of whatever he'd felt in those last moments. Peering closer, I saw his hide was kind of peeling up in places, and the eyes that had once been bright had a milky translucence like cataracts. A ripe, musty smell hung about him, as if there might be something rotting deep inside. I backed off, the hair on my arms rising. I wasn't having Horace in my room, no matter how many lists Nick made. He could put him out with the recycling if he didn't want him.

And that's when I saw it.

Under the deer head was Nick's desk, and it was back to the old mess. Books everywhere, most of the covers tattered and torn. Pens, a highlighter with the lid off, balled-up sheets of paper, a dictionary lying open . . .

We'd always been taught never to read other people's stuff, but schoolwork didn't count. Curious, I shifted the dictionary so I could get a closer look at the scrawl underneath. It was a poem — Nick's version of the magazine contribution I hadn't got to first base with yet, I guessed. Nick and poetry? Half-grinning, I read the first line, and the grin froze.

The poem was scrawled in black pen with ugly-looking strokes that had ripped through in places to the page below. There were words half-finished and heaps of crossing-out.

Frowning, I pieced it together:

Your silent promise fills my mind:
One thought, one dream, one fantasy.
My hunger fills the hollow hours of day,
The sleepless wilderness of night.

It wasn't half bad . . . didn't rhyme, but like Mrs Holland said, it sure came from the heart. It was either about food, or old Nick was secretly in love. But who with? He didn't have a girlfriend I knew of. Guiltily I skimmed on, hoping maybe he'd slip in a name, something that'd give me a clue who it could be.

Lines, words, phrases leapt out, savage as pit-bulls:

My lips search for your nipple,
Cold as despair,
Drink deep of your fatal feast.
You taste of metal, oil, eternity.
My fingers probe
Clumsy with desire,
Fumbling for the touch
That will release you . . .

Jeez! This was hard-core! Whoever she was, she sure wasn't someone you'd want to bring home to Mum. I pictured a female Goth, all leather and piercings and truckloads of that black eye-stuff, drugged up to the gills. What had Katie said? *I thought your brother was the bad boy of the family.* She had that right. Hopefully Nick hadn't really done all this stuff. Knowing it went way beyond schoolwork, that I was totally out of line, I couldn't resist one final glance:

Its length hard and relentless
Heavy as lead between my legs . . .

Man! *Nick!* I was dumbstruck and secretly impressed. You didn't have to be a genius to figure out what Nick was talking about.

201

Somewhere a door slammed, making me jump like a rabbit. Quick as lightning I shoved the dictionary back over to hide the page, hoping Nick wouldn't notice it had been moved. He wouldn't want Mum seeing it, that was for sure. She'd have a conniption. Was he crazy, leaving dynamite like that around? He couldn't submit it to the school magazine, not unless he wanted to get himself expelled. It was red-hot, X-rated. Nick — my brother!

It just went to show, you never know what's going on in someone else's head.

High country

Friday night, and all the gear was piled in the hallway ready for the morning, only Dad's rifle and our toothbrushes needing to be added. The pile seemed huge, considering Dad had insisted we packed light. 'You need to be warm and dry, Son. Clean is for girls' blouses,' he muttered, too low for Mum to hear.

She had her half-moon specs on, concentrating on the button she was sewing back onto Dad's camo jacket. Knowing Mum heard most things, especially ones she wasn't meant to, I expected her to give a me private, amused Mum-glance: the kind that always made me feel we were in a secret alliance against the rest of the world. But she didn't, just snipped the thread, smoothed the faded fabric almost regretfully, and held it out to Dad. 'Here you go, Rambo,' was all she said.

We'd be leaving early, before anyone else was up. Dad could wake any time he set his mind to, an old trick from his firefighting days. I set my alarm for five a.m. and lay staring at the luminous dial, listening to the gentle *chug*, *chug*, *chug* of the second hand making its way round. I had the strangest feeling inside, part excitement, part dread. Mum had once called the McLeod family tradition of a father/son hunt a 'rite of passage'. She said it was how primitive societies marked the transition from childhood to being an adult: 'We have them for all the important milestones of our lives, if you think about it: birth, marriage, death.'

I didn't know if she'd told Nick the same thing when it was his turn; whether he'd needed to be told. He'd always had a gut-level understanding of the stuff that came so naturally to Dad. Nick had gone off two years ago a gangly, goofy kid, and come back just two days later . . . different. Changed, forever, in a way I instantly recognised but didn't understand.

It was as if he'd crossed an invisible boundary into a world where I didn't belong.

But after tomorrow I would. After I'd killed my deer.

Excitement jerked me awake five minutes before my alarm went off. Maybe I had inherited one of Dad's genes after all, I thought as I shivered into my clothes and pulled on my shoes, fumbling with the laces. My finger gave a sullen twinge, reminding me to be careful. Though the splint felt clumsy I could still do most things: take notes in class, even photographs; it wouldn't stop me firing a rifle. Dad stuck his head round my door, cheeks rough with stubble, and gave an approving grunt. He had the heavy green gun bag in one hand, a cup of coffee in the other. 'Five minutes,' he said gruffly, his eyes as bright as I'd ever seen them.

We packed the truck, saying little, working quietly so as not to wake the neighbours. The air was thin and icy, with a brittle edge that echoed the frosting of stars overhead.

Dad swung into the driver's seat and started up to warm the engine and de-mist the windscreen before we set off. I opened my door and was halfway in before I had a sudden thought. 'I'll be right back,' I told him.

Grumbling, he gave me the key so I could let myself back in. He'd think I needed to make a last visit to the toilet, but I didn't.

I tiptoed through the sleeping house, past Nick's room to Muddle's half-open door. I crept inside. There she lay, blankets kicked off like always, bum in the air and knees tucked under, fists either side of her head the way she'd slept ever since she was born. I breathed in the special smell of her: baby powder and the pink lotion Mum washed her hair with; sweet, sleep-scented sweat; creases and dimples and softness, and the damp, ammonia warmth of nappy. I didn't touch her, just stood and looked at her for one last long moment before turning and padding silently out again.

We'd said goodbye to Mum last night. 'You men will be up way before me tomorrow,' she told us with a smile.

Mum wanted this to be Dad's time, man's time — but there was no way he could have got up and dressed without waking her. Not Dad. I went to the end door and opened it a crack. 'Mum?' I breathed.

'Good morning, Pippin.' I could hear the smile in her voice.

In the dim light from the street outside I could just make out her face on the pillow. 'I came to say goodbye,' I whispered.

'Goodbye, darling.' I bent and kissed her cheek, buttery from her special face cream. 'Have fun. Take care.'

Suddenly I didn't want to go. I knelt so I could put my arms round her properly and gave her a big hug, puffy with duvet. 'I love you, Mum.'

I was halfway through the door when she stopped me. 'Pippin . . .' But now I was itching to be on the road. I hovered in the doorway, mentally hopping from foot to foot.

'Don't change.'

I gave her a grin and was gone.

After much discussion Dad and I had agreed to head back to

Rickety Bridge. It wasn't an area Dad had hunted before, but rumour had it there were red deer there — and stags with a good rack of antlers, which is what we were after, were hard to come by these days. 'Though this is the time of year to get 'em,' said Dad, winding his window down so he could stick his elbow out into the rushing darkness. 'The rut: the roar. Mid-March on, when the stags go looking for hinds and broadcast what's on their mind to anyone who'll listen. Us, in this case, eh, Son?'

I knew most of it already: the autumn rut is famous for being the best and most exciting time to hunt. By then the stags' antlers have lost their velvet softness and are fully developed, magnificent and lethal. This is the time stags leave their traditional bachelor territory and move into the rutting grounds; their guard down, they're mean and cantankerous and spoiling for a fight. By mimicking the roar they use to challenge other stags you can lure them within range, using their own natural instincts against them. If a stag mistakes a hunter for a rival deer there's no doubt who will win — before the stag even realises a fight is on.

Dad was in his element on the long drive, more open and chatty than usual. I felt I was being drawn into a magic fellowship, a brotherhood whose doors had been closed to me till now. It seemed no time at all before we were bowling through the little town that had taken hours to reach before, roaring past kids on battered mountain bikes outside the corner store, past the fish and chip shop, drab in the morning sunlight, the tiny police station, the garage, the Legoland church, and out onto the open road again.

I wouldn't have recognised the turnoff, but Dad was driving slowly now with the map open on his lap and soon we were bumping along the unsealed road towards the river. The going was more rugged than I remembered, even in the four-wheel-drive, but at last the familiar series of hairpin bends took us downhill to where the glint of water shone between the trees. Dad manoeuvred the truck over the wobbly bridge with one casual hand on the wheel, the jaunty set of his moustache and crinkled eyes signalling his approval more clearly than words.

'Five-star accommodation, eh, Son?' Dad said as we humped armloads of gear into the smaller of the two empty huts; then he spread out the special topographical map on the dusty bonnet of the truck and we studied it. 'Three things you look for,' he told me: 'shelter, areas of the sort of vegetation deer like, and places where they've been found in the past. They're creatures of habit — where you find them one year is where you'll likely find 'em the next. We'll also be looking for sign — tracks, droppings, rubbings. Wallows — where they rub their coats in the mud to get rid of ticks, especially in the rut.

'There's a four-wheel-drive track here.' Dad indicated an orange-and-white-striped line criss-crossing the maze of brown contours. 'It'll make our job easier. We'll drive to this spur, then move up by foot over the ridge and hunt the tops along the bush line. If we have no luck there, we'll move lower tomorrow and do a bit of bush stalking, see what we can fossick out. Sound good?'

It did sound good, and for the first few hours it felt good. Every moment I expected to see the periscope head and mayfly-wing ears of a deer pop up over the ridge ahead. Dad said to hunt in silence even though we were heading upwind, and it felt good to have his solid, reassuring back ahead of me and my own freewheeling thoughts for company.

By mid-afternoon we still hadn't seen hair or hide of any deer and I was tired, thirsty and — though I'd rather have died than admit it — bored. We were picking our way between clumps of tussock, going either steeply up or steeply down, and the ground was treacherous with tiny stones that skidded and slithered under my feet.

Now and then we'd stop and hunker down in the tussock, or find a knobbly rock to perch on, like sitting on a cheese-grater. Dad would put a finger to his lips to signal utter silence — again — and we'd watch and listen. Out would come a muesli bar or a banana and the water bottles and Dad's home-made 'roarer': a piece of old radiator hose with two 90-degree bends. He'd put it to his lips and groan into it like someone with terminal guts-ache: five or six short grunting roars. He let me have a go, but my roars didn't have quite the same authority. 'All down to experience, Son,' he told me with a wink. 'Practice makes perfect, as the old stag said to the spiker.'

But even Dad's roars got no response, other than the faintest suggestion of an echo.

At last, when we were heading back towards the truck, Dad gave a sudden grunt of satisfaction and beckoned me closer. 'See here, Son?' There was a trampled nest in among the tussock where the ground had been churned up, gouge marks clearly visible among clumps of dark turds that looked alarmingly human. 'Pig rootings. They lie up in the bracken during the day, then come out and dig for roots at night. So there are wild pigs about if nothing else. Maybe we'll bag us a porker instead, eh?'

'Maybe.' I imagined a black boar rushing out at us from the undergrowth, grunting, tusks gleaming. Imagined Nick: 'Great trophy, Pigsqueak! Just the thing for an oink like you!' I'd never hear the end of it. Except it wouldn't be like that. Not now, not with Nick the way he was. He'd look at it dully, then turn away.

Staring down at the pig rootings I felt the weight of the

world settle back on my shoulders. Nick . . . the poem I hadn't even started, due Monday . . . the photography assignment I'd missed because of my appointment with the orthopaedic surgeon.

I hunched off my pack and dug inside for my camera. This was my chance to make up for lost time. The topic was 'Nature' and I'd expected our trip to be full of photo opportunities: herds of deer grazing in dappled clearings, lichen-covered logs and hollow treetrunks with ferns unfurling from their mossy depths. So far there'd been nothing except barren high country slopes, and I wasn't sure I had the skill to capture their stark beauty on camera, but pig rootings were a different matter.

Dad waited approvingly while I focused and shot, wishing for the zillionth time I had a digital. Glancing at the tiny display I saw to my dismay there were only a few exposures left. One frame only, then. I'd better save the others in case we actually saw a pig.

But I knew we weren't going to see one, or a deer. The still, sunny afternoon and shimmering emptiness of the slopes and sky had the simplicity of a primitive Eden where complex things — good and evil — hadn't been created yet.

And I was right. Apart from birds, two distant rabbits and each other, the pig rootings were the closest we came to any living thing all day.

The stag

I'd imagined that evening by the campfire would be the perfect time to tell Dad about Nick and the drugs. But once our bacon and baked beans had been eaten and Dad was sipping his second beer, I found myself putting it off yet again. This time was mine. The whole Nick thing was like a sleeping monster: once it had been woken it wouldn't roll over and go back to sleep again. It would devour everything — maybe even cut our hunting trip short with Dad rampaging home to confront him.

One more day wouldn't matter. I'd tell Dad in the car on the way home; that would be the time.

Dad reached into the cooler and pulled out another can, frosty with condensation. 'Here you go, Son,' he said gruffly. 'Reckon you're man enough to share a beer with your old Dad. Make it last, eh?' We drank a toast to fathers and sons; to hunters, past, present and future. Then the talk turned to my subject choices for school, and my chances of being picked for the National team next year. Dad showed me the Southern Cross and Orion, and we talked about the stars and time and eternity, and how small we both felt under the great bowl of black sky. Dad drained his can, stretched and yawned and stirred up the fire. 'With the bush so dry, we'd better make sure it's out before we head for our sleeping bags,' he told me. 'What say we sleep under the stars tonight?' Then he started on hunts — times long gone, with Sarge and other friends I'd never heard of, story after story unfurling in the flickering firelight. For the first time I realised how deeply Dad cared about the bush, about nature and conservation and even the deer he hunted, and how much he knew.

Lying staring up at the stars I found myself wondering why, if Dad loved the bush and the creatures of the wild, he wanted to kill them. I hadn't asked, but I knew what he would say. He'd tell me deer were an introduced species. He'd talk about overpopulation, about the damage they did to the environment, and how if hunters didn't shoot them the Department of Conservation would drop poison by helicopter, which was way worse. I'd heard it all a million times.

I could understand why deer had to be killed. But what I couldn't understand — what seemed to be entirely missing in me — was whatever made you want to be the one who shot them, who pulled the trigger and saw them fall. Shooting a target was one thing; shooting something living was different. Way different.

Earlier we'd watched a huge yellow moon rise like a hot-air balloon over the treetops on the far side of the river. It had shrunk and brightened on its climb through the night sky, and now it shone like a burnished coin in the darkness. I imagined myself lining up the cross-hairs, dead centre, pulling the trigger, seeing the shards of silver fly. There were dimpled craters on its bright surface, almost like bullet-holes . . .

On the far side of the clearing I could hear the shuffling of a hedgehog grubbing for bugs in the undergrowth. Hoping to catch a glimpse of him I rolled over, snuggling deeper into my sleeping bag. My thoughts drifted, sleep nibbling at the edges of my mind . . . Horace, Katie, Beattie, Lee . . .

the photo I'd take tomorrow . . . the poem I'd write . . . the one Nick had written. It had been a love poem, but though I couldn't remember the words it seemed to me now that it had been almost more about despair. Nick wasn't acting like someone in love. He was silent, morose. Wounded . . . in danger. The shock of that last thought jerked me wide awake again, my skin prickling with a premonition of disaster. At the same moment, almost as if it had been conjured up by my own imaginings, an electrifying shriek pierced the night. Over and over it sliced through the silence, half whistle, half scream. From closer at hand an answer came: a harsher volley like the creaking of a rusty door before silence fell again.

Dad gave a sudden snort, sat up with a startled 'Eh?', then flopped down and went back to sleep.

Lucky him, I thought. I'm going to stay awake all night.

And slept.

Dad's snoring woke me in the grey dawn. Ignoring it was hopeless: leaning up on one elbow I looked across and saw him, nose to the sky, mouth open. He wasn't about to wake. I slid out of my sleeping bag, still in my clothes from last night, grabbed my daypack and an apple and tiptoed down the path.

I knew exactly where I was going. Back to the swimming hole, scene of the near-disaster of the climbing trip. To lay some ghosts or find some truths, or even just the inspiration I needed to write something for Mrs Holland: something from the heart.

As I rounded the familiar corner the birds were stirring in the trees, their first tentative chirping and the steady fall of the water the only sounds to break the silence. Grey rock reared up from gun-metal water to oyster sky; moment

212

by moment trees were materialising like a photograph developing in shades of grey. The cliff I'd fallen from loomed tall as a skyscraper.

I settled myself on Gabriel's rock and opened my pack. It was heavier than it should have been; there was something in the bottom. Trust me to be lugging all kinds of stuff I didn't need. I peered into the depths, frowning. It was a rope: a climbing rope from that last redpoint climb with Buzz. I'd shoved it in my bag meaning to give it back to Rob and forgotten about it. Well, I wouldn't need it now. I ran my fingers regretfully over its nubbled smoothness, feeling the strength and promise in the sleek, sleeping coils. Extra weight or not, it felt good to have it along, like a friend or a lucky talisman. I found my camera, notebook and pen, rolled over onto my elbows facing the water and waited for inspiration.

It came from the far side of the pool, where a low bank sloped gently down to meet the water. Above it the sky was lightening to the colour of mushroom, the undersides of the ragged clouds streaked with gold.

I don't know what made me look up from the first words I was fumbling towards — a sound perhaps, or the suggestion of movement. Instantly I knew there was something there, though I couldn't see it. I stared at where the bush straggled in an untidy line almost to the water's edge, willing the invisible creature to take form . . . and then there it was, stepping silently out from the shelter of the trees so suddenly I forgot to breathe.

A stag. A red stag, regal and magnificent. Though he was way across the water something about the clarity of the morning light seemed to magnify him, bring him almost close enough to touch, every detail as clear as if I were watching him through a telescopic lens. I could see the

213

crust of mud on the coarse hair under his neck, the misty double plume of his breath, the liquid depth of his eyes . . . the distinctive wedge-shaped area of longer, curly fluff on the bridge of his muzzle. His nose, held high to taste the air, had the gloss of a caramel toffee. The light breeze drifting over the water brought the faintest of sounds: the scrape of hoof on stone, a swishing gurgle as he stepped into the water. I could smell him now: the wild, gamey scent of a stag in rut.

Calm and unhurried, he looked round once before lowering his head to drink, his ears alert for the least vibration in the air. Watching him, still scarcely daring to breathe, I could almost feel the weight of his antlers, the balance of them, their proud curve and smooth, honed perfection. There was something about the way he carried himself, an arrogance, that told me he was a young stag, a king in waiting.

He dipped his muzzle into the water and I could see his throat pulsing with each long swallow, hear the rhythmic sucking as he drank. Little ripples spread towards me over the water; before they reached me he lifted his head again to listen, the crystal drops caught on the long hairs of his chin gleaming like gems as they trembled and fell.

Behind him the sun had risen silently over the far horizon, a burning ball that was cupped for that long moment in the cradle of his antlers. I felt my hand creep towards my camera, slip it out of its case. I raised it slowly, slowly . . . adjusted the focus and the shutter speed. Took a shallow breath and lifted it to my eye, positioning the stag in the centre of the frame. My finger felt for the shutter, tightened — and shot.

There was the minutest metallic *click* and the stag plunged backwards, throwing his head up, every sinew tensed and ready to run. He stood frozen, his focus locked on me as intensely as a laser, tension rising from him like steam. The sense of wild vitality he radiated was so strong it was almost visible, a life force so potent it left me trembling.

Don't be afraid, I wanted to whisper. *I would never hurt you.*

He stared at me for what seemed an eternity, then swift as a shadow, silent as smoke, he turned and vanished the way he had come.

I didn't tell Dad.

The hunt

'So,' said Dad, 'today's the day. We leave the vehicle, then walk due east to get some distance. Hunt back into the wind in the afternoon, then head home with a truck full of venison and a trophy for your wall. We'll hunt the river valley today: see what we can find grazing on the flats near the water. What d'you say?'

'Didn't you say something about bush stalking?' I muttered guiltily.

Dad shot me an approving glance. 'So you've been listening,' he grunted. 'Yup, bush stalking's the most productive hunting method, but it's also the trickiest. Sunny day like today with a light easterly breeze, there'll likely be deer feeding in the beech forest; as the day goes on they'll move up towards their beds high in the bush. We'll follow 'em, stop often, look, listen, even smell. Roar every now and again; see what we can flush out. Come on then: let's hit the trail.'

We put a good distance between ourselves and the camp before we even left the truck. By mid-morning we'd doubled back and were hunting into the wind towards the campsite, moving in single file through the beech forest along a rough contour path. I'd imagined we'd sneak along like kids playing cops and robbers, but Dad said it was best to imitate the deer's own style of walking: steady and rhythmic, neither fast nor slow, giving you time to look round for sign rather than having to watch every step you took on the rough terrain. At the beginning of the day Dad had been bluff and positive, but as the hours wore on and we saw nothing he gradually fell silent. By mid-afternoon he was scowling and muttering about 'clowns who start false rumours and send folks off on wild goose chases', and by early evening I could tell by the slump of his shoulders and his gloomy silence he'd pretty much given up hope of finding anything.

I'd used two of my last three photos ages ago, on a waterfall and a spotted toadstool. I was saving the last one just in case. Now I was mooching along contentedly in Dad's wake, shuffling lines for my poem like a jigsaw puzzle in my mind. It would be about the stag, I'd decided: I'd call it *Stag at Sunrise*, unless a better title came to me later.

The track was level, the ground spongy underfoot, the air cool and green. As we walked the sun glinted through the canopy of tiny leaves above us like a strobe, dusty sunbeams glancing off the shiny leaves of shrubs and drenching the lacy fountains of ferns with light. Tender tendrils of grass grew alongside the track among pincushions of moss; fallen tree trunks criss-crossed the bush on either side, decayed and overgrown. Sound was everywhere: rushing water, birdsong, the white noise of insects blending with the muted hum of bees.

I was starting to feel hungry. Just as I was wondering whether I'd be able to persuade Dad to visit the fish and chip shop on the way home I saw him stop and check his watch. He turned to face me, looking glum. 'Well, Son,' he said, 'I'm sorry. I haven't seen a trace of deer all day. If they were here once, they aren't now. Still, there'll be other times, eh?'

He dug in his pocket, fished out a squashed-looking Mars bar and handed it over; dug again looking for another, and came out with the roarer. Gave it, then me, a quizzical glance. 'What say we have one more try? Last blast.'

'OK.' I had that same feeling of complete and utter deerlessness I'd had the day before; it was hours since I'd seen the stag, and I knew he'd be long gone.

'Here you go then,' said Dad. 'Give it your best shot: show us what you're made of.'

I finished the chocolate and wiped my mouth on my sleeve. Took a deep breath and put my lips to the opening of the pipe, then made a long, low farting sound with as much volume as I could generate. More for Dad's sake than anything I waited a second and listened before handing the roarer regretfully back.

That's when we heard it. Deep, resonant and unmistakable: an answering bellow from the bush below.

Dad latched onto my arm with a grip like a vice. 'Holy *cow!*' he breathed, eyes blazing. 'Did you hear that? *Now* we're cooking with gas! We'll sneak up on him, see how close we can get. But first . . .' Dad unshouldered the rifle; I saw the glint of copper casings and heard the lethal snick of metal as he loaded the magazine. I knew most hunters prefer to stalk with a half-closed bolt — the gun's still safe, but can be made ready to fire in seconds without the give-away click of the safety catch being released.

My guts were quaking. 'D-do I roar again?' I quavered.

'No,' whispered Dad. 'He's too close. Roar again and he'll rumble you — or figure you for a more dominant male and scarper. We know where he is. I'll carry the rifle; you grab hold of a shrub now and then and give it a good shake — he'll think it's another stag thrashing the bushes with his antlers. Don't worry if you make a bit of noise; stags in rut are clumsy buggers. And remember: we make one hundred per cent positive ID before we even think of taking a shot.

218

Could be another hunter roaring, stalking us.'

My adrenaline level, already off the radar, jumped another notch. I reached for the nearest bush and gave it a tentative shake. Dad nodded once, teeth gleaming under his moustache. 'That's the way. No more talking.' He touched my shoulder briefly, then turned and we headed off down the slope.

Five minutes later we were in deep bush with visibility down to a few metres. Every sense was raw with the effort of looking, listening, smelling, tasting the air. My heart beat slow as a drum, my blood thick and hot. This was it: the primitive bloodlust that drove hunters out again and again to watch, wait, stalk, kill. I'd thought it was missing in me, but now, with our quarry almost close enough to touch, it had me in its grip.

Half a pace ahead Dad paused, holding up one hand in a signal I responded to without thought. We crouched, still as stone. And then it came: a mashing, rending sound so close we were almost on top of it. A breath of breeze stirred that now-familiar rank smell into my nostrils: I drank it in deep. Then came the muffled plod of a footfall, then another. My blood congealed in my veins. How close was he?

There was the heavy rustle of a big body shoving through leaves, the cracking of a branch. Then it came again: the electrifying, full-throated roar of the stag, at point-blank range.

In utter silence Dad edged away from me, gesturing me to follow. Testing each footfall I shadowed him, side-stepping to where the trees opened to a leafy tunnel like the porthole of a ship: an almost circular window to the secret world of the stag.

I froze, staring, shoulder to shoulder with Dad.

He was less than 20 metres away, spotlit by a watery shaft

of sunlight. He was even more massive than I remembered, his antlers a curving bowl of branching bone, his coat smooth and dappled-looking in the mottled shade.

Something tapped my arm. Dad was passing me the rifle, showing me that here was where I should stand, here where I should rest my hand to shoot.

I took the rifle, my mouth dry. My heart was kicking in my chest with hollow jerks that made me feel sick. Adrenaline hummed in my ears.

The rifle felt heavier than I remembered, but its weight stopped my hands from shaking. I eased into position, resting my forehand on the branch, the barrel nestled snugly in my palm, the splinted middle finger stiff and straight against the steel. My sharpened senses registered every detail: the sooty furring of mould on the branch, the golden strands fine as hair each ending in a glistening drop of honeydew . . . but always, always, my hunter's eye was fixed on the stag.

He tossed his head, thrashing it up and down; rubbed his forehead against a sapling till I heard it creak, then lashed the undergrowth with his antlers and urinated, a gushing stream that frothed into the forest floor. Then with a series of low grunts he shambled round to face us, his neck extended as if he were about to roar again. I glanced at Dad; he gave a microscopic nod.

Holding the rifle steady as rock I sighted down the scope. I saw a tangle of leaves, a splintered tree trunk, a rotten, crumbling branch . . . where was he? I swivelled the barrel a millimetre and he leapt into view, shockingly close. His head filled my vision, his antlers cut off by the circular frame of the scope. I could see a tiny furrowed scar on his forehead, green-stained froth in the fold of his mouth where he'd been browsing on the tender leaves . . . the downy triangle of curls above his toffee-coloured nose.

I slid the bolt into place with the tiniest of clicks.

For the second time that day the stag heard a soft, metallic *snick*. His head twitched up, his ears flicking forward like radar dishes, his dark eyes gazing straight down the sights of the rifle into mine. There was no hint of fear, only liquid curiosity and perhaps the smallest hint of recognition, though I knew that was my imagination. *You again.*

Yes, me.

The rifle was steady, balanced in my hands. The butt was tight against my shoulder. My aim was straight and true, the cross-hairs dead centre, right between his eyes. He wouldn't feel a thing.

I could read Dad's mind beside me clear as day: *Now, Son — do it now! You'll never have a better shot!*

Was this what it took to become a man?

The forest held its breath.

I adjusted my aim a hair's-breadth, tightened my finger on the trigger, and fired.

The river

The barrel jerked up, the butt kicked and the roar of the rifle blew the forest apart. Sight and hearing fused into a single sense, exploding into overload.

The rotten branch beside the stag's head disintegrated in a shower of splinters. There was an eruption of energy too fast for the eye to follow, a flash of white, the crashing of foliage as a hundred kilograms of brute power and panic bolted to safety. Long before the echoes of the shot had died away the clearing was empty.

I lowered the rifle, my ears ringing.

When at last Dad spoke I wondered if the sound of the shot had deafened me, or if Dad's voice could really be so soft.

'So.'

'Dad,' I whispered, 'I'm sorry. I couldn't do it.' Until the moment my finger tightened on the trigger I'd thought maybe I could. But then I remembered the Coke bottle at the firing range, saw the life, the light in those liquid-dark eyes. That's when I knew: I couldn't shoot the stag any more than I could shoot the moon.

Even then, in the last millisecond before the rifle fired, part of me planned to pretend I'd tried: tried, and missed. But before the vibrations died away I knew that wasn't going to happen. I'd made my choice, finally and forever: life over death. I'd stand by it, no matter what it took.

Part of that choice was having the courage to look Dad in

222

the eye. Slowly I turned my head and raised my eyes to his. But he wasn't looking at me. He was staring at the empty glade, his face unreadable.

'Dad?' I held out the rifle. The smell of gunpowder hung in the air like wood smoke, with a chemical tang that caught in my throat. The forest was utterly silent. 'I'm sorry,' I said again. 'It . . .' I was groping for words, some way to make him understand. 'It was too beautiful.'

At last Dad turned his head. His face seemed carved from some hard material, all flat planes and harsh, etched lines. His eyes were cold as flint. 'I knew you'd never make a hunter.'

Dad took the rifle and stepped away to unload before slinging it over his shoulder. There was a density to his silence that made it more eloquent than words. He took a step uphill towards the track, then hesitated as if he was about to say something. But without meeting my eyes he gave a tiny shrug and turned away.

I followed, the distance between us solid as a wall. There was no going back. Dad would never take me hunting again; I'd never want to go. Yet again Dad had given me a chance to prove myself; yet again I'd failed him.

Dimly as a fading dream, the parallel reality played out in my mind's eye. The hollow *thock* of the bullet striking bone, the explosion of blood, the carcass on the forest floor, just so much meat and bone. The dead weight of the stag's head as I hefted it, the jaw sagging, for the ritual photograph.

Somewhere, far away by now, the stag was moving swiftly through the trees at a high-stepping trot, adrenaline surging through his veins.

Some men might need to kill to come of age. Not me. For me, the moment of clarity when I knew the only shot I'd ever take was with a camera . . . that was the moment I'd become a man: my own man, the only kind I ever wanted to be.

Dad hurried ahead of me along the path, anger in every rigid line, every clumsy footfall. His limp was worse, like always when he was mad. He was walking fast, glaring straight ahead, stumbling every now and then on the uneven ground. *Let's get this over with*, his body language growled. *Might as well never have come.*

He might think he was keeping a lid on his feelings, but he wasn't fooling anyone. He reminded me of Mum's pressure cooker: steam hissing out of his ears, pressure building till he was ready to explode. Meanwhile, he couldn't get away from me fast enough. Struggling to keep up I saw him trip and almost fall, then plunge on.

I was watching him when it happened. The path was sloping gradually downwards, winding through the trees; then just ahead it bent abruptly to the right, the gloom of the forest brightening to a wide window of grey air and a watery murmur that told me the river was nearby.

Dad reached the bend, striding out, eyes front, thoughts who knew where. His stiff leg swung wide to take the turn and misjudged, his foot coming down heavily on the cushion of moss to the left of the path. His leg seemed to buckle as he lurched and pitched forward, arms flailing; then with a sliding rush of falling earth he was gone.

It happened quicker than thought — too fast for me to begin to process what had happened.

I froze, staring at the emptiness where he had been, numb with disbelief. But it could only have been seconds before I crept cautiously forward, taking in the gaping cleft of freshly broken earth, pale and wounded, its edges crumbling, tiny avalanches of sandy soil still skittering down. I inched my way down the path, closer to the place he'd fallen; saw how steeply the ground dropped to meet the river way below. Across the ravine I could see the curve of the cliff-edge as it followed the course of the waterway, how erosion had undercut the ground to leave an overhanging lip of earth that looked completely solid from above. But it wasn't. Just left of where the path dog-legged to avoid the ravine the ground was an unstable platform less that a metre deep: a crumbling booby-trap overhanging the abyss below, concealing the nothingness Dad plunged into when it disintegrated beneath his weight.

But I was different. Light, pre-warned, and very careful. Keeping to the path I crept forward, then lowered myself to hands and knees and crawled to the edge, weight well back, scarcely daring to breathe. The place where Dad had broken through had left a bite-shaped fissure I could see through.

My stomach turned over. Way below Dad lay sprawled in the shallows of the river like a broken puppet, white-faced and motionless.

I was shaking, paralysed, but my mind was racing. From what I could see of the cliff-face across the gorge it looked sandy and unstable. I couldn't climb down; it wouldn't be safe. Yet I had to reach Dad, see how badly he was hurt, get him out of the water before the rain came and the river rose. Then I'd go for help. How? I'd worry about that later. Right now I had one priority: Dad.

In seconds I was fumbling in my pack for the climbing rope: the rope I thought I'd never need. After a quick scan of the cliff edge I found what I was looking for: a sturdy sapling, rock-solid, with a smooth trunk. A few deft twists, a firm tug and one end of the rope was securely tied on with a double figure-eight loop. I tossed the other end over the edge, my guts giving a queasy squirm as it unfurled and fell.

Would it be long enough? I peered down and saw it dangling a couple of feet from the bottom. So far, so good. Because of the undercut the first bit would be most dangerous: the edge could give way, stones and earth fall on me or Dad, and I'd be relying solely on the rope for purchase. But I had no choice.

I swivelled feet-first to the drop, grabbed the rope and wormed my way over. For a moment I was half-on, half-off the rim and felt it shift beneath me; then the rope sliced through the soft earth, caught on firmer rock beneath and held. I slithered into space and down, clutching the rope, my hands on fire. Too late I wished I'd thought of padding the edge of the precipice to reduce rub on the rope . . . then the cliff face sloped out to meet me and I half-slid, half-scrambled my way to the bottom.

I ran to Dad, shaking like jelly, hands raw with rope-burn, my finger throbbing under the splint. I knelt in the shallow water by Dad's head and touched his cheek. It was cold as stone. 'Dad?' I said urgently. 'Dad!' Nothing; not a flicker of response. His head was lying in the icy water, his dark hair wet and slick as a seal. His clothing — jacket, shirt beneath — was soaked. My eyes moved downwards and my blood froze. Dad's leg, his bad leg, was bent at an impossible angle, twisted the wrong way.

I felt sick. Help — I had to get help. But first I had to move him out of the water. I was scared his neck might be injured, or his back. In ways I was scared even to touch him after that first contact, that terrifying coldness. But I had to; I couldn't leave him there. Already the wind had changed, bringing a misty dampness that told me the cold front was on the way. He'd freeze, or drown when the river came up.

If he wasn't already dead.

I put my cheek to his mouth to check for breath, but my

226

skin was numb and I couldn't feel a thing; probed the putty-cold skin of his neck, not knowing where to look, till at last I felt the faint flicker of a pulse. I stared down, remembering him sleeping in just this same pose this morning, face to the sky, mouth ajar, moustache bristling. Then he'd been snoring like a chainsaw, indestructible. Now he was distant and unreachable, as if all his energy was focused somewhere deep inside.

'Dad,' I whispered, though I knew he couldn't hear me, 'Dad, I have to try to move you. Don't let your neck be broken. Don't die.'

I sloshed into the water and got my hands under his shoulders, grabbed a double handful of wet jacket for grip, and heaved. A stab of pain shot up my arm but I ignored it. I heaved and tugged over and over with desperate, spasmodic lunges till Dad's torso was clear of the water. He was heavy as a sack of stones, his head lolling uselessly and his eyes a crack open as if he was play-acting, or peeking in a game of hide-and-seek. I wanted to close them with my fingers, like you do with dead people, but I didn't dare.

I went round behind him and rocked and shoved till he rolled over. There was a poster in the Igloo showing CPR and the recovery position: on your side with top leg bent. I hauled at Dad till he looked as much like the picture as I could remember. Then I noticed he was still wearing his backpack. It was soaked and sorry-looking but the tough canvas was still intact. Unzipping it I found a swag of gear I'd never dreamed we had: pocket knife, flashlight, waterproof matches, compass, first-aid kit, rain gear, a beanie and gloves, even a lightweight emergency blanket. Travel light, huh, Dad? I thought as I manhandled the beanie and gloves on and wrapped the blanket round him, rain gear over the top and tucked in tight. Dad might seem rugged and macho,

227

but he didn't cut corners when it came to the stuff that really mattered.

I looked at the rifle lying beside him. Firearm safety had been drummed into us since we were small, and it didn't seem right to leave it. Picking it up, I saw the wood of the butt was scuffed by the fall, but otherwise it seemed undamaged. It weighed a ton. I couldn't take it with me; it would be hard enough making it back up the cliff. After a moment's thought I burrowed under the blanket and dug in Dad's pack for the cartridges, then remembered something Dad always did before he stashed the rifle in the safe. Holding the trigger back I slid the entire bolt out and put it carefully in the front pocket of my pack along with the spare rounds. Without the firing mechanism the rifle was safe to leave.

I was at the foot of the cliff when I realised something else was niggling at my mind, something I'd forgotten. Then I had it. The map . . . and the car keys. My guts quaked at the thought, but I crunched back over the pebbles and found them.

And there was something else, even more important. I bent and kissed Dad's cheek, prickly with stubble. 'I'll be back soon, Dad,' I told him, trying to sound confident and in control. Still I half expected him to leap up, dust himself off and bellow, 'Well done, Son! You passed with flying colours!' But he didn't stir.

As I turned back towards the cliff I'd never felt more alone.

Hell's doorstep

The surface of the cliff had most likely been sand millions of years ago, but pressure and the forces of time had compacted it into stone; now it was rock hard and abrasive as sandpaper, creamy gold interspersed with horizontal bands of ochre. Random terms from long-ago geography lessons drifted through my mind: metamorphic rock? Striations? I remembered thinking it was stuff I'd never need to know. I could see that that the darker bands were harder than the pale ones: wind and rain had worn them away unevenly, leaving a ladder of rock with shallow rungs that might possibly give me purchase enough to reach the top, even with my broken finger.

Moments later I was on my way up, moving with a smooth, steady rhythm. The climb wasn't difficult, but I was cold and tired and scared, and within seconds my finger felt like it was being twisted off with a pair of pliers. I shut my mind to the pain and pressed on, keeping my weight over my feet to reduce the strain on my hands. I didn't dare think about the drop, or the fact I wasn't wearing a harness and had no rope other than the thin nylon lifeline beside me. Though I wasn't touching it I clung to the knowledge it was there. If I slipped I might just have time to grab it.

It seemed a lifetime before I glanced up to find the overhang almost within reach. Here the rock was softer, coarse grains crumbling beneath my fingers. The underside of the shelf was crusty with earth, cobwebs and interwoven

229

roots; the rope, which had been steadily retreating further behind me as I climbed, now trailed down an arm's-length from the cliff face. Checking that my feet were secure and my handhold firm I reached back for it, terrified of losing my balance and falling, felt my fingers brush against it before it swung away. Cursing under my breath I swiped at it again, tapping it till the rhythm of the back-swing brought it within reach. I grabbed it and pulled it close, tucking it between my legs and winding my left leg round it for torsion. Now came the moment of truth. There was no way I could use my climbing skills to negotiate the crumbling overhang above me. I was going to have to trust the rope, the invisible knot above me, the dwindling strength in my arms. If I fell now I'd be dead — Dad and me both.

I took a deep breath and swung out over the void, twirling helplessly, my feet kicking in space. Desperately I twisted the rope between them, feeling myself slither downwards before my grip caught and I was clawing up hand-over-hand, my broken finger screaming as it tried to bend with the others against the splint. I grabbed a handful of earth, what should have been solid crumbling to nothing as my fingers raked through it, soil cascading into my eyes and gaping mouth. I squeezed my eyes shut, spitting, gasping as I groped blindly for the rope. But the channel it had gouged through the soft lip of earth was too narrow, the nylon embedded too deep. Now, when I needed it most, the rope was gone. With a sickening rush of fear I flung one arm, then the other up and over the ledge in a desperate dyno, grappling for something, anything to hold.

My fingers hooked into the narrow gutter the rope had carved, held for a second and then began to slide. I used the momentary traction to haul myself up, levering my torso further onto what I prayed was solid ground, scrabbling for a handhold, something, anything . . . But I felt myself slither helplessly backward, dragged down by my own body weight as invisible blades of grass tore away under my fingers.

Then my good left hand snagged something tough as twine: a skinny root that gave, then held. With a final convulsion I heaved my lower body up, jack-knifing with a strength I never knew I had, eyes staring, breath sobbing. I had one knee over, felt the ledge quake . . . and then I was rolling, scrambling on hands and knees away from the edge as if the cliff were a living thing that might pounce after me and drag me back.

The dusty 4x4 had never looked as good as when I rounded the final bend and saw it there, waiting as patiently as an old carthorse by the side of the gravel road where Dad had parked it a zillion years ago.

The sight of the truck brought me face to face with the reality I'd been trying to ignore. Like it or not, I was going to have to drive for help — me, who'd never driven anything bigger than a go-cart.

Dumping my pack on the dusty bonnet, I found my water bottle and had a long drink, scanning the horizon. Low, sullen cloud was almost touching the treetops; away down the valley I could see the road snaking through buff-coloured farmland before it plunged back into the trees again. A curl of smoke rose up to meet the clouds — a farmhouse, or a farmer burning off stubble in his fields? *He'd have to be crazy in this drought* . . .

Reluctantly I turned back to the truck. A twist of dread at what lay ahead was tightening inside me, but I knew what I had to do. Dad had a key-ring like a jailer, but eventually I found the right key and unlocked the driver's door, threw my pack in the back and slid on in, half-expecting Dad to pop up out of nowhere like a jack-in-the-box and demand to know just what the hell I thought I was playing at.

I took a deep breath and pushed the key into the lock. Then, heart banging like a jack-hammer, I turned it. The truck gave a coughing leap forward as if someone had given it a zap with a cattle-prod, then stalled.

What was wrong? Why wasn't it behaving like it did for Dad? I didn't dare try again — what if it didn't stop next time and smashed into the trees ahead?

Get a grip, Pip — don't be such a baby. Think! Tune in that damn brain of yours to someplace useful!

The driving lessons I'd been on with Dad and Nick . . . I could remember Dad's voice growling orders, Nick's responses, sullen and defensive. But could I remember what Dad had actually said? Without warning Dad's voice barked at me out of the static, gruff as a sergeant-major on parade: *Start her up in neutral, dammit!*

Where was neutral? I took hold of the gear-stick and gave it a tentative wiggle, but it didn't want to budge. Then I remembered: the clutch! But which of the three pedals was it? The one on the right was the accelerator, I knew . . . Cautiously I poked at the other two with my foot. The left one pushed down furthest; there was a diagram on the gear lever and when I moved it again it slid smoothly from one position to the next. Way to go! There was a wobbly dislocated feeling somewhere in the middle; praying it was neutral, I turned the key again. The engine caught and settled to a contented purr, happy as a cat.

OK . . . Clutch in, foot trembling, and into first. Clutch out, slowly, slowly — I could hear Dad's warning growl: *I said slowly, dammit!*

The truck lurched again and stalled. Not slow enough.

It never seemed as hard as this when Dad was doing it. Oh yeah: the handbrake!

Five minutes later I was bunny-hopping down the road, weaving left and right like some crazy drunk — but I was doing it: I was driving.

I crawled along in first gear, the engine whining, my courage growing with every turn of the wheels. I decided to risk a change into second; I'd never get anywhere at this rate. 'The clutch and the accelerator act like a see-saw, Nicholas,' I remembered Dad lecturing in one of his more patient moments. 'When one comes up, the other goes down.'

Up came the accelerator, down went the clutch, and the truck lurched into second gear. Move over, Michael Schumacher! But now we were hurtling towards the next bend, going way too fast — I stamped down on the brake and the wheels locked, the truck skidding and slewing on the loose gravel. I jerked my foot off both pedals and the truck steadied; sick and sweating I coaxed it round the corner. A soothing monologue was playing out in my head: *Easy does it, slow and steady, that's the way. You're doing great . . .*

By the time I'd wound down to the farmland I was driving like a pro — a bit jerky, a little haphazard in the steering department, but making steady progress. If it hadn't been for the thought of Dad lodged heavy as a stone in my chest I'd almost have been enjoying myself.

With my eyes fixed like Superglue on the road ahead I was barely aware of the mushroom of smoke on my left, thicker now and closer. I bowled along, the trees thinning to nothing, golden stubble stretching away on either side. Soon I'd be back at the campsite, then just the last stretch into town and I'd be home and hosed.

Starting to relax, to believe I could really do this — save Dad and be a hero — I eased the truck round the next bend.

Afterwards, replaying what happened in my mind, I couldn't believe that till I was round the corner I didn't know what I was driving into; had absolutely no idea it was even there.

And it was only afterwards that I pieced together what must have happened. The fire in the farmer's field had been driven hard up to the road by the breeze. The road curved in a shallow horseshoe, trapping the blaze with the wind at its back, fierce as a wild animal at bay.

It wanted something to burn, and the only thing there was me.

Fireman's son

My first response was a kind of startled double-take: *Smoke?*
— followed instantly by a surge of horror.

It was smoke — smoke like I'd never imagined. Smoke
that seethed with evil purpose like some kind of malevolent
creature from a horror movie, black and thick as tar, billowing across the road in front of me in an impenetrable pall.

I was blinded. I couldn't see, couldn't *see* . . .

My legs were trembling, shaking in a dumb parody of
fear. My foot on the accelerator wobbled and shook; the
truck jiggered and almost stalled.

Now the smoke wasn't only in front of me, it was behind
me too. Behind me, in front, and on every side.

Shit! my brain yelled. *SHIT!*

The steering wheel had turned greasy with sweat. I was
driving blind, driving in darkness — solid, swirling, lethal
as poison gas, darkness no headlight could penetrate.

The truck was jerking along making a ghastly pinking
sound. Pure adrenaline was racing through my veins, honing
every sense razor-sharp, making every action automatic.
My foot shoved down the clutch and my hand snapped the
gears from third to second before we stalled.

Turn back! my brain screamed. But I couldn't. To turn
back I'd have to slow down, stop, reverse, do all sorts of
stuff I didn't know how to.

And there wasn't just smoke. There was fire.

Flames — orange and red and purple and gold — danced

through the roiling blackness around me, licking at the passenger side. Heat pressed at me through the closed window as if the truck was being blasted by a flame-thrower; fine black ash pattered on the windscreen like confetti. All round me was the sound of the fire: a munching, gobbling crackle like tinfoil being crumpled.

Stop! screamed my brain. *Stop before it's too late!* But it was already too late. I couldn't stop. If I did, the petrol tank would explode. I cringed back into my seat, a mental picture of the safety sign at our local garage flashing through my mind: no cigarettes, no running engines, no cellphones, even, in case a spark ignited the petrol fumes. And I was driving through the middle of a roaring fire, only a paper-thin sheet of red-hot metal between the petrol tank and the flames.

The tyres . . . I imagined them oozing, softening, melting into black puddles that stuck the truck to the road, trapping it like an insect in amber, wriggling and helpless, engine racing, going nowhere. Already I could feel the truck's grip on the invisible road softening, becoming squashier, more yielding; could see the flames licking the black rubber, catching in a flickering rim of blue fire like on the Christmas pudding, gobbling its way deeper, brighter with every turn of the wheels.

What if something was coming the other way? We'd crash head-on, have to stop, petrol would spill . . .

Then run! screamed my brain. *Run! Run away!* Could I? Should I? Should I throw open my door and jump, race through the smoke and pray the fire hadn't spread to the other side of the road? I could see myself ducking and dodging like a soldier under enemy fire, throwing myself flat with my arms over my head as the truck exploded in a fireball behind me.

My hand fumbled of its own accord for the door handle, slipped, gripped, eased the door open the merest fraction. Smoky air whirled in: a choking gust of blackened grass and the sickening barbecue-smell of a zillion tiny cremated corpses. I retched, bending instinctively forward . . . and that's when I saw it. The driver's side was leeward of the wind, protected from the worst of the smoke by the bulk of the truck. And low down, between the floor of the truck and the open door, I could just make out a pale wedge of road.

One hand holding the door ajar, the other slippery with sweat on the steering wheel, my stinging eyes glued to the faint line that was the edge of the road, I crept on through the fire. Praying I wouldn't stall, praying I wouldn't veer into the flames, praying the truck wouldn't explode. Praying that somehow I'd get out of this time-warp nightmare and back to the still, safe afternoon I had to believe still existed somewhere.

Suddenly the smoke was thinner, then thinner still; daylight dimmed the flames, light and air fading them to ghosts, then nothing. The air cleared and brightened. As quickly as it had come the fire was behind me. A pale, straight ribbon of country road unpeeled in front of me in the fading dusk.

It was over, and now I was shaking so hard I couldn't drive. My hands, arms, legs were jerking, rattling my teeth like castanets. I wobbled to the verge and the truck burped and stalled, but it didn't matter. Nothing mattered. I laid my head on the steering wheel, too drained to cry or think or breathe. For a long time I just sat there, being alive.

Eventually I straightened and took a deep, shuddering breath. Risked a glance in the rear view mirror, almost afraid of what I might see. But there was nothing there, nothing to show it hadn't all been some kind of crazy dream. Nothing except a transparent curtain of what looked like mist drifting harmlessly on the wind, and a few curls of ash under the wipers.

At the policeman's signal I ran across the grass, ducking from the wash of the rotor, and scrambled up into the seat beside the pilot. 'Here you go,' he said, his voice almost drowned by the whine of the engine. He was holding out a headset like the one I'd worn at the range; I pulled it on, and instantly the racket faded to a background hum. 'Better?' The pilot's voice spoke inside my head and I nodded, taking everything in at once: the small mike joined to the headset so I could talk back to him, the dizzying array of lights, gauges and dials on the instrument console, the two men belted into the seats behind us.

The pilot was holding out his hand, relaxed and friendly. He didn't look like a rescue helicopter pilot, I thought: not much older than Nick, but with a steadiness in his eyes that instantly made me trust him. 'You're Pip, right? I'm Ivan, and in the back we've got Lofty and Luke, our paramedics.' He stretched past me and shut my door, then nodded at the seatbelt hanging beside it. 'Put that on and we'll be off. Don't want to keep your old man waiting any longer than we have to, do we?' He gave me a grin and a wink, and I felt suddenly certain everything was going to be OK.

'See this?' You'd have thought we were heading off on a joyride instead of a life-or-death rescue mission. 'It's the GPS — the Global Positioning System.' It looked more like a Gameboy to me: a small flat display screen in front of our seats. Ivan was pushing buttons while he talked. 'We key in the coordinates you figured out with the guys at the police station, then we press 'Enter' and the GPS draws a line between us and our destination. We follow the line and bingo: there's your dad. Simple, huh?'

I found myself grinning back at him. He was right, it did seem simple — and it was good to know the information I'd given the police would help us find Dad quickly. In the time it took the helicopter to arrive I'd drunk two mugs of hot cocoa and wolfed down almost a whole packet of chocolate biscuits, working out exactly where Dad was on my map between bites. The cops had relayed the information to the pilot by radio so he'd know where he was headed, but they were taking me along as insurance, just in case I'd got it wrong. I wasn't complaining.

'All set? Then let's go.' I'd expected a massive upward thrust, but the huge machine lifted off the ground so gently I didn't even realise we'd taken off, hovering lightly as a soap bubble just over the H of the landing pad. I couldn't see the rotor — it was turning so fast it was just a flicker like heat haze in the air above us. The cops gave a cross between a salute and a wave and turned back into the station house, Ivan shifted his hand a fraction and we were rising effortlessly through the air, the chopper climbing smoothly forward, then banking over a line of trees and away.

With one eye on the controls and one on the terrain below us Ivan chatted away about hunting by helicopter in the old days, the deer we'd seen and hadn't seen, the kind of rifle we'd been using. Other stuff came through the headphones too: the robot-voice of the weather report and Ivan's exchanges with the controller back at base — the relaxed shorthand of guys who knew their job and had done it together a zillion times. I half-listened, watching the angel's-view vista of mountains unfolding below me.

The distance it had taken me nearly an hour to cover by

truck took less than ten minutes. Peering down I could see the site of the fire: a bald black rectangle of field bordered by a strip of road. The wind had dropped; there was no smoke now, just the faintest haze of blue in the still air. A truck scooted down a narrow farm track towards the red roof of the farmhouse, trailing a plume of dust; I could pick out the black-and-white speck of a dog in the back. The farmer who'd lit that fire was going home for his dinner.

Moments later we were slaloming down the river gorge as it wound between the mountains, flying low, skimming the treetops and almost brushing the rocky elbows of the spurs and ridges on either side. The river unfurled below, a shimmering snake of silver. We banked round a bend, the last rays of the sun flashing off the water like a mirror, treetops skidding past close enough to touch — and then I saw him in the distance, a still black spot on the river bank.

'There he is!' I yelled, deafening Ivan through the head-phones. 'There's Dad!'

'I see him.' The tiny dot grew by the second as we homed in on it as smoothly as if we were sliding down an invisible flying fox. It mushroomed from a dot to a comma to a bundle to Dad, lying shrouded and still just as I'd left him hours before.

The helicopter pressed itself down onto the stony river bed, dust flying and ripples skittering away across the surface of the water. Before the whine of the rotors had died I was fumbling for the catch on my seatbelt, wrenching open my door and tumbling out, crossing the space between us at a stumbling run, thumping down on my knees on the hard stones and throwing my arms round him, pressing my warm face against his. Dad had always been a powerhouse of energy, radiating heat, constantly in motion; now his skin felt cold and lifeless, smelling of mist and stone. 'We're here, Dad — me and the rescue guys. We're taking you home.'

I stared down at his face, willing him to wake. I wanted a sign, not just that he was going to be OK, but that this alien figure lying so pale and still was really him, my Dad.

His eyelashes flickered and his eyes drifted open, searched, found mine and held, the tired shadow of a smile down deep. His lips moved under his moustache. I bent close to catch the faint thread of his words, but it was only later, on the way to hospital, that I realised what Dad had said.

'Good man.'

Spot the difference

Dad drifted in and out of consciousness on the flight to hospital. He'd had a bad bang on the head from when he'd fallen and his leg was broken, but nothing a night in hospital and a few weeks in a cast wouldn't fix, Lofty told me cheerfully.

Dad spoke to me once more before he was wheeled away down the hospital corridor. He reached out and gripped my hand, squeezing so hard my fingers crackled like rice bubbles. 'Nick,' he whispered. 'Get Nick.'

Nick? Why did Dad want Nick? Had the medic been wrong? I'd watched enough TV soaps to know there's only one reason people want their family summoned to their bedside. 'Why, Dad?' I croaked. 'Are you . . . are you going to . . .'

Dad's voice was paper-thin, but with an intensity that told me what he was saying was important — more important than anything. 'Don't worry, you won't get rid of me that easy. I've been doing some thinking up there in the mountains.' Cold and alone, in pain, not knowing where I was or when I'd be back, if ever . . . he'd had plenty of time. 'There's something I need to say to your brother. Something I need to say to my boy.'

Looking down at his face I had the strongest feeling that if Dad and Nick could only have a chance to be together things might still turn out OK. In spite of the knowledge I'd been carrying forever like a yoke on my shoulders; in

242

spite of the dark feeling of foreboding that shadowed every thought of my brother, every mention of his name.

I'd go home and fetch Nick and the two of them would talk — really talk, the way they hadn't for as long as I could remember — and everything would be fixed.

It was never too late.

Then Mum was there with Madeline on her hip and Mrs Wood clucking round them like a broody chook, and Muddle was reaching out and clinging onto me like a banana-scented octopus and Mum was bending over the trolley and giving Dad a long, embarrassing kiss — the kind of kiss I thought you weren't allowed to give injured people in hospitals with the nurses watching — and there wasn't time to think about anything.

Mum turned, sweeping me and Muddle into a two-for-the-price-of-one hug and then pushing me away, still somehow managing to hold on tight. 'Well!' There were tears in her eyes and a smile on her face, though the smile wobbled a bit at the edges. 'You boys . . .'

Then Dad was wheeled away down the shiny corridor with Mum hurrying beside him and Mrs Wood was fussing Muddle and me into Mum's car, nattering away non-stop about how thankful she was she only had daughters, and what I needed was a long hot bath and a good night's sleep, and she'd take Madeline back to her house and I was to be sure and give her a call once Nick and I were ready and she'd run us back to the hospital to be together, because family was all that mattered at times like these.

I sat in the back letting the wave of talk wash over me, aching for home and silence. Mrs Wood pulled up outside our house with a jerk, two wheels on the footpath, and I heaved myself out and unloaded the gear we'd bundled into the boot: the backpacks, the armful of damp waterproofs and clammy blanket, the rifle. The police would get the camping stuff and the truck back to town for us within the next few days. 'All part of the service, son,' they'd told me cheerfully. 'Do it more often than solving crimes in this neck of the woods.'

'Now you take care with that gun, young Pip,' Mrs Wood cautioned me, handing over Mum's keys and backing hastily away.

'It's OK, Mrs Wood,' I told her with a lopsided grin, glad Mum was more streetwise where guy-stuff was concerned. I felt in the front pocket of my pack to check I still had the bolt and held it up for her to see. 'It's totally harmless without this.' But I could tell she wasn't convinced.

I dumped the gear in the entrance porch while I tried the door, thumbing the bell a couple of times in case Nick was holed up inside, then unlocked and carted the stuff inside, piling it on the kitchen floor. I hung the keys on the holder beside Dad's Igloo key, propped the rifle in the corner and put the bolt and ammo on the table with the pile of unopened mail. I'd lock it away once I'd had my shower.

I rapped on Nick's door on my way to the bathroom, opened it a crack and peeped in, but the silence told me it was empty. Wherever he was, he'd be home by suppertime. I closed the door, crossed to the bathroom and stripped, turned on the taps till the water ran steaming-hot, then sidled in, the cleansing cascade of water flowing over me.

I could have stayed there forever, but I thought I heard a door slam, the subtle change of pressure that meant someone had come home. Not someone: Nick. I shampooed my hair and soaped myself, rinsed, then reluctantly turned the shower off and shuffled out, dried myself and pulled on the clean sweatshirt and jeans I'd left ready.

I was hungry enough to eat a mammoth, wool and all. I'd

tell Nick what had happened, then grab something to eat before we headed to the hospital. For the first time I felt a twinge of apprehension: what kind of state would Nick be in?

I padded down the passage, the carpet nubbly under my bare feet, the strangely empty feeling of the house seeping deeper under my skin. I thought I'd left Nick's door shut, but now it was open a crack, the room beyond in darkness. 'Nick?' I rapped once and pushed the door open. 'Nick?'

The room was empty. Horace's head jutted from the wall, shadowy and indistinct, axe-shaped in the gloom. Light gleamed off his glass eye as if he was watching me slyly, secretly, waiting for me to leave. I had a sudden sense that the moment I was gone he'd move, perhaps just the tiniest twitch of an ear as it strained to catch a sound only he could hear: the memory of a shot, an echo locked deep in his long-dead brain.

The house felt hollow with emptiness.

I walked slowly through to the kitchen, picturing Nick at the table tilted back on his favourite chair, scoffing handfuls of cereal straight from the pack.

He wasn't there.

I poked my head round to the living room, but he wasn't there either.

'Nick?' I said to the empty house. Then again, knowing no-one would answer: 'Nick?'

I must have been wrong. Heard a window bang, or the Woods' back door.

I was about to cross to the pantry when I noticed the mail. Someone had rifled through the pile: before it had been neat and four-square; now it was fanned over the table like a hand of cards.

Someone had been here. Nick — it could only be Nick.

I went back to his room and snapped on the light. It was stark, tidy, impersonal as a motel room, empty. Except for one thing. A paper on the bed: a letter.

I crossed and picked it up, my eyes skimming the envelope that lay beside it, the familiar Igloo logo, the top ripped and gaping, the neatly typed address: *Mr and Mrs J McLeod, Private and Confidential* . . .

Then the letter, words stamping themselves on my brain: *We regret to inform you . . . your son Nicholas . . . suspended from his duties . . . avoid police involvement . . . pending further investigation . . .*

The letter fluttered onto the bed upside-down. Something was scrawled on the back in Nick's black writing, angular as fishhooks.

I'm sorry I opened your letter. I'm sorry for everything. Tell Pip it wasn't his fault.

Me? Why was Nick dragging me into this? How could any strife he got himself into be my fault? My mind staggered like a drunk, battling to make sense of what I'd read. Nick must have done something — sold drugs to someone — at the Igloo. Whatever it was, it blew the fragile eggshell of my secret wide apart. Everything was smashed, but everything was in the open too. And now he was sorry. Yeah, right!

But though in my head I was acting out a kind of world-weary cynicism, it wasn't what I was really feeling: emotions too complicated to confront or understand, even deep inside myself. Horror, pity, exhaustion . . . something I couldn't find a name for, and only later, much later, realised was grief. All I could hear, over and over in my head, were those two words, ones I hadn't heard Nick say since he was a little kid: *I'm sorry* . . .

I left the letter where it lay and went slowly back into the kitchen. I had the strangest feeling of unreality, like a person in a dream. A feeling of dislocation, as if something was out of place, something was wrong. As if there was something I wasn't understanding, something I wasn't seeing. I stood in the doorway, trying to identify the feeling in the silence of the empty house.

The kitchen . . . it was as if everything was in its place, yet slightly skewed, like one of those 'spot the difference' puzzles in the comics we'd loved as kids. At first glance the two pictures seemed identical, but when you looked closely, compared, you'd see the laces were missing on the boots, the spike gone from the end of the umbrella, the numbers missing on the clock.

Something was wrong. Something was missing.

Nick . . . and something else.

Then I realised what it was.

The bolt and ammo were missing from the table.

The rifle was missing from the corner.

The keys were missing from the hook.

Everything fell into place in a split second of clarity, and the world turned to ice.

I ran.

Nick

I didn't need to think where to go. I knew. There was another key missing from the hook — the Igloo key.

Mum's car was gone from the footpath. I didn't think to call Mrs Wood, to hammer on her door. She had no place in this.

I wrenched open the garage door and grabbed my bike, dragged it outside and kicked my leg over. The tyres skidded, then caught: I threw myself down the drive and into the street, round the corner and onto the long, winding road that scrolled down the hill. There was no sign of Mum's car, but I knew there wouldn't be. Nick was long gone.

I snapped the bike into lowest gear and pedalled like a madman, whipping round the corners, legs flying to catch up with the terminal velocity of the steep gradient, chasing gravity as it scooped the bike away from me and down. I wasn't wearing my helmet; the wind flew through my hair and stung my eyes to tears, but I didn't care. All I cared about was Nick. All of me — every atom — was bent on getting to the Igloo before it was too late.

At last I reached the flat, and now my legs could work, my muscles stretch and scream with the turbo-charge of adrenaline hammering in my blood. I felt the burn as I rode faster, faster, dodging cars at traffic lights, ducking pedestrians, passing other cyclists as if they were standing still. My bike and I were welded into a single entity, a bionic fusion of muscle and steel, anguish and fear.

I didn't stop, didn't slow. Swung round the last corner and threw myself down the final straight, legs driving, skidding through the gate of the Igloo on a pressure-wave of power.

My brain took an instant snapshot: the huge signboard — CLOSED FOR RENOVATIONS — the parking lot, deserted except for one lone car, buttercup-yellow, parked up beside the service door. Mum's. In seconds I was beside it, dropping the bike, running to the steel fire door. My heart was jerking under my ribs and I realised I was crying, sobbing . . . it was the way Nick had parked the car, so carefully, dead centre between the lines as if he was doing his driver's test.

A prayer without words filled my mind: *Let him have left the door unlocked . . . let me be in time . . .*

I put both hands on the cold metal and shoved. It didn't budge. Put my shoulder to it and heaved, praying for a sudden give, a yielding creak as it swung open under my weight . . . nothing. I hammered with my fists, kicking it, punching, swearing, sobbing: *Nick! Nick!*

He was in there. Him and the rifle, *its silent promise filling his mind, cold as despair,* just like his poem said.

There had to be another door, a door the admin people used, a door Nick had searched for and found. It was there on the other side of the building: an inconspicuous entrance with a sign saying *Staff Only,* open just a crack. I pushed; it swung away from me and I edged inside. It was dark. My eyes would adjust, given time, but time was the one thing I didn't have.

The wedge of light from the open door showed a whiteboard with columns and names, times . . . a computer-printed notice: SECURITY BEGINS WITH YOU. Beside it hung a rubber torch. I flicked it on, following its dusty beam down the passageway and into the echoing cavern of the main arena. I picked my way through, hurrying, eyes raking the darkness for Nick, my whole being cringing from the sound I dreaded to hear.

I jagged the torch over buckets, ladders, ticker-tape, the debris of building work in progress. He could be anywhere, but he was nowhere.

Then suddenly I knew I was wrong: there was only one place Nick could be. Because this wasn't just about Nick. It was about me too; about Nick and me. *Tell Pip it's not his fault* . . . It was about brothers and rivalry. Success and failure. Life and death.

The climbing gym.

I broke into a stumbling run. I ran past the netting of the sports courts into the dark passage to the gym. Down the familiar corridor, knowing every step by heart, feeling the vastness of the amphitheatre and looming height of the climbing walls open up in front of me. My mind flashed back to that other time so long ago . . . to those insane, solitary, magical moments on the sheer wall of the Midnight Run.

The wavering beam of the torch seemed to find its own way to the start of the climb, skating across the floor to the base of the wall. It drew me after it like a magnet, my feet padding its wake, mesmerised, reluctant. I took a breath to say his name, *Nick?* — but the word stopped in my throat.

The light from the torch fell on a shape at the foot of the wall. For a moment the shape was everyone, everything: Dad's still figure on the river bank; my own broken body if Rob hadn't come in time to talk me down from the darkness at the top of the wall.

The shape was Nick, my brother.

The beam played on the wall behind him like Madeline's blow-paint picture, some trick of light dispersing it into a frozen explosion of bruised colours: Nick's still body the dark centre, spattering to purplish-grey streaked with

250

crimson, then midnight blue, and finally blackness.

I was too late.

'Nick?' I whispered. The word caught on a sob, hanging in the still air among the invisible building-site smells of epoxy and paint and dust.

Then I realised. If the rifle had been fired it would be here in the gym, thick and reeking: the metal smell of gunsmoke, the harsh corrugations of sound still trembling in the shattered air. *It's not the bullet itself that does the damage, but the hydraulic shock the bullet causes . . .*

I ran the last few steps to Nick. He was curled like a kitten, one hand held up to his chest like a fern frond, the other hugging the rifle to him like a toy.

I fell to my knees and pulled him to me, sobbing the same words over and over: 'Nicky, Nicky, don't do it, you'll hurt yourself, please don't hurt yourself . . .'

I held him close as I could, hugging, hanging on tight — tight enough to keep him here with me in the circle of light, safe from the darkness beyond.

It was a long time before I felt his body unfurl, before he finally looked at me, his eyes empty hollows: eye sockets in a skeleton, bullet-holes in the moon. 'I couldn't do it.' His voice was so low I could hardly hear him. 'I didn't have the guts. I can't even do this right.'

What could I say to him? I knew I needed to say something, let him know I was there, always, trying to understand. 'It . . . it's not about guts or failure or courage. It's about doing the best you can. It doesn't take courage to give up; it takes courage to carry on.'

But he needed more from me: a rope to hold on to and drag himself up with, out of the dark pit he was trapped in and back into the real world. Dad's words just a few days before swam into my mind: *Focus on the little things, and the big ones will take care of themselves.* And then I remembered the message I had for him — Dad's message. *The little things . . .*

I searched my mind, groping for the right words in the darkness. 'Nick, listen. Dad's been hurt. He's going to be OK, but he's asking for you. He . . . he wants you; needs you.'

Nick stared up at me as blankly if I was speaking some foreign language, and for a moment I thought I'd lost him. Then slowly, as if his tongue was swollen, he repeated the words: 'Dad? Needs *me*?'

A new look came over his face, like shadow shifting to light with the movement of the sun: the exact same expression it used to get when we were kids and Mum cornered him and had a good scrub with a flannel: a look of disbelief, cleansed and dazed and scoured clean.

'Yes, he does. We all do,' I told him. 'Come on, Nick. It's time to go.'

Epilogue

'This is . . . this is . . .' Dad cleared his throat and looked at Mum for help.

'This is a celebration of your coming of age,' said Mum, taking his hand. 'It comes with love from both of us.'

Slowly and carefully I unwrapped the flat package.

It was my photo of the stag, blown up big and framed, with my poem printed underneath. It was way cool. It's up on my wall now — my version of Horace, I guess — and it's going to stay there.

As for the real Horace, he's long gone. There's a poster of Anna Kournikova above Nick's desk now, not that he's ever there to see it. I pop my head round the door every now and again to give her the once-over, just so she doesn't feel neglected. She's pretty hot, but not as hot as Jessica Parker, the new girl in photography club.

But my favourite picture of all is the one on the mantelpiece in the living room. No frills, no Highlands track tops, just the three of us on the beach. Me with my nose peeling from a day in the sun on one side, Nick with his washboard ribs and sand in his hair on the other. And Dad in between, an arm round each of us, grinning fit to bust.

It's taken time and hard work to get where we are now. Counselling, talking, listening, and most of all, understanding. Dad's different these days — softer, slower, gentler. And guess what? He's busy writing a handbook for the Igloo, with a bit of help from Mum where the spelling and stuff goes. But the ideas are all Dad's, and they come from the heart. He reads us bits every now and then, in this real proud, radio announcer's voice. It's called *Fair Play Begins on the Sidelines*.

I didn't ask what Dad said to Nick in the hospital, and they never told me. But I guess I know. Something that's been part of my life as far back as I can remember . . . something I lost sight of just when it mattered most.

The name of the tree.

SHOOTING THE MOON

Monarch of the mountains
You cradle the rising sun in your antlers,
A beating heart held between cupped hands
And offered to the bloodstained sky.

Every new dawn is a blazing trophy
In a game where life is the only prize;
Each day is a victory as you stand proud
Staring the future in the eye.

Shooting the moon
Will not kill the night;
The darkness can only be vanquished
By the dawning light.

Philip McLeod, age 14½